"You look beautiful tonight."

It wasn't what he wanted to say, but he couldn't seem to help himself. Not when her eyes were so wide, their color so deep and dark above her sculpted cheeks. Not when her long honey-colored hair was blowing wild and free in the evening breeze.

"Thanks. You look absolutely ridiculous in that jacket. Where on earth did you get it?"

"I found it in a thrift shop," he told her. "Five dollars. I couldn't resist."

Lonny tore his eyes from her face, and they settled on the rise of her breasts, two soft, round swells shaping the bodice of her dress. He knew that she couldn't be wearing a bra in a backless dress, and the understanding rocked him. Sammy, his buddy, his good old pal, had breasts.

ABOUT THE AUTHOR

Judith Arnold says she can't remember ever not being a writer. She wrote her first story at age six and pursued a successful career as a playwright after getting her master's degree from Brown University. Judith, who now devotes herself to writing full-time, also pens novels under the pseudonym Ariel Berk. She and her husband and two sons live in Connecticut.

Books by Judith Arnold

HARLEQUIN AMERICAN ROMANCE

HARLEQUIN TEMPTATION

Don't miss any of our special offers. Write to us at the following address for information on our newest releases.

Harlequin Reader Service
901 Fuhrmann Blvd., P.O. Box 1397, Buffalo, NY 14240
Canadian address: P.O. Box 603,
Fort Erie, Ont. L2A 5X3

Best Friends
Judith Arnold

TORONTO • NEW YORK • LONDON
AMSTERDAM • PARIS • SYDNEY • HAMBURG
STOCKHOLM • ATHENS • TOKYO • MILAN

Published March 1987

First printing January 1987

ISBN 0-373-16189-1

Chapter One

Samantha watched Lonny move confidently along the roof, as graceful and surefooted as a cat. His knees and ankles were flexed to accommodate the roof's steep slope, but he didn't wobble or flail or struggle for balance. He stood straight, his hands on his hips, and made an unhurried inspection of the shingles that slanted upward to the peak of the roof. He seemed oblivious of the height and the precariousness of his perch, of the glaring strength of the midday July sun and of the white rental Chevette Samantha had just steered to a halt by the curb in front of the weathered Victorian house atop which he was working.

Even though she'd known Lonny for close to ten years, Samantha still marveled at his lean grace. The first time she'd ever seen him had been at a college mixer, where he had distinguished himself as the only male in the room who looked good when he danced. In fact, he'd looked fantastic, his long legs slightly parted, his feet stepping naturally to the rhythm of the song, his arms relaxed and his smile contagious. Over the years, whenever she'd seen him playing softball or basketball, swimming, sprawling out on her bed in her dormitory room to tell her his sad stories of unrequited love, she'd always been conscious of the streamlined length of his body and the fluidity of his movements.

She'd been chunky and clumsy for most of her life, and Lonny's lithe physique had enthralled her.

Samantha was no longer chunky and clumsy. But she couldn't imagine herself striding breezily across a roof three towering stories above terra firma, as Lonny was now doing. He smiled as he worked—that same confident smile he wore when he danced, when he played ball, even when he was busy confessing the details of his various heartaches to Samantha. Lonny's enchantingly warm smile was as much a part of him as his flesh, his mind, and his energy.

He wore sneakers and well-faded blue jeans. He'd removed his shirt and draped it over the railing of the unpainted second-floor deck that abutted the eastern wall of the house, facing the ocean. His hair was longer than it had been in March, the last time Samantha had seen him. It was still thick and straight, as black as tar, combed behind his ears and dropping to the base of his neck in the back. He held it off his face with a red bandanna tied in a headband above his eyebrows. His exposed chest, a hairless expanse of taut, deeply bronzed skin, glistened with perspiration.

Watching Lonny work, Samantha found herself remembering those first few years of their friendship, when she'd harbored an enormous crush on him. Talk about unrequited love! Surely one of the most painful situations a woman could endure was to be told by the man she loved that he considered her his best friend. The last thing Samantha had wanted to be was Lonny's pal—except that to be his pal was better than nothing, so she'd accepted what she could get.

But then to have him confide in her about his chronic despair over Moira Davis, Samantha's freshman-year roommate, who had absolutely no interest in returning Lonny's affections... Well, all right, Moira had intermittently returned his affections, but not his adoration. And after one or another of Moira and Lonny's frequent spats, Lonny would come to Samantha, wail over his most recent psychic bruises, and expect her to sympathize and bolster his battered ego.

She did of course. That was what best friends were for.

This time, however, they were reversing roles. Samantha was the bruised one, and Lonny had promised to nurse her back to emotional health. "You sound horrible," he had commented during their last few telephone calls. When she had told him why she sounded horrible, he demanded that she come and visit him. "Spend a week here in Spring Lake," he insisted. "You must be entitled to some vacation time this summer. Come on down, and I'll take care of you. Between me and the ocean air, you'll be feeling much better in a few days."

She was sure she would. Lonny had always had a knack for cheering her up. And she'd lived in Manhattan long enough to know that breathing the clean, salty air of the New Jersey shore would be a welcome treat for her lungs. Although she'd never visited Spring Lake before, she fell in love with the cozy seaside village the instant she drove past its quaint downtown area along a tree-shaded street of massive, charming houses, which ended at Ocean Avenue, the broad road that bordered the town's pristine beach. Lonny's house was on a side street just one lot removed from Ocean Avenue, and the beach and the boardwalk were visible from the curb where Samantha had parked. She was certain the view would be spectacular from the second-floor deck—to say nothing of the roof.

She saw Lonny leap down to the deck and land lightly on his feet, and she shook her head in amazement. If she'd attempted that jump, she'd have landed on her neck and wound up paralyzed. It wasn't until Lonny reached the deck railing to get his shirt that he spotted Samantha leaning against the bumper of the rented car. His eyes lit up, and he smiled and waved.

Samantha returned his wave and stood up straight. The brisk coastal breeze caught her hair and blew it back from her face. She rarely wore it loose; although she refused to cut off the long, wavy honey-colored mane, she usually deferred to style and professional sensibility by coiling it in a demure knot at the nape of her neck. But for a vacation week at the shore, she had no need to look like a consummate businesswoman. So she literally let her hair down, and she didn't bother to enhance her heart-shaped face with makeup. Her attire was equally informal: a baggy short-sleeved blouse that featured a pattern of brightly colored mynah birds and jungle flora, an above-the-knees denim skirt, and flat leather sandals. Even when she'd been twenty pounds overweight, Samantha had enjoyed dressing flamboyantly. One of the drawbacks of her job as a product manager at LaBelle Cosmetics was that she had to dress like a grown-up for work.

"Hey, Sammy!" Lonny called down to her. He swabbed at his face with his shirt, wiping the sheen of sweat from his cheeks and chin. His features were appealingly harsh: the high brow, rugged jaw, and large, straight nose set off surprisingly gentle light brown eyes with thick fringes of eyelash. Lonny's maternal grandfather had been Spanish, which explained not only his dark coloring but also his hybrid name—Richard Alonzo Reed. But even with his exotic lineage, Samantha couldn't help thinking of Lonny as a purebred WASP, a privileged blueblood from the right side of the tracks. His grandfather had probably been a Spanish count or duke or some such thing.

"Hey, yourself," she called up to him. "If the roof's about to cave in, I'm going to find myself a hotel room for the week."

"The roof is not going to cave in," Lonny promised. "And I didn't knock myself out setting up a brand-new guest bedroom for you just for the fun of it. You're staying here, pal, whether you like it or not. Don't go away," he concluded before climbing through an open window and disappearing into the house.

Grinning, Samantha pulled her suitcase from the rear seat of the car and started up the paved walk to the wide veranda that extended across the front and sides of the house. When she'd been cruising through the neighborhood in search of Lonny's address, she'd noticed that most of the houses located near the water featured verandas.

She was impressed that Lonny's house had such a superb location. The last time he'd seen Samantha, on one of his brief jaunts to New York City, he'd told her he'd bought the house dirt cheap because of its state of disrepair. Restoring dilapidated old buildings was his profession, and the faded yellow Victorian was the third house in Spring Lake that he and his partners had purchased for renovation and eventual resale. However, the enthusiastic way that Lonny had described the house to her when she'd last seen him made her suspect that this was one house he might choose to keep for himself. Given its proximity to the ocean, she could understand why.

By the time she reached the top step of the veranda, he was swinging open the front door. He'd removed his bandanna, rinsed his face, and donned a fresh shirt, which he was in the process of buttoning as he joined her on the porch. Leaving the shirt half undone, he engulfed Samantha in a bear hug. "Hey, Sammy, how are you?" he greeted her before planting an exuberant kiss on her cheek. His arms tightened around her for a moment, then released her. "*Where* are you?" he asked, stepping back to appraise her. "Have you lost weight?"

"No," she fibbed. She had lost a couple of pounds during the past few months, but she didn't consider that worth mentioning. "I haven't been a tubbo for years now, Lonny. I wish you'd get used to the fact that I'm normal size."

"You're not," Lonny argued, raking back a thick lock of hair that had flopped onto his forehead. He studied her carefully as he finished closing his shirt. "You're skinny, Sam. And pale, too. You look like hell."

"Thanks a heap," she said with a laugh. She was used to brutal honesty from Lonny, and she was too touched by his concern to be insulted by his criticism. "After an hour-and-a-half drive from the city in a car that doesn't have air-conditioning, I think I'm entitled to look a bit worn out."

Lonny continued to scrutinize her. He opened his mouth to speak, then reconsidered and offered her one of his easy smiles instead. Samantha knew Lonny well enough to guess what he'd been about to say: that she was looking worn out not because of a long hot drive but because her personal life was a mess and she was doing a lousy job of coping with it. She was glad he didn't say it, though. She wanted a chance to unwind and refresh herself from her trip before she had to contend with any more of Lonny's tactlessness.

"Come on in. I've reserved the royal suite for you," he said, hoisting up her suitcase and opening the screened front door for her. She followed him through a parlor, furnished with a scratched coffee table and a few cushions tossed randomly about the newly buffed parquet floor, to a staircase that had been recently stripped and refinished. The faint odor of fresh paint was overwhelmed by the ocean's lush fragrance, which wafted through the open windows to permeate the house.

At the top of the stairs, Lonny escorted Samantha down the hallway to a door and opened it. She stepped into a room wallpapered in faded lavender paper, with yellowed roller shades hung above the two windows and a single-size mattress placed on a straw mat against one wall. "This is the royal suite?" She sniffed with pretended disdain.

"It's got a bed, which is more than I can say for most of the other bedrooms on this floor," Lonny defended the room. "Plus an ocean view." He set her suitcase down by the closet door and grinned mischievously. "The only other bedroom that has furniture in it is my room," he warned her. "Take your choice, woman: comfort or safety."

Samantha guffawed. Lonny was the safest man she could think of. Even if circumstances forced her to sleep in his bed, she knew she'd be totally safe with him. At one time, back in her college days, that comprehension had sorely disappointed her, but not anymore. By now she had learned that a best friend, no matter how attractive one might consider him, was worth far more than a lover, and that a man so trustworthy that one could share his bed without any complications developing was a rare friend indeed. She knew that Lonny knew that, too. Despite his wicked teasing, he'd never risk their friendship on anything as ephemeral as sex.

"I take it the royal suite doesn't have a private bath?" Samantha asked, drifting to the window to check out the view.

"Across the hall," Lonny directed her. "It looks awful, but it's clean. I'll be downstairs opening up a couple of brewskies, so don't take forever." Before Samantha could respond, Lonny had vanished down the hall.

She laughed again. Already his presence was cheering her up. Although she usually didn't like to be ordered around, she knew that Lonny's take-charge behavior was his strategy to keep her from wallowing in the self-pity that had gripped her ever since she and Stephen had broken up. Like a bossy nurse, Lonny would whip her into shape with his unflagging good humor and compassion…and a few beers, which he insisted on calling "brewskies," like an overgrown college kid.

She crossed the hall to the bathroom and discovered that Lonny's description of it had been accurate. The sink basin was discolored, the toilet seat was cracked, and the wall behind the claw-legged bathtub was mottled with water stains. Above the sink hung a mirror in desperate need of resilvering.

But the shabby condition of the mirror couldn't explain the wan appearance of Samantha's reflection in it. She preferred the way she looked when she wasn't wearing makeup, but as an employee of a cosmetics firm, she felt obliged to wear it most of the time. She was glad for her rare opportunities, like today, to leave her eyelashes their usual spidery blond shade and her lips their true pink color. Yet her pallor and the gray shadows underlining her round brown eyes were not her usual coloring by any means. They were a mark of the wearying sadness she'd been trying, without success, to fight off for months.

Sighing, she brushed out her hair, then splashed cold water onto her cheeks, pinched some color into them and forced a smile. She'd listened to Lonny's tales of woe about his love life countless times, but she wasn't used to sharing her own with anyone, not even with Lonny. It would do her good to unburden herself to him in the way he'd unburdened himself so many times to her, but given her lack of experience in the art of unburdening, she decided she'd be best off smiling as much as possible throughout the ordeal.

As he'd promised, Lonny was waiting at the foot of the stairs with two cold bottles of beer in his hands. "Shall we have the cocktail hour on the porch?" he inquired with a genteel bow.

Samantha nodded. July was much milder in Spring Lake than in New York, where the sidewalks hugged the heat and the air trapped by the skyscrapers became stagnant and stale. Lonny led her out the front door and around to the ocean side of the house. A wooden two-seat swing dangled from the veranda's overhang. They sat side by side on the swing, and Lonny handed her one of the open beer bottles.

"Should we drink a toast?" Samantha asked.

Lonny raised his bottle. "Here's to your coming to the shore to visit me more often, so I don't have to travel to New York all the time."

Samantha scowled. "Number one, you don't travel to New York all the time—maybe half a dozen times a year. Number two, you love New York."

"Only because you're there," Lonny claimed.

Samantha's frown dissolved, although she made light of his compliment. "Sure. I'm there, and so's Broadway, Greenwich Village, the Central Park Zoo, the Guggenheim Museum—"

"Well, you're right up there with the Guggenheim and the zoo," Lonny pointed out. "That's pretty exalted company." At her skeptical grin, he shrugged and lifted his bottle again. "All right. Here's to happiness."

"To happiness," Samantha chimed in, tapping her bottle against his before sipping.

Lonny stretched his long legs to the porch railing and pushed against it, causing the swing to rock gently. "How's work?" he asked.

"Going well," Samantha said, gazing toward the beach. From where they sat, she could see the seam where the pulsing slate-gray water met the pale blue of the fading afternoon sky. It was an infinitely nicer sight than the grungy air shaft her midtown office overlooked. She was grateful to have any window at all in her office; given her youth and her lack of seniority at the firm, she was lucky to have an outer office. But still, she wouldn't mind having a job that would enable her to look out at the ocean instead of an air shaft.

"Lots of painted ladies keeping you in caviar?" Lonny hazarded.

"Not caviar, but my line is doing well," she told him, then took another sip of beer. "I don't want to talk about work. This is supposed to be a vacation."

"This isn't a vacation," Lonny reminded her. "It's therapy."

Samantha groaned. "I hope the only therapy you have in mind is water therapy. I intend to spend the better part of each day on the beach."

"That'll do for starters," Lonny confirmed. "Then we're going to fatten you up, analyze your id, and introduce you to some eligible bachelors I happen to know."

Samantha socked him playfully on the arm. "If that's what you've got planned, Lonny, I'm driving back home tonight. One thing I don't need right now is a new romance."

"Who said anything about a new romance?" Lonny protested. "I was thinking you ought to have some good clean fun. Short-term, no commitments, no obligations. How long were you and Stephen together, anyway?"

"Too long," Samantha grunted.

"Four years?"

"Three years. This past year doesn't count. He's been in Denver since September."

"Yeah, but you didn't break up until April," Lonny reminded her.

"I don't think you can consider two people who are fifteen hundred miles apart *together*," Samantha commented dryly. "Huge telephone bills do not a relationship make."

"But you were still seeing each other," Lonny noted.

"Sure," Samantha muttered. She struggled to shape another smile, then gave up. She couldn't smile when she and Lonny were discussing something as miserable as her prolonged breakup with Stephen. "We saw each other at Thanksgiving, which we spent with my father and without a minute of privacy, and Stephen told me he loved me and missed me. Then we saw each other just after Christmas, when Stephen gave me a hideous green sweater and mentioned that even though he loved me and missed me, he was dating other women and he thought I should date other men because it would enrich our relationship. Then we saw each other last April, and he told me that he missed me so much he was thinking of inviting some oil baron's daughter to move in with him. Sure, we've been seeing each other."

"Really?" Lonny's eyes grew wide. "He invited an oil baron's daughter to move in with him?"

Samantha shook her head and picked at the label on the wet bottle of beer. "He asked me if I'd like to meet her, though. He said that he thought we'd like each other, and that he was sure that it would enrich our relationship if we met. I told him to take me to the airport." She tasted the salt of tears welling up in her throat, but swallowed them back down. She was sick and tired of feeling sorry for herself. "I must have been crazy to think Stephen and I could keep our relationship alive when we were living so far from each other. You know how men are, Lonny. Two weeks without regular sex and their personalities mutate."

Lonny tossed back his head and roared with laughter. "Oh, Sammy, I thought it took three weeks, at least. Look at me—I've gone two weeks without on more than one occasion, and I haven't mutated."

"But you've never gone three weeks without," Samantha guessed.

Lonny effected a grave pose. "Three weeks? Never, Sam, never."

"Men," she snorted. "You're all alike."

Lonny knew better than to take her comment seriously. "Fact is, Sammy, I never thought Stephen was the one for you. I'm amazed that you two stuck it out as long as you did, whether or not you count this last year. I only met the guy a couple of times, and I won't deny that he had his charms. But he obviously wasn't your one and only."

"Oh?" Samantha eyed Lonny curiously. "What makes you say that?"

Lonny reflected for a moment, then took a long sip of beer. "He was a martini drinker."

"I'm a martini drinker, too, sometimes," Samantha remarked.

"Only when you were with him," Lonny pointed out. "Beer is much healthier than martinis. He was a bad influence on you."

"He was a good influence on me," Samantha argued. "Martinis are less fattening that beer."

Lonny leaned away from her to view her. "And look at you now. Underweight."

"I've never been underweight in my life, today included," Samantha correctd him. "Anyway, I thought Stephen and I made a terrific match. He was bright, good-looking, pleasant company. Our backgrounds were similar, and our jobs, and we had similar goals in life. If he hadn't been transferred to Denver, we'd probably be married by now."

"And what a solid marriage it would have been," Lonny said sarcastically. "The guy is gone for all of three months, and he's already dating other women. If you'd gotten married to him, Sam, he probably would have suggested on your honeymoom that he should see other women and you should see other men in order to enrich the marriage.''

Samantha exhaled and turned from Lonny. She focused on the horizon for several minutes, collecting her thoughts. Lonny was right: Stephen wasn't the ''one and only'' for her. She no longer loved him, and if she was honest with herself she'd have to admit that she didn't even miss him anymore. What she missed was the nearly four years of her life she'd devoted to him, the routines and rituals she'd established with him, the dependability of knowing that she was one half of a couple, and he was the other half. It wasn't losing Stephen that hurt as much as losing a pattern of living with which she'd grown content and complacent.

She wished she could explain that to Lonny. She wished that by explaining her sadness she could dispel it. But she didn't know how to verbalize her feelings without sounding maudlin or pathetic. Instead, like an idiot, she was singing Stephen's praises, defending him to Lonny. She hadn't wrangled a week of vacation time, rented a car, and driven all the way from New York City to Spring Lake just to tell her good friend that Stephen really was a wonderful man even though he'd shattered her world.

''Well,'' she murmured, ''if this is your idea of therapy, Lonny, I don't want to know what your idea of eligible bachelors is.'' She took a long draft of beer, then set the bottle on the whitewashed planks at her feet and stood. ''I'm going to take a walk to that little gazebo on the boardwalk,'' she said, pointing out the roofed extension that jutted from the boardwalk toward the water, providing a modicum of shelter for the boardwalk's strollers and joggers. ''When I get back, we're going to talk about something jolly, like food.'' Before Lonny could stop her, she was off the veranda and heading down the street to the beach.

Watching as she ambled down the sidewalk toward Ocean Avenue, Lonny decided that she really didn't look underweight. Slim, yes. Skinny, no. He'd come to terms with the fact that there was less of Samantha Janek now than there had been back in their college days. Not that he had ever considered her fat, although she'd always referred to herself as "tubbo" and "porker" and other such self-deprecating names. He used to think of her as...sturdy, that was it. Big and sturdy, strong enough to lean on.

Today, however, she looked almost lost in her oversize shirt, so slight, so fragile beneath the folds of gaudy cotton. He liked her shirt, and especially her skirt, which ended in a straight hem a good two inches above her knee. Like most men, Lonny regretted the demise of the miniskirt, and he was all in favor of its revival. Samantha's skirt wasn't quite short enough to be a miniskirt, but it revealed her knees and an enticing sliver of thigh above them. She had great legs, he realized. For a shortish woman, she seemed disproportionately leggy.

He leaned back in the swing and grinned. Rarely did he think of his buddy Sammy in the context of appearance. When people knewn each other as long and as well as he and Samantha had known each other, they stopped *seeing* each other. For Lonny, that had happened after he'd known Samantha just a few months. The rapport they shared had developed almost immediately, and once it had, Lonny had stopped thinking of Samantha as a girl and thought of her as a friend. She would talk about her thunder thighs and her big butt; she'd make sardonic cracks about tying a red flag to her shoulders and wearing a sign that read Caution—Wide Load. Lonny never paid much attention to her snide comments about her weight, though. It was simply the way Sammy was, always making jokes, laughing away whatever was bothering her.

She wasn't laughing away her troubles at the moment. Lonny's smile faded, and he ran his index finger thoughtfully over the damp green glass of his beer bottle as he contemplated Samantha's dispirited state. It wasn't like her to be depressed. He'd never known her to be gloomy before, and he was worried.

The last time he'd seen her had been just before she'd flown to Denver for what turned out to be her final visit with Stephen. She'd been edgy about the trip, and in retrospect Lonny recognized that she must have known things were not going to go well between her and her boyfriend. But Lonny had been so excited about the decrepit Victorian in Spring Lake he'd just put a binder on that he hadn't given Samantha much of a chance to discuss her problems. He'd swept through Manhattan on his way to his parents' house in Tarrytown, met Samantha for lunch and ranted for a full hour and a half about the incredible beach house he was on the verge of purchasing, and about his plans for refurbishing it. Samantha had been dressed in one of her sweet little working-woman dresses, with her hair pulled back into that schoolmarm bun she always wore in New York, and her feet jammed into a pair of high-heeled pumps that looked like the sort of shoes his mother might wear to a country club dance. She'd picked at her pesto and said, "It sounds nice," and, "I bet you're thrilled," at all the appropriate moments.

Already things had been going badly for her, already she'd been losing her appetite, losing weight. And he'd been so full of himself and his dream house by the shore that he hadn't even noticed at the time.

He hadn't been aware of her sadness because he wasn't used to it. He wasn't used to Sammy falling apart on him. Her old lover wasn't worth falling apart over. Samantha Janek was too tough to be disheartened by a little twerp with a big ego who waltzed off to Denver because he'd rather earn a larger salary than remain in the same city with the woman he supposedly loved.

Lonny had said as much during several of their telephone conversations. Samantha had agreed, had told Lonny he was absolutely right...until the next time he spoke to her and she sounded just as disheartened, and the time after that, until finally Lonny had insisted that she come to Spring Lake.

He had looked forward to her visit with curiosity as well as concern. He didn't know what to expect. It seemed impossible that Samantha might need to lean on him. Or on anyone. She was too strong.

She had reached the gazebo on the boardwalk and was peering out over the railing, studying the incoming tide. The ocean breeze tugged her hair in all directions, and the late afternoon sun sifted through the long tresses, seeking the red-and-blond highlights in their tawny depths. Lonny had always considered Samantha beautiful, but now that he was actually *seeing* her for the first time in ages, he was astonished to find that she *was* beautiful. Even if he hadn't known who she was, even if she were a total stranger he'd just happened to notice on the boardwalk, he'd consider her beautiful.

Carl Dunlap would surely think so, Lonny mused as he watched Samantha turn from the ocean and stroll slowly along the boardwalk to the ramp leading down to the sidewalk. A successful realtor with whom Lonny frequently did business, Carl seemed like Samantha's sort of guy, the kind of man who savored his professional achievements and respected intelligent, equally successful women like Samantha. The dinner outing Lonny had scheduled for the

following evening would make for an interesting double date: Carl and Samantha were two hotshot business types, and then there were Lonny, an overeducated handyman with not a single pair of wingtips to his name, and Marcy, a clerk in a silkscreen T-shirt shop. Lonny had been dating Marcy on and off for a couple of months. She was pretty flaky, as scattered as Samantha was ambitious. But Lonny found her amusing and companionable. He suspected that Samantha would, too.

Samantha was returning to the house, and he stood to welcome her. Once again he was struck by the unfamiliar delicacy of her appearance. He'd never thought of her as "Caution—Wide Load," but he'd always pictured her cheeks as round and pinchable, the way they'd been back in college. They weren't round anymore. They were elegantly hollow, her eyes large and soulful above the well-defined bones. Her neck was slender, her shoulders pronounced beneath the blousy shirt, and her legs... Once again, Lonny found himself unabashedly admiring her legs.

"Hey, gorgeous," he called to her as she started up the walk to the veranda. "What do you think of our beach?"

"It looks very sandy," she quipped.

"If you're a good girl, maybe I'll take you there tomorrow."

Samantha faked a scowl. "Oh, so you make me drive all the way down here, and *then* you start laying down the rules. You might have warned me I'd have to be a good girl before I made the trip."

Lonny slung his arm around her shoulders and gave her a squeeze. "I tell you what," he proposed, "I'll take you to the beach tomorrow if you promise to be a good girl afterward."

"Why?" Samantha asked warily. "What happens afterward?"

"You're going to have dinner with an eligible bachelor."

She pressed her lips together. "I hope the eligible bachelor you're referring to is you, Lonny. I'm not interested in meeting any new men at the moment."

Lonny assessed her dry tone of voice and decided not to be discouraged by it. "One bachelor, Sam. I think you'll like him. He's your type—rich, civilized, washes behind his ears. Good-looking, too."

"Is that my type?" Samantha posed.

Lonny shrugged. "Anyway, I've already made reservations for you and him and me and a lady for dinner at a spiffy restaurant, so you're stuck. It's just one night, Sammy. Who knows? Maybe you'll even like him."

Samantha shook her head. Lonny had never set her up with any of his friends before. He'd frequently asked her to set him up with her friends—Moira Davis in particular, but also other women he'd catch sight of in her dormitory. "Who's that?" he used to ask whenever a cute new face appeared in the dining room or the lounge. "Who's that, is she unattached, and what are my odds?"

She had never revealed to him how much those questions had anguished her. Why was he interested in every woman in the world but Samantha, she used to cry to herself. Why did he want her to introduce him to everyone else when she was so in love with him? Just because she was on the plump side, a lower-class girl at an elite Ivy League university, lacking the prep-school sophistication of people like Lonny or Moira...

Of course, Lonny had often told Samantha that he loved her. She didn't quite believe him then, but she did now.

Moira was history to Lonny, and so were Jennifer Collins, Tracy Aldridge, Lisbeth Mumford, and all the other pretty, slender dormmates Samantha had arranged for him to meet. Lonny's infatuations had faded from his life a long time ago, but his friendship with Samantha endured.

So now, after all these years, he was going to return the many favors she'd done him by setting her up with a rich, civilized, good-looking bachelor with clean ears. "Do I really have to go on this blind date?" she asked, already resigned to the idea.

Lonny handed her her half-consumed beer. "You'll thank me for it, Sammy," he swore.

"You mean I'm going to fall madly in love with the guy?"

"I mean, you're going to enjoy yourself and forget about falling madly in love for the time being. It's better not to fall madly in love with someone so soon after you've just fallen madly out of love with someone else."

"I take it I'm in the presence of an expert," she said with a cynical sniff.

"You are indeed," Lonny assured her. "How many times have I fallen madly out of love? If anyone should know about these things, it's me. But enough about that," he resolved, sliding his arm around her shoulders again and ushering her to the front door. "I seem to recall your requesting that we talk about something jolly, like food."

"One of my favorite subjects," Samantha concurred. "If you really want to boost my spirits, let's talk chocolate."

"Chocolate," Lonny contemplated, strolling with her through the house to the kitchen at the rear of the building. "How about chocolate-covered ants for supper tonight?"

"Ants are *not* jolly," she argued, unable to stifle her laughter. Lonny's arm tightened around her, and he dropped a light kiss onto the crown of her head.

His unwanted matchmaking notwithstanding, Samantha was glad she'd come to Spring Lake to be with Lonny. For the first time in months, thanks to him, she was laughing again.

Chapter Two

The beach was surprisingly empty, given that it was Sunday. Lonny had explained that, even on the weekends, Spring Lake never attracted sun-worshiping hordes the way the more developed nearby towns of Asbury Park or Seaside Heights did, with their boardwalk arcades and amusement parks. Which was just fine, as far as Samantha was concerned. She didn't want to have to fight off a mob in defense of a few square inches of sand.

Rolling onto her stomach, she cushioned her head with her folded arms and closed her eyes. Even though she'd slept sinfully late that morning, the warmth of the sun and the steady rhythm of the surf threatened to lull her back to sleep. The noontime heat seemed to add pounds to her arms and legs, making them feel unnaturally heavy. She nestled her bikini-clad body deeper into the sand and sighed languorously.

Lonny had already left the house by the time Samantha had emerged from the "royal suite" with a stiff neck, courtesy of the thin mattress on the floor that had served as her bed. She found his note on the kitchen table and read it. "Had some business to take care of this morning. If you're not here when I get back, I'll find you at the beach. Help yourself to whatever's in the fridge—except for the chocolate-covered ants. I'm saving them for supper. Lonny.'' Samantha had breakfasted on a navel orange and a cup of instant coffee, then slipped on her swimsuit, took a towel from the linen closet, and headed for the beach.

She assumed that the business Lonny had to take care of was actual work-type business. As far as Samantha could tell, the profession of renovating old houses had little to do with calendars. It relied more on such variables as the weather and the specific needs of the clients. Since Lonny was spending much of his time fixing up the Victorian house he'd decided to keep for himself, he had to attend to money-making ventures at odd hours, like Sunday mornings.

Last night they'd talked at length about the house. Lonny had never owned a house before, at least not one he didn't plan to resell as soon as he made it livable. Originally he and his partners had planned to resell the Victorian just as they'd resold most of their properties, but when Lonny decided he wanted to keep the house, his partners sold their shares to him. It was much too large a house for Lonny, but he adored it.

He had taken Samantha on an animated tour of the place, describing to her the improvements he intended to make. The drafty parlor would be fitted with thermopane windows, and the kitchen would be equipped eventually with modern appliances. The dreary dining room would be painted a cheerful blue. The wall between two tiny rooms upstairs would be torn down, opening the space into an airy sitting room, and a door leading out to the upstairs deck Lonny had already built would be added so he wouldn't have to climb through a window to get outside. His enthusiasm was infectious; before long, Samantha could visualize the house as it would look when he was done refurbishing it. Much too large for him, agreed, but too wonderful to part with. By the time he was done showing her around, she found herself nearly unable to bear the thought of returning to her cramped one-bedroom apartment in Manhattan.

Spring Lake had been a summer retreat at one time for wealthy city dwellers. Samantha could easily understand the need to escape the heat and the hectic pace of New York every now and then. But she couldn't imagine herself giving up the life she had there, even though her apartment was tiny.

She'd worked hard for what she had, studying for her advanced business degree at night while she toiled as an assistant to an assistant at LaBelle Cosmetics during the day. She'd won her current position not because she was related to the right people—or sleeping with the right people—but because she had designed an ingenious marketing strategy for the company's new line of brightly colored eye cosmetics. "We can call it 'Artist's Eyes,'" she'd proposed. "We can have the shadow colors arranged on a tray resembling a miniature artist's palette, with paintbrush-shaped applicators. We can do the eyeliners like watercolors, and the shadows like oils. We can package them in containers shaped like berets, with splotches of paint on them." Her confidence and gutsiness had persuaded the head of marketing to give her concept a try, and when the line outsold all projections in its first year, Samantha found herself with a promotion and an office overlooking the air shaft.

The position entailed a great deal of responsibility, but being saddled with responsibility was worth the prestige and power that came with the job—to say nothing of the generous salary. Not that Samantha was money-hungry, but she was honest enough to admit that she liked the monthly check the company gave her. She liked gazing at the big computer-printed number on it before she deposited it at the bank. Money didn't go far in New York, but she earned enough to live comfortably, to eat and dress well, to forget about scrimping. She liked being a "have" instead of a "have-not." The novelty hadn't worn off yet.

"Sam?" An unfamiliar baritone boomed from the boardwalk and broke into her thoughts. "*That's* Sam?"

She craned her neck to peer upward. The sun glared against the white sand, and she had to squint to make out the two male figures leaning over the boardwalk's steel railing and staring at her. By the time her eyes adjusted enough for her to recognize Lonny, he was shouting, "Hey, pal, you'd better watch out. You're shriveling up like a strip of bacon in a microwave."

She twisted to inspect her shoulder, which showed only the faintest glimmer of pink, and grunted at his exaggeration. By the time she turned back to the boardwalk, the two men had ducked under the railing and leaped to the sand. Lonny wore a pair of cutoffs faded to near-white, and a dark blue T-shirt. His lithe build contrasted vividly with that of his husky companion, whose body appeared to have been carved from a granite boulder. The man was shirtless beneath a pair of baggy denim overalls, and Samantha focused for a moment on the hulking shoulders and muscular chest visible under the bib of his trousers. He seemed to be around Lonny's age, thirty or so, with a thick shock of straw-colored hair and broad, pleasant features.

"Good God," he roared as he loped across the beach to Samantha. "Lonny keeps telling me about his buddy Sam. He never told me that his buddy Sam happened to look like a million bucks in a bikini."

Her cheeks colored slightly at the man's playfully lewd compliment. Although she enjoyed the flattery, she hoped that the man wasn't the blind date Lonny had promised her. Lonny had sworn that the man would be her type, and big blond beefcakes definitely weren't her type. This big blond beefcake did have a nice smile, though, and she had no difficulty returning it.

"Sammy, this is Jack Rogan, one of my partners. Jack, Samantha Janek. And I'll thank you to stop ogling her."

"I wouldn't be ogling her if she wasn't worth ogling," Jack retorted gleefully. "Why the hell didn't you tell me Sam was a girl?"

"I'm not a girl," Samantha objected, her smile cool now. "I'm a woman."

"Absolutely," Jack hastily agreed. "One hundred percent. No argument there."

She laughed at his unrestrained flirting. She wasn't used to exchanging banter with men as stereotypically handsome as Jack, even if her taste in the opposite sex generally ran to refined executives with lean builds. Jack, she decided, looked like what she'd expect a construction worker to look like: all muscle, all heft and bulk. To her mind, Lonny looked more like a man who might wield a clipboard than one who might wield a hammer. Seeing him prance about his house's roof the previous afternoon had done nothing to erase her image of him as an intellectual exuberantly playacting the role of construction worker.

"He talks about you all the time," Jack revealed, dropping onto the sand beside Samantha's towel. "Says you work for some makeup company. I've got to admit, I always wondered whether a guy who worked for a makeup company might be a little funny, you know?" He turned accusingly to Lonny. "Why didn't you tell me she was a girl? You wanted to keep her all to yourself, is that it?"

"Samantha isn't the sort of woman to be kept, whether by me or by anyone else," Lonny remarked dryly. He lowered himself to sit on Samantha's other side, crossing his legs Indian-style and grinning. "How's the therapy going?" he asked her as he tugged off his T-shirt.

"Very well, actually," she reported. The hour or so she'd spent on the beach had rendered her more relaxed than she'd felt in months.

"We were just down the road a way, checking out a property in Point Pleasant," Lonny related. "When I told Jack you were here for a visit, he decided he wanted to meet you. Please accept my apologies."

Samantha chuckled. "No need to apologize for your charming colleague," she said before bestowing Jack with a winsome smile. As long as she knew he wasn't one of the eligible bachelors Lonny planned to foist upon her, she could enjoy Jack's aggressive flirting. "So Lonny talks about me all the time," she mused aloud. "What does he say, other than that I work for a cosmetics firm?"

Jack shoved back a clump of sweat-damp yellow hair with one of his large hands. "That you live in New York, that you're raking in the dough, that you went to college with him, that you love food and know all the best restaurants in Manhattan."

"Is that what you told him?" Samantha questioned Lonny.

"Is *what* what I told him?"

"That I love food. Honestly, Lonny, I wish you'd stop thinking of me as the bottomless pit."

"I never thought of you that way," Lonny defended himself. "You thought of yourself that way. But face it, Sammy, you do love food."

"Hey, don't knock food," Jack added, inspecting Samantha's prone body with relish. "Whatever you're eating, sweetheart, it's landing in the right places. How long are you planning to be in town, anyway?"

"Just as long as my therapy takes," Samantha said, shooting Lonny a sidelong glance.

He smiled hesitantly, absorbing her private joke but choosing not to respond to it. "I'm going swimming," he announced abruptly, tossing down his shirt and hoisting himself to his feet. He kicked off his sneakers and jogged down to the water.

Samantha sat up and watched Lonny test the foamy waves with his feet. Without pausing to get used to the ocean's temperature, he charged through the water until it reached his hips, then executed a dive through a curling roll of surf.

Lonny was a talented swimmer. He'd starred on the swim team at college, and Samantha and Moira used to attend most of the home meets to watch him compete. Ten years later, Samantha still marveled at his grace and strength in the water, at the lissome power of his body as he mastered the ocean's treacherous pull.

Yet his sudden decision to go swimming by himself unsettled her. She wondered whether he thought he was doing her a favor by leaving her and Jack alone, whether Jack was indeed one of the eligible bachelors Lonny wanted her to meet. If that was the case, however, he would have departed with a discreet smile and a wink. He wouldn't have just bolted for the water.

He had seemed almost angry with her. Or maybe with Jack. She couldn't guess why. Later she'd have to ask Lonny what he was up to once they were alone again. Cheering her up and helping her to recover from the breakup with Stephen was fine, but Lonny didn't have to be so mysterious about his strategy. As far as she was concerned, the "water therapy"—snoozing on the beach beneath the sun and shriveling up like a strip of bacon, if necessary—was all she wanted right now. That, and Lonny's friendship.

HE WASN'T ANGRY, really. Groping for footing beneath the churning waves, Lonny slicked back his hair and gulped in a deep breath of air. That had been stupid, running off like that, leaving Sammy alone with Jack. Stupid and rude.

He blinked the salt water from his eyes and gazed back at the beach, where his two friends were sharing a laugh about something. Samantha's slender body was clearly framed by the orange towel she'd spread beneath herself. Her skin was beginning to toast, her city pallor giving way to an attractive pink color. Her swimsuit was dark green, not flashy, calling attention to the parts of her anatomy that it covered in the most subtle fashion. Her legs looked ridiculously long, gloriously long.

He could think of no good reason that Jack's flirting should bother him. But it did. He didn't like the idea of a hunk of hormones like Jack Rogan spinning his lines to snare Samantha. Not that Lonny viewed her like a baby sister in need of his protection, not that he expected her to be a nun, not that he doubted her ability to fend off Jack if she chose to, but...damn it, she was *his* friend, Lonny's friend, his best friend. Jack had no right to be staring at the skimpy bra of her bikini that way.

Pivoting, Lonny scanned the horizon for the next breaker and dove beneath it. The water roared in his ears and tore furiously at his body, then released him with a buoyant nudge toward the surface. He shook his head clear and spun back to the shore to spy on Samantha again. How different she looked today than she had the first time he'd gone to the beach with her, nine and a half years ago. Time was supposed to wreak havoc on women, but in Samantha's case— well, she *had* been a bit plump in those days, he'd grant that, and not exactly coordinated, but he'd always considered her cute.

She wasn't cute anymore. She was nine and a half years older, and definitely not cute.

She'd been cute the February day they'd gone to Narragansett, bundled up like Eskimos, and romped on the desolate sand. It hadn't been the way he'd intended to go to the beach with her, but in retrospect, he had to admit that it had been one of the best days of his life.

Lonny had always loved the water. Growing up in Tarrytown, he had learned to swim at the country club pool, but he preferred swimming in what he called "real" water, the town's lakes, or the ocean during the two weeks every summer that his family vacationed at Cape Cod. "Real" water was water that didn't reflect the bright turquoise of a swimming pool's walls or smell of chlorine.

So he'd been delighted when Brad Hunter invited the gang to spend their spring break at his uncle's villa on Cable Beach in the Bahamas. There had been ten of them, Lonny and Brad and a few other guys from the dorm, Samantha and a few other girls, and of course Moira Davis, Lonny's beloved. They'd all had a long, tiring school term, suffering through one of New England's most brutal winters on record—to say nothing of their brutal classes—and they were more than ready for a week of nothing but sun and sand and the clearest, bluest water to be found outside a swimming pool. More important than the water would be the company, of course. Lonny's college friends were the closest friends he'd ever had. He couldn't imagine a better group of people with whom to share a beachside house.

When Moira told Lonny that Samantha wouldn't be joining them on the trip, he was appalled. "Why not?" he asked. "What's wrong with her?"

Moira shrugged and tossed back her sleek black hair. "I guess she just doesn't want to," she supposed. "I told her it was going to be a terrific time, but she said she'd pass on it. Maybe she just doesn't feel like going."

Lonny refused to believe that. He marched across campus to the dormitory where Moira and Samantha lived, took the stairs two at a time to their floor, and stormed down the hall to their room. He pounded on the door, then listened for Samantha's muffled voice through the thick wood. "Yeah? Who's there?"

"It's Lonny," he said, swinging open the door without waiting for permission to enter. He slammed the door shut behind him, glowered at the disheveled round-cheeked woman hunched over her desk, and said, "Why the hell aren't you going to Cable Beach? Everybody's going."

She threw down the yellow highlighter pen with which she'd been marking passages in a textbook and stared up at Lonny. Her dark eyes glistened, and her lips parted, but instead of answering him directly, she turned back to her book. "Everybody's *not* going, Lonny," she contradicted him. "I'm not."

"Why not?" he demanded to know.

She lifted her highlighter pen, then put it down again. "It... My father expects me to spend the vacation with him."

"Like hell he does," Lonny disputed her, unzipping his parka and sprawling across her bed. Even though he was desperately in love with Moira, he never sat on Moira's bed, let alone lay on it. On those few occasions that she deigned to make love with him, it was always in his bed, in his room, not in hers.

"Sammy," he said, "you told me your father is dating some woman and couldn't care less whether you went home or not." Samantha's father had been widowed when Samantha was twelve years old. She had told Lonny that whenever her father became involved with a woman, he tended to lose interest in his children. He worked hard, he provided for their material needs as best he could, but he didn't want to be bothered with them beyond that. Samantha had had a dreary winter vacation because her father had spent nearly the entire time with his latest flame.

"That was at Christmas," Samantha explained, her voice soft and wavering.

"You mean, he isn't dating her anymore?"

"I mean, I'm spending the spring break with him," Samantha answered more firmly. "My choice."

"No dice," Lonny argued. "I don't believe you."

Samantha didn't speak for several minutes. When she finally rotated in her chair to face him, her expression was plaintive, her eyes once again glistening. "Look, Lonny, I *can't* go to the Bahamas, okay? I'd like to, but I can't. Now, could you please remove your carcass from my room so I can finish reading this chapter? Macroeconomics waits for no man."

"Or woman," Lonny agreed, plumping Samantha's pillow and sinking his head more comfortably against it. "Tell me the truth. Why can't you go?"

"I don't want to talk about it."

"I won't tell anyone," Lonny vowed. "I won't even tell Moira. Come on, what is it? You get airsick?"

"Of course not," she answered.

"You don't like the tropics? You don't like piña coladas?"

"I've never been to the tropics," she countered. "I've never had a piña colada. Lonny, isn't it obvious? You know me better than anyone else. You know why I can't go, so let's just drop it."

His eyes opened wider. If he did know her better than anyone else did, then why didn't he know why she couldn't go to the Bahamas? He suddenly felt very inadequate. "I missed something, Sammy," he said contritely. "Spell it out for me."

"M-o-n-e-y," she obliged, then grimaced.

He paused to gauge how serious she was. "It's not going to cost that much, Sam—"

"To someone who has a lot of money, it's not going to cost much," she snapped. "To me, it's going to cost a fortune. I'm not like the rest of you, Lonny. I'm here on a scholarship, I'm working my way through school, and I haven't got money to spend on vacations in the Bahamas. Maybe a few hundred dollars isn't much money to you, but to me it's more than I can afford." Her frown deepened. "Is it asking too much of you, Lonny, to remember that not everyone came into this world with a healthy portfolio of blue-chip stocks waiting for them? To you, popping down to the Bahamas for a week is taken for granted. To me, it would mean no books for next semester, no new clothes, no movies, no plays, no ice-cream sundaes at the Ivy Room— which would probably be for the best, considering the inflated state of my rear end, but still..."

Lonny sat up straight. He knew that Samantha came from more humble origins than he. He knew that, unlike the rest of his friends, she had grown up in a working-class environment in Pittsburgh, where her father worked in a steel mill and she was assigned the role of raising her younger brothers and maintaining the house. He knew that she was in college thanks to a complicated package of scholarships and loans, and that she had to work Thursday evenings and Saturday mornings in the library to cover the cost of her textbooks and typing paper. But a week in the Bahamas— even a scholarship student deserved that much.

"I'll pay your way," he said impulsively.

Samantha's jaw went slack. She looked positively astounded. Lonny considered what he'd said and decided it was the right thing to say. He wanted her to be in the Bahamas with him. He wanted her along for the trip that much. How would he survive the week if Moira chose to jilt him for the umpteenth time and Samantha wasn't there for him to cry to?

When Samantha's silence extended beyond a minute, he repeated the offer. "I'll pay your way, Sammy. Please come."

"Be serious," Samantha said.

"I *am* being serious. I can afford it, Sammy. To each according to his needs, from each according to his ability, and all that."

"Somehow, quoting Karl Marx doesn't seem appropriate in this context," Samantha quipped. But her eyes were glistening once more, and she was unable to blink the tears away. "Lonny, I can't let you pay my way. I'm not going to take money from you."

"Why not?" he persisted.

"I'm not going to be your charity." She sighed, reached for her highlighter pen and fidgeted nervously with it. "I *can't* take money from you, Lonny. We're friends. All right? I just can't, that's all."

Lonny gazed at her. She began to cry, a muted weeping that caused everything to go soft inside him. He'd never seen Samantha cry before—and he'd never felt so personally at fault for it. How insufferably arrogant he must have sounded, offering to pay her way. Samantha had too much pride to accept his gesture; he should have realized that before he shot off his mouth. He should have thought of her feelings instead of his own.

Yet it was still unnerving to witness Samantha's vulnerability. He hadn't been aware that she suffered from feelings of inferiority when she compared herself to their affluent friends. He didn't view her background as something that made her inferior, but maybe she did. He should have been more sensitive about it.

"I tell you what, then," he said, hoping to ameliorate the situation. "If I can't get you to Cable Beach, can I get you to Narragansett Beach?"

"What?"

"Narragansett Beach," he reiterated, naming one of the public beaches on Rhode Island's south shore, a half-hour drive from the Brown campus. "How's next Sunday for you?"

"Too cold," she said, smiling slightly and sniffling. "It's February, Lonny."

"What's the matter? You aren't tough enough?"

"I'm not dumb enough. I'm not going to the beach in February."

"Yes, you are," Lonny stated. "I'll take you if I've got to carry you over my shoulder."

"You'll give yourself a hernia if you do," Samantha warned.

But she went with him to Narragansett Beach that weekend. Dressed in a sweat suit, a turtleneck under the hooded gray sweatshirt and a stocking cap on her head, Samantha allowed him to drive her to the abandoned stretch of coastline. They played catch with a football, and Samantha fumbled the ball the few times she came close to catching it. They played Frisbee, and Samantha threw the plastic disk into the icy waves, forcing Lonny to strip off his boots and socks and wade, howling and roaring curses, into the water to retrieve it. They didn't leave the beach until the frigid air had their noses red and their bones aching, and they stopped at a diner for hot chocolate on their way home.

Three weeks later, Lonny flew south to Nassau with the rest of his friends. Moira spent the week displaying her luscious body, in a collection of crocheted string bikinis, on the patio's lounge chairs, reading random volumes of *Remembrance of Things Past* and sipping rum punch from a co-

conut-shaped mug she'd found behind the bar in Brad's uncle's den. She refused to muss her hair by playing volleyball on the beach; she had no interest in snorkeling or waterskiing. She was resplendently feminine and lovely, and whenever Lonny wasn't exerting himself trying to get her into bed with him, he found himself wishing Samantha was there so he could have some fun with her, playing football and Frisbee and chasing her errant throws into the water. If Samantha were there, she'd help Lonny to knock Moira off her high horse. They'd drag the gorgeous, slender raven-haired heartbreaker onto the beach and fill her delectably shaped belly button with sand until she begged for mercy.

If Samantha had been there, Lonny would have had somebody to talk to. Instead, he'd spent the week aching for Moira and talking to himself.

They had been all so young then, Moira and Samantha eighteen, Lonny barely twenty. Now Moira was divorced, living in a luxury condominium on Chicago's North Shore and working as social director at a hotel, scheduling wedding receptions, sweet-sixteen parties and debuts in the sumptuous banquet halls. Samantha maintained a correspondence with her former roommate, and kept Lonny posted about Moira. Yet Lonny had little more than a passing curiosity about the woman for whom he'd once sworn his undying love. He never would have imagined during those hazy, windswept days on Cable Beach so long ago that his love for Moira could ebb while his affection for Samantha grew stronger.

Perhaps he could convince Samantha that her problem with Stephen would resolve itself the same way. The man would eventually vanish from her thoughts. She'd get over him. And she'd still have Lonny's friendship. The important things in life had a way of lasting.

She and Jack Rogan were engrossed in a conversation when Lonny waded out of the water and returned to them. Or at least Samantha was engrossed in the conversation. Jack had drawn his knees up toward his chest and was resting his chin in his hands, a pose carefully designed to convey that he was hanging on her every word.

"He's beginning to nod off," Lonny whispered to Samantha. "Move your butt—I need the towel."

"I'm not beginning to nod off," Jack protested.

"You should have brought your own towel," Samantha scolded Lonny, sliding the orange towel out from under her.

"This is my own towel," Lonny pointed out, running the cloth over his dripping hair. "You stole it from my own linen closet, in my own house."

"She's been telling me about life in the fast lane in New York," Jack said, proving that he'd been paying attention to Samantha's monologue. "I don't know why we're knocking ourselves out here rewiring old firetraps when we could be living the life of ease in the Big Apple. All you've got to do is say, 'Let's make red eyeliner and call it *The Morning After*,' and they pay you big money and give you your own secretary. Did you know that Sammy has her own secretary?"

"You want a secretary?" Lonny asked. "I'll give you one for Christmas."

Jack's eyes sparkled wickedly. "Can I pick out the one I want?" he asked. His naughty grin dissolved into a smile full of awe as he turned back to Samantha. "I mean it, Lonny. This lady is living one hell of a life in New York. Prestige job, prestige salary, and I'll bet you she's never smashed her fingernail with a hammer."

"Not at work, I haven't," Samantha agreed. "But when it comes to hanging pictures in my apartment, I'm a disaster."

"So hire someone to hang your pictures for you," Jack suggested. "In fact, hire me. We can make a weekend of it."

Samantha laughed and turned to Lonny. "Jack never lets up, does he?" she said with mock helplessness. "I'm glad you came to rescue me."

Whatever irritation Lonny had felt earlier dissipated completely. "Of course I'll rescue you," he played along. "I only wish I didn't feel like a ninety-eight pound weakling around Mr. Big here." Tossing down the towel, he stood and hoisted Samantha into his arms. She was lighter than he'd expected, and even though she giggled and flailed her limbs, he had no difficulty carrying her across the sand to the water's edge.

"What are you doing?" she shrieked as he sloshed into the shallow water.

"Rescuing you from Jack," he reminded her. "What do you weigh, Sammy? You feel so light."

"A smart woman never discusses her weight with anyone," Samantha responded. "I'm a smart woman."

"If you're so smart, what are you doing in the arms of someone who's about to drop you into the ocean?"

"You wouldn't dare," Samantha muttered, tightening her hands around his neck for good measure.

"Wouldn't I?"

"Lonny, we only have one towel between us," she said, her smile fading. "And you've already gotten it all wet."

"We're half a block from my house, which has many dry towels inside it," he countered. "It wouldn't kill either of us to walk half a block wet."

She felt more than light in his arms, he decided. She felt good. His right arm curved naturally around the arch of her ribs, and his left held her well-toned legs. Her torso rested against his naked chest, her skin warm and smooth next to his, and gusts of wind blew the tawny waves of her hair over his shoulder and along his chin and cheek. He was torn between the desire to hurl her unceremoniously into the water and the desire to continue holding her. He stood, his legs apart for balance, his feet firmly planted as the briny water swirled around him, and continued to cradle her body in his arms.

Her eyes searched his face, sensing that his teasing mischief had left him. "What's going on, Lonny?" she asked quietly. "What are you thinking about?"

He gazed at her and smiled his relaxed, casual smile. "I'm remembering the time the gang went to the Bahamas and you didn't come along," he told her.

She seemed startled, clearly not having expected that answer. She laughed. "If this was how you spent the week, dangling defenseless women above the water and threatening to dunk them, then I'm glad I didn't come."

"Like hell," he refuted her. "If you had come, you would have been the only woman there who wouldn't have minded getting dunked. You would have been the only one who wouldn't have minded getting her hair wet, even if it meant you wouldn't look perfectly chic at dinnertime. You would have loved getting dunked, Sammy, and then you would have turned around and dunked whoever had dunked you."

"Which probably would have been you, Richard Alonzo," she presumed. "I was never as friendly with Brad and those other guys as I was with you. Only best friends have the nerve to dunk each other."

Lonny's fingers moved over her skin, caressing the soft flesh of her underarm. He was her best friend, but he still hadn't been able to summon up the nerve to dunk her. "Sammy," he murmured tentatively.

"What?"

He pondered his words for a moment before speaking. "Remember when we went to Narragansett instead, just the two of us, in February?"

She closed her eyes and reminisced. A low laugh escaped her. "Frostbite," she recalled. "I remember being absolutely sure I'd gotten frostbite on the tip of my nose. You made me stop for cocoa on the way back to school. You told me cocoa was a surefire cure for frostbite of the nose."

"I figured if I filled you up with enough chocolate, you'd stop bitching about how if your nose fell off it would be my fault." He smiled gently. "What I remember was that we had a fantastic time together that day."

Samantha's smile reflected the tenderness in Lonny's. "Yes. We had a fantastic time."

He held her above the frothing water for an instant more, then pivoted and walked back to the sand. There he lowered her to her feet. "I'll let you off this time, kiddo," he said. "Next time I might not be so kind."

She adopted his light tone. "If you're expecting gratitude, pal, think again."

"Hey, I rescued you from Jack, didn't I? Surely you ought to be thankful for that."

"Uh-huh," she snorted. "First you led him to me, then you abandoned me to him, and then, after a refreshing swim, you got around to rescuing me. And for what? If my memory hasn't failed me, the next thing on the agenda is some god-awful blind date you've got lined up for this evening."

"You're going to like Carl," Lonny predicted.

"And if I don't?"

Smiling, Samantha turned and sauntered back to Jack, who was waiting impatiently for her to return. Lonny lingered, observing the way her feet sank into the sand with each step, forcing her hips to move back and forth in an undignified shuffle. Her arms twitched at her sides, not swinging in a natural rhythm but fighting the air to keep her body upright.

There might be a lot less of Samantha than there used to be, but she still was pretty klutzy. And Lonny loved her for it.

Chapter Three

"Artist's Eyes," said Carl.

Samantha smiled politely at the man seated next to her on one of the oversize cushions on the floor of Lonny's sparsely furnished parlor. In his mid-thirties, with short curly brown hair and a neatly trimmed mustache, Carl Dunlap was handsome in a polished, conventional way. He wore an impeccable navy blue blazer over a crisp white button-down shirt, starched khaki trousers and cordovan loafers. Although there was little physical resemblance between him and Stephen, Carl's style reminded Samantha of her former boyfriend. No question about it, Carl was her type.

That wasn't to say that she was thrilled about this double date Lonny had arranged. But she would survive it, possibly even enjoy it. At the absolute worst, she could count on a decent dinner at an elegant restaurant to salvage the evening.

She'd brought a couple of dresses to Spring Lake with her, assuming that she and Lonny would eat out once or twice during her visit. The one she had on now, a gauzy white sundress with a halter top and open back, showed off the color she'd acquired from her day at the beach. Although her skin tone was more pink than golden, the rosy glow of her slight sunburn was a vast improvement over the pallid hue she'd had when she arrived the day before.

"That's right," she said in response to Carl's conversational gambit. "They're eye cosmetics in brash, vivid colors. Originally they were intended just for teenagers, but the marketing program we developed helped to broaden their appeal. Lots of young women, even professional women, are wearing Artist's Eyes cosmetics now."

"And all thanks to you," Carl said with obvious admiration.

"Heavens, no!" She laughed. "It's an excellent product. If it weren't, nobody would buy it, no matter how clever our marketing strategy was."

"Come now," he argued good-naturedly. "How many brands of cosmetics are there? The only thing that makes a woman buy one brand over another is the advertising, don't you think?"

She conceded with a grin. "I guess so. As Charles Revson put it, 'In the factory we make cosmetics. In the store we sell hope.'"

"If you're selling hope, I'm buying," Lonny announced as he bounded down the stairs and into the parlor. He had on a pair of pleated white slacks and a madras blazer so hopelessly outdated that it actually looked chic. He had washed and combed his hair, and while it was still unfashionably long, the shaggy black fringe seemed a suitable complement to his strange jacket. Lonny definitely wasn't a polished, conventional man, but Samantha warmed instantly at his arrival.

"If you're buying what I'm selling," she teased him, "you're going to raise a lot of eyebrows."

"Raising eyebrows is one of my favorite activities. Well," he said, pulling his keys from his pocket, "if you two think you can be trusted alone for a few minutes, I'm going to pick up Marcy. When I get back, we'll move on to the restaurant."

"We'll be fine," Carl assured him, waving him toward the door.

"I didn't ask if you'd be fine. I asked if you could be trusted. Those are two distinctly different matters, Carl," Lonny contended with a chuckle. "I'll be back soon." He hurried outside, letting the screen door clap shut behind him.

An awkward silence settled over the room. Samantha rearranged her legs as demurely as she could on the cushion and smiled politely again. "Do you know Marcy?" she asked Carl.

"You could say we're neighbors," Carl replied. "Her store is across the street from my realty office."

"What kind of store does she own?"

His smile contained more than a hint of condescension. "They sell personalized T-shirts. She doesn't own it, though. She just works there."

Samantha nodded and turned her attention to her skirt, draping it more carefully over her knees. She didn't like Carl's attitude toward Lonny's date. Even if Carl owned his own real estate firm and the woman was only a salesclerk in a T-shirt shop, Marcy deserved his respect—especially since she was Lonny's companion for the evening. An almost maternal protectiveness about Lonny gripped Samantha. She resented Carl for implying that Marcy's occupation was less than acceptable. If Lonny had chosen Marcy as his date, Samantha would respect the woman, no matter what she did for a living.

"So, you know Lonny through your real estate business," she said, figuring it best to change the subject.

"I've put together some deals for him," Carl responded. "He's very gifted at what he does. He seems to be the brains of his outfit: he can walk through the paperwork of buying and reselling houses with a real flair. If he ever gets tired of physical labor, I'd be glad to put him to work in my office."

If Lonny's other partner was anything like Jack Rogan, Samantha could easily believe that Lonny was the brains of the outfit. His Ivy League diploma was only the most superficial proof of his intelligence; Samantha's long years of friendship with him had convinced her that he was blessed with a keen mind. He was a man who had made physical labor his career not out of need but out of choice.

She tried to picture Lonny as a real estate salesman, and the image made her chuckle. He would probably arrive at work in a garish madras blazer, his long hair covering the collar of his shirt, and he'd shock all but the most tolerant of clients. Then, when he took them to see a house, he'd probably scale the walls to show them the finer points of the roof's structure. No, she couldn't see him working for Carl Dunlap. His elite pedigree notwithstanding, Richard Alonzo Reed would never be suited to a high-power desk job like Carl's—or like her own.

As if he could read her mind, Carl asked, "Tell me more about your work at LaBelle Cosmetics. If these Artist's Eyes products are geared to young professional women, how come you aren't wearing them?"

Samantha shrugged. "I'm on vacation."

"Even on vacation, I should think you'd want to set an example for others. If the product is that attractive, you ought to be wearing it, shouldn't you?"

"Well, it's...it *is* pretty brash," she admitted, then grinned. "If you'd like, I'll put some on."

"Sure," Carl encouraged her. "Let me see what a pretty young professional woman looks like with Artist's Eyes."

"I'll be right back," Samantha promised, rising to her feet and moving to the stairs.

She headed for the bathroom across the hall from her room and shut herself inside. She had brought some Artist's Eyes products with her because, as Carl himself had pointed out, sometimes a product manager had to set an example.

She opened the two beret-shaped trays, one containing oil-based shadows in brilliant primary and secondary colors, the other containing black, brown, blue, green, silver and gold pats of eyeliner. Before selecting a color, she examined her reflection in the flawed mirror above the sink. In all honesty, she thought she looked much better without her eyes slathered with paint. She really didn't want to wear any of the stuff.

But what the hell. This date was a one-shot deal, and she frankly found Carl to be a bit of a snob. If he was her type, then maybe she was in danger of becoming one herself. Perhaps now was the time to counter whatever incipient snobbery might be lurking inside her.

She lifted the eye shadow applicator and traced a thin purple line on her left eyelid, extending the color beyond the outer corner of her eye. Grinning impishly, she added another thin line, this one of blue, and another of lime green. By the time she was done, she had transformed the skin between the lashes and eyebrow of her left eye into a rainbow.

"Perfect," she whispered, deciding to leave her right eye untouched. "No, not quite perfect." She rolled the bristles of the eyeliner brush into a point and deftly outlined her left eye with a narrow line of gold, which she thickened at the corner of her eye, beneath the edge of the rainbow. She batted her eye several times to make certain that the liner was dry, then chuckled. She looked utterly outlandish. But what the hell, she repeated to herself. If Lonny could wear a 1960s madras blazer, then she could wear a rainbow, complete with its requisite pot of gold.

She stowed her cosmetics in her toiletries bag and opened the bathroom door in time to hear Lonny's voice and that of a woman at the foot of the stairs. Inhaling deeply, she descended to greet them.

"Oh, wow!" Lonny hooted, taking note of the novel addition to Samantha's face. "I love it. Don't you love it, Marcy?"

The woman at his side gaped for a moment at Samantha, then smiled feebly. "How . . . interesting," she managed.

Marcy herself was beautiful. Samantha shook her head in tacit acknowledgment of Lonny's talent for courting stunningly beautiful women. Marcy's perfectly balanced features were framed by a shimmering mane of blond hair, and her figure, visible beneath a clinging cotton knit dress, curved in and out in all the right places. It was the sort of build Samantha would have sold her soul for. After years of battle with the bathroom scale, she had learned the sorry arithmetic of her own body: every pound she gained was added to her rear end and her hips, and every pound she lost was subtracted from her bustline and her face.

"Interesting is right," Carl chimed in as he joined the others at the foot of the stairs. He gawked at Samantha for a long moment, clearly disconcerted by her flamboyant makeup. "*Professional* women wear it like that?"

"You're looking at a professional woman now," Samantha reminded him.

"Well, yes, I'll vote with Marcy. It's very interesting," he said tactfully.

"My mother always told me that if you don't like something you should say it's interesting," Marcy remarked, undermining her attempt at diplomacy.

"My mother told me plenty of garbage," Lonny said. "And I made it a point not to listen to her. If you ask me, Sammy, you look spectacular. Shall we go?"

Carl suggested that they all travel in his roomy Buick, rather than dividing up and driving to the restaurant in two vehicles. Samantha was surprised that Lonny quickly agreed to the arrangement. She had assumed that he would want some more time alone with Marcy. Granted, his compact pickup wasn't the most romantic transportation in the world, but if Marcy was the sort to mind trucks, Lonny would never have asked her out in the first place.

Maybe he wanted to travel in the Buick for Samantha's sake. He knew she wasn't overjoyed about this blind date; maybe he felt he ought to stick close to her until she began to feel comfortable about it.

She was glad Lonny and Marcy were in the car with her and Carl, because it freed her of the obligation to talk. As it turned out, even if she'd wanted to talk, she would have had to fight for the chance. Marcy monopolized the conversation. "Lonny tells me you're his best friend, Samantha. I think that's so neat, having a best friend of the opposite sex. I did once—no, twice. Two of my best friends were guys, but with one, when I was seven years old he moved away and I never saw him again, and with the other, we started sleeping together and that ruined everything. I wasn't seven years old then, of course. But that's the trouble with having a best friend who's a guy—you wind up sleeping with him and bingo, there goes the friendship. You aren't sleeping with Lonny, are you, Samantha?"

"I...uh..."

"It's none of my business, of course. But I guess if you were, you wouldn't be best friends. Take my advice, Samantha, don't sleep with Lonny. Really. Going to bed with him isn't worth ruining a good friendship."

"I'm not sure," Lonny broke in with a laugh, "but I think I've just been insulted."

"I didn't mean it as an insult," Marcy swore. "All I meant was—"

"I'm sure Samantha knows what you meant, Marcy," Carl interrupted. "I'm also sure she doesn't wish to discuss her sex life with you."

Samantha didn't wish to discuss her sex life with Marcy, but more than that, she didn't want Carl behaving as if she were unable to speak for herself. Although as it turned out, she *couldn't* speak for herself. By the time she opened her mouth, Marcy was prattling on again.

"It's just that friendship is a precious thing, that's all I meant. Sex isn't so precious, if you ask me."

"I'm definitely insulted now!" Lonny yelped.

Marcy pressed ahead, ignoring him. "Now, friendship...at the moment I've got three best friends. No, make that two. I'm not talking to one of them right now. But she's a woman. They all are. So there's no way I could ruin the friendship by going to bed with them. You know what I mean?"

"You're coming across loud and clear," Carl grunted.

"Lonny says you live in New York City," Marcy continued. "It must be hard to be best friends with someone who lives in another state."

Samantha seized the opportunity to speak. "As a matter of fact, it works out quite well," she said. "That way, if we're not talking to each other, we aren't aware of it."

Marcy wasn't sure what to make of Samantha's ironic comment. She turned to Lonny for an explanation, and he did his best to smother his laughter. "We phone each other a lot," he explained.

"Is that very popular in New York, Samantha?"

"What?" she questioned. "Phoning your friends? It's all the rage."

"No, I mean what you did to your eye. That rainbow."

"Oh." Samantha had almost forgotten about her rainbow-adorned eyelid. "No, I don't think it's particularly popular. It's just something I felt like doing."

She pulled down the sun visor and studied her reflection in the vanity mirror attached to it. Her eye looked positively weird, but such weirdness seemed appropriate tonight. The mere thought of going on a blind date struck Samantha as weird. She couldn't remember the last time she'd had to make small talk with a strange man; in the years she'd been with Stephen, she hadn't had to face the difficult task of striking up a social conversation with a stranger. That was one of the things she liked about being with Stephen—no need to meet men, no need to have well-meaning friends arranging dates for her. Now that she and Stephen were apart, the ghastly process of meeting men would have to start all over again. She shuddered.

"Look," Lonny said, touching her shoulder over the back of the seat. "Out on the horizon. There's a cruise liner. Can you see it?"

Samantha didn't care much about cruise ships, and Lonny knew she didn't. But he was sensitive enough to recognize that her mind had wandered in a depressing direction, and he was doing his best to distract her. "I see it, yes," she told him before twisting in the seat to face him. She smiled in thanks.

"I'd love to take a cruise," Marcy mentioned to no one in particular. "Traveling to exotic ports, dancing and drinking champagne all night, meeting all those rich men..."

"There are plenty of rich men in Spring Lake," Carl pointed out, his tone insinuating he considered himself one of them.

"I already know them all," Marcy said glumly. Lonny laughed again.

They arrived at the restaurant. It was a seafood place, its dining room boasting a wall of glass overlooking the ocean. The table reserved for them offered a splendid view of the water, which was filled with pleasure boats returning to their moorings for the evening. In the distance, the slow-moving cruise liner was silhouetted against the pale evening sky. Sea gulls wheeled and cawed above the boardwalk, where two young men with surfboards rested after a hard day tackling the waves.

Samantha was impressed by the discretion of the maître d' and the waiter, neither of whom made any indication that they were startled by her makeup. For that matter, they didn't appear to be startled by Lonny's madras jacket, either. Samantha wondered whether he wore the jacket because, like her, he was anticipating that the evening would be weird.

They all ordered, and Carl selected a '76 Rhine from the wine list. "Seventy-six was a much better year for Rhines than seventy-five," he reported. "I'm not sure why that is, but there you have it."

Samantha contained the urge to shudder again. Stephen had been a wine connoisseur, boning up on the vintages, describing wines as "fruity" or "lively" or "unpretentious." Samantha used to wish she could trade her unpretentious wine for an unpretentious Stephen. She had always forgiven him for his pedantic lectures, naturally. But when she heard such nonsense emerging from Carl, she realized how silly it sounded.

"Just last week I took a listing on a house with a marvelous wine cellar in it," Carl continued. "The owner built it himself. Do you build wine cellars, Lonny?"

"If a client wanted one, I'm sure I could build one," Lonny answered. "But being a beer drinker myself, I'm not into wine cellars. As long as a house has a refrigerator big enough to hold two six-packs, I consider it well-equipped in the booze department."

"I love wine myself," Marcy commented. "The trouble with most refrigerators is that if you put a jug of wine in, it takes up the whole top shelf so you have no room for anything else."

"People with wine cellars don't buy wine in jugs," Carl said superciliously.

"People who don't buy wine in jugs are nerds, if you ask me," Marcy retorted.

"Nobody asked you," Carl muttered.

Samantha caught Lonny's eye and bit her lip to keep from snickering. Lonny also seemed to be fighting the urge to laugh. She wondered whether he'd deliberately arranged this double date because he'd known that Carl and Marcy would antagonize each other. Samantha decided that watching the two of them trade barbs was much more entertaining than trying to engage Carl in a serious conversation.

She would have preferred to let Marcy keep Carl occupied, but he took the arrival of the waiter with their salads as an excuse to turn his attention back to Samantha. "How did you happen to enter the field of cosmetics, anyway?" he asked her, his gaze flitting to her decorated eye. "Was it simply that you're a woman who likes to wear makeup?"

Samantha checked the impulse to tell him that she rarely wore more than lipstick and a subtle touch of shadow and mascara on her eyes. Let him think that she spent the better part of her life peering out from beneath rainbows. "It was mostly a matter of luck,'' she answered honestly. ''When I graduated from college, all I had to show for myself was a bachelor's degree in economics. So I took a job as a glorified secretary at LaBelle. It paid more than any of the other glorified-secretary jobs I was offered.''

Carl glanced at Lonny for a moment, then turned back to Samantha. ''Why did I have the impression that you've got a business degree?''

''I have an M.B.A.,'' she told him. ''I earned it at night while I was working at LaBelle.''

''How industrious,'' Carl praised her, his arrogant tone causing her to wince inwardly. She might have thought he was her type when he'd first entered Lonny's house, looking so dapper and exhibiting the sort of confidence and class she liked in a man, but after less than an hour in his company, she found him insufferably smug. Was Lonny trying to tell her something by setting her up with Carl? Was Lonny trying to convey his disapproval about the kind of men she was attracted to? She shot him a probing look, but he was staring out at the ocean and didn't notice.

''I should think it would have been easier to go straight to business school after college, and skip the glorified secretary job,'' Carl mused aloud.

''It would have been,'' Samantha concurred tartly, ''but that option wasn't available to me. I had a fortune in college loans to pay off, and even though they would have been deferred while I did graduate work, I would've had to take out even more loans to cover the business school tuition. I didn't have any wealthy relatives willing to foot the bills for me.'' She almost added that she would bet good money Carl *did* have wealthy relatives.

''I'm sure your education is worth more to you because you paid for it yourself,'' Carl deduced in a pious voice. ''You should be thankful you had the opportunity to put yourself through school. I can think of few pursuits more ennobling.''

Samantha shot Lonny another look. This time he was paying close attention to her, his eyes inscrutable as he awaited her response. She fashioned a chilly smile as she faced Carl. ''To tell the truth, Carl, it wasn't ennobling at all. It was a first class pain in the—''

''We're in mixed company,'' Lonny cut her off, once more wrestling with his laughter. ''Watch your tongue.''

''I just want the man to realize that there's nothing noble about me, including my language,'' she said, her grin widening. ''I hated having to put myself through school. It made me envious of all the kids whose parents were footing the bills. The only people who think being broke is ennobling are people who have lots of money themselves.''

''Who needs college, anyway?'' Marcy posed. ''I've dropped out of college twice, and I'm doing just fine.''

''That's a matter of opinion,'' Carl shot back.

Marcy turned her dazzling smile on Lonny and Samantha. ''Did you know Carl and I used to date? When was it, Carl, two years ago? We weren't best friends, of course.''

''Of course,'' Lonny said with a chuckle.

''You, Marcy, are the perfect argument for the value of a college education,'' Carl scoffed. ''No matter who's paying for it.''

Ignoring Carl, Marcy leaned toward Samantha. ''If you'd like,'' she confided, ''I can tell you whatever you need to know about Carl.''

''I think I already know whatever I need to know about him,'' Samantha assured her.

''He's really a nice guy,'' Marcy insisted. ''We used to argue about wine all the time, but other than that—''

''Other than that, we argued about everything else,'' Carl reminded her.

Marcy laughed. "But we had some good times, too. Carl used to take me for long drives to look at his listings. I used to design cute T-shirts for him to wear. Remember that shirt I made for you, Carl—it read: Realtors do it a LOT. Do you still have that shirt?"

Carl appeared apoplectic. He was spared from having to respond to her question by the waiter, who approached with their entrees. Samantha attempted to focus on her stuffed shrimp, but she was having too much trouble trying to suppress her laughter. Tonight was definitely weird enough to warrant the rainbow she'd painted on her eyelid.

She heard Lonny's subdued laugh and raised her eyes to him. He gave her an apologetic shrug at the way the evening was progressing, and she winked to reassure him that she wasn't at all upset by Marcy's revelation. Carl was a man who needed his feathers ruffled, and Marcy was clearly a born feather-ruffler. Their antipathy notwithstanding, Samantha thought they made a much better couple than either she and Carl or Lonny and Marcy made.

Over dinner, the conversation drifted to innocuous subjects: the damage the area beaches had suffered the previous autumn from a hurricane; the zoning battle a hotel chain was waging to build a high-rise resort in Spring Lake—Carl was, unsurprisingly, in favor of the hotel, Lonny against it, Marcy neutral—and a discussion of the prospects in the upcoming football season for the Giants and the Jets. Lonny regaled the group with a description of the college football games he, Samantha and their group of friends used to attend, and she didn't protest when he shared with Carl and Marcy the tale of the ice-cream-eating competition he and Samantha had once waged, in honor of a big win at a homecoming game, to see who could eat the most hot-fudge sundaes in a week. Lonny had paid for all of the sundaes, and Samantha had won the contest. In her college days, she'd been able to wolf down enormous quantities of junk food. Her pudgy figure had attested to that.

Now she was hard pressed to finish the generous portion of shrimp she'd been served, and when her dinner companions decided to order dessert, she declined, choosing only to sip her remaining wine while they gorged on rich pastries. No matter how bombastic Carl had been about '76 Rhines, the wine in her glass was delicious, and she considered it a satisfying conclusion to her meal.

"Why don't we take a walk on the boardwalk?" she suggested once the men were done settling the bill. "I'm stuffed—I could use a walk to work down all that food."

"All what food?" Lonny reproached her. "You hardly ate anything."

"I ate like a pig," Marcy declared boastfully. Samantha eyed the magnificently proportioned woman and pursed her lips. She'd never seen a pig with a twenty-three-inch waist before. If she did, she'd probably be moved to kick it.

The sun had set during their meal, but the sky still held a residual light when they emerged from the restaurant and crossed the street to the boardwalk. With gentlemanly propriety, Carl slipped Samantha's hand through the crook in his elbow and ushered her along the rough-hewn walkway far enough ahead of Lonny and Marcy to afford both couples some privacy. "How long were you and Marcy an item?" Samantha asked as soon as Marcy was out of earshot.

Apparently, Carl's history with Marcy was not the topic he would have chosen for their stroll. He did his best not to react negatively to Samantha's indiscreet question. "I'd hardly call us an 'item,'" he objected. "We went out once or twice. Certainly you can see how mismatched we are."

"Mismatched?" Samantha shook her head. "You're two attractive people, and the sparks fly when you're together. I bet you had some lively times with her."

"Lively," he echoed, contemplating the term. "Marcy is a twit, but, yes, I suppose she's lively."

"She isn't a twit," Samantha argued. "Lonny doesn't date twits."

"I take it you're on intimate terms with Lonny's social life?" he asked sardonically.

"Not intimate terms," Samantha granted, "but I know his taste. When we were in college—even after he graduated, and he hung around Providence for an extra couple of years while I was still in school—I was his primary social secretary. He was always asking me to set him up with my classmates. I know what he looks for in a woman. Twittiness is definitely not at the top of his list."

Carl meditated in silence for a while. "Does he know what you look for in a man?" he asked.

She cast a quick look up at Carl, then shrugged. A one-shot deal, she reminded herself, deciding that she had nothing to lose by being honest with him. "The man I was seeing for three years was a lot like you."

"Oh?" Carl appeared intrigued. "In what way?"

"Good-looking, sure of himself, ambitious in business, unfailingly polite." She ruminated for a moment. "A bit self-centered, and his sense of humor needed some fine-tuning."

Carl's mustache twitched as he worked his mouth around a suitable reply to her blunt criticism. "What makes you think my sense of humor needs fine-tuning?"

"Oh, come on. 'Realtors do it a LOT?' I think that's hilarious. You seemed horrified when Marcy mentioned the T-shirt. You ought to laugh some more," she resolved. "I wish my ex-boyfriend had a better sense of humor. He was always so damned earnest."

"Earnestness is a fine characteristic," Carl observed.

"You probably think it's noble," Samantha grumbled. She stopped walking, rotated to view the water, and grinned. Maybe she had been too earnest lately, but after seeing that trait magnified in Carl, she was determined to try not to take herself so seriously anymore. When she took herself seriously, she wound up thinking about the time she'd wasted being in love with Stephen. It was better to laugh every now and then, to paint rainbows over one's eye and say, "what the hell."

Before Carl could stop her, she shed her sandals, slid beneath the boardwalk's railing, and jumped down to the sand below. He froze in place, unsure of how to stop her, and watched as she darted to the water's edge and splashed in up to her shins.

Lonny stopped to watch her, too. In the waning light she was just a vibrant spot of white against the darkening water. But he didn't need to see her to know what she looked like: alive and ebullient, a sprite with her own personal rainbow glowing above one sparkling eye.

Something had gone wrong with this blind date, he pondered. But something had also gone very right with it. He couldn't care less about Marcy's past with Carl, although he found the idea of it kind of amusing. Someone as correct and well-bred as Carl needed a flaky run-at-the-mouth lady like Marcy to compensate for his own starchiness.

But Lonny had thought Samantha would be crazy about Carl. Not crazy enough to fall in love with him—Lonny believed her when she claimed she wasn't interested in romance so soon after her breakup with Stephen—but crazy enough to be taken by his aura of achievement. Wasn't that what Samantha revered most in Stephen, in all men? Wasn't she looking for someone like herself, someone who wanted to make good and climb into the upper-class world that had once locked her out? Wasn't that what she wanted?

If it was, then why had she painted her face so whimsically? Why was she romping in the waves, splashing water all over her expensive white dress like an intoxicated adolescent? Lonny didn't really care why. He was too transfixed by the sight to care.

It was a pretty dress, much prettier than the stodgy business outfits he usually saw her in in New York. He hadn't had a chance to tell her before Carl had arrived at his house, but he thought she looked wonderful with her back and shoulders exposed, and her collarbones. He'd never paid much attention to her collarbones before. Then again, he'd never paid much attention to the silken lines of her back, the delicate bones of her shoulders, the stalky length of her legs, the sweet radiance of her face....

A bizarre sensation crept over him, similar to the sensation he'd felt that afternoon when Jack Rogan had been drooling all over Samantha, and when Lonny had carried her off and held her in his arms above the water. The sensation was quite familiar to him, but he was unnerved by it.

He wanted Samantha. His Sammy, his buddy, his best friend. He wanted her as he'd never wanted a woman before.

"Carl looks like he's going to have a cow," Marcy said before erupting in robust laughter. "He used to hate when I did things like that."

"Things like what?" Lonny asked, dazed by his sudden discovery.

"Taking off and jumping into the water. I never did that, of course, but once, when we were driving home from some property he wanted to show me in Monmouth, I made him stop the car, and I got out and climbed a tree to pick an apple. I thought he'd have a cow then, too. He kept screaming about how I was going to get thrown in jail for stealing an apple.''

"And here you are to tell about it," Lonny said. His mind drifted to what Marcy had said earlier, about the dangers of sleeping with one's best friend. She was right. She might be flaky, but she had a functioning brain. He couldn't have Samantha, not the way he wanted her. He ought to kill the notion right now.

"I think he likes her," Marcy said, referring to Carl.

"I think he still likes you," Lonny countered.

Marcy mulled over that possibility and shrugged. "You'd never get him to admit to it. He wouldn't even admit to it when we were seeing each other. He took me to this real estate brokers' convention once, and at the banquet he introduced me to everybody there as his secretary.''

"The creep," Lonny snorted. "I hope you told him off."

"I did better than that," Marcy bragged. "I dumped my glass of wine over his head. He had a conniption. He complained it was lousy wine, and he couldn't bear the thought of bringing his suit to the cleaners reeking of such a lousy wine.''

Lonny laughed. "If he really liked her," he said with a nod in Samantha's direction, "he'd be chasing her across the sand right now." Simply verbalizing the thought gave it an appealing resonance, and in a trice Lonny sprang over the railing, landing with feline grace on his feet, and raced toward Samantha. He paused just inches from the water's edge.

By the time he reached her, she had stopped splashing and was simply standing ankle-deep in the water, gazing out at the horizon. She turned at his approach, smiled mysteriously, and then directed her gaze back to the water again.

"Looking for the cruise liner?" he asked.

"I don't know what I'm looking for," she confessed.

Me, he pleaded silently, then scowled. *Bad idea. It won't work.* "Is this sort of behavior acceptable for product managers at LaBelle Cosmetics?" he inquired.

"Is wearing rainbows over your eye acceptable for product managers at LaBelle Cosmetics?" she returned. "Lonny, the important question is, is Carl Dunlap really my type?"

"I thought you'd like him," Lonny said. "He reminds me a lot of Stephen."

"I don't like Stephen," she pointed out.

"But you wouldn't mind finding a suitable replacement for him."

"I never said that," she protested, then grinned. "This water is freezing."

"Then come out," he advised her.

She picked her way onto the sand. Lonny's gaze fell to her feet, which were now caked with white sand. They were small feet, he noticed. Small, and incredibly dainty. He sucked in his breath and raised his eyes to her face. "Did I tell you you look beautiful tonight?" he said. It wasn't what he wanted to say, but he couldn't seem to help himself. Not when her eyes were so wide, their color so deep and dark above her sculpted cheeks. Not when her long, honey-colored hair was blowing wild and free in the evening breeze.

"I don't think so," she said lightly. "So go ahead, tell me. I love to hear it."

"You look beautiful," he complied.

"Thanks. You look absolutely ridiculous in that jacket. Where on earth did you get it?"

"I found it in a thrift shop," he told her. "Five dollars. I couldn't resist."

"I like this water therapy," she remarked. "I think I'm beginning to feel the effects."

Oh, God, so am I, Lonny muttered beneath his breath. He tore his eyes from her face, and they settled on the rise of her breasts, two soft, round swells shaping the bodice of her dress. He knew that she couldn't be wearing a bra in a backless dress, and the understanding rocked him. Sammy, his buddy, his good old pal, had breasts. "I think we'd better go back," he said quietly, the strain audible in his voice.

"I guess I ought to thank you for setting up this date," Samantha said as she willingly followed Lonny back up the beach to the boardwalk. "Something tells me Carl isn't going to thank you at all."

"I've made Carl plenty of money," Lonny commented. "He thanks me constantly."

"But he won't thank you for tonight."

"Who cares?"

Carl and Marcy were waiting together by the railing. Lonny gripped Samantha's waist to boost her up. As he heaved her upward, Carl grabbed her hands. She placed her feet on the wood and wiggled under the railing. "I'll crawl around and meet you on the other side," Lonny said before disappearing into the narrow crawl space beneath the boardwalk. Within a few seconds he reappeared, standing in the tall grass on the street side of the boardwalk.

Carl was mute as they crossed the road to the car. Marcy more than made up for him, rambling at length about the forces of wine and about how full moons brought out the lunacy in people. Lonny casually mentioned that the moon hadn't risen yet, and even if it had, a full moon was two weeks off. Marcy wasn't fazed by this news. "I figure, if a full moon can make people fully insane, then a half-moon can make them half-insane. So, on only one night a month can you count on everybody to be sane."

"Oh? Maybe a new moon makes people newly insane," Lonny proposed.

"Gee, I never thought of that," Marcy exclaimed. "You may be onto something, Lonny. Newly insane, huh? I'll have to rework my whole theory."

When they neared Lonny's house, Carl offered to drive Marcy home. There wasn't any question of his wanting to spend more time with Samantha, at least not then. Lonny supposed that if Carl liked Samantha, as Marcy seemed to think he did, he could always invite her out for another evening, just the two of them. He doubted that Samantha would accept such an invitation, however, and that thought pleased him.

No. A bad idea. He'd invited her to Spring Lake to help her recuperate, not to complicate her life further. To do anything to jeopardize their friendship would be incredibly stupid, and he loved her too much to follow through on his half-moon, half-insane desire for her.

He loved Samantha. That alone was all the reason he needed to keep himself from doing anything as foolish as *loving* her.

Chapter Four

Lonny eased open his window, unlatched the screen and climbed out onto the deck. One of these days he'd have to construct a proper door to the deck, but he hadn't yet decided which room to put it in. Probably the room Samantha was sleeping in. He'd like to have a door from his own bedroom to the deck, but that would require visitors to traipse through the master bedroom to use the deck, and he didn't want that.

Maybe he'd build two doors. Or maybe he'd simply continue to use the window. He took a perverse pleasure in climbing through the window—it made him feel like a cat burglar.

He'd donned his jeans and a plaid cotton shirt before climbing outside, but he didn't bother to button the shirt. Instead, he rolled up the sleeves and let the brisk shore breeze wash over his chest and forearms as he tiptoed to the railing and surveyed the sky. The moon hung low over the roofs of the houses to the south. It was a few days more than half-full, which, he decided, gave him license to be slightly more than half-insane. A faint summer haze reduced its silver brilliance, giving it a surreal soft focus.

It wasn't quite midnight, but the town was still. No traffic moved on Ocean Avenue; no pedestrians promenaded along the boardwalk. In Seaside Heights, where he used to rent an apartment, the boardwalk would be swarming even at this late hour, the arcades aglow with neon lights and the raucous noise of rock music and video games roiling the atmosphere. Seaside Heights had been a fun place to live for a few years, but Lonny preferred the serenity of Spring Lake. Maybe it was sign of his maturity that he was happy to trade the hurly-burly of Seaside Heights' nightlife for the tranquillity of Spring Lake, where the only sound to break the dark silence was the constant whisper of the ocean.

Water therapy was what Samantha needed, not sexual therapy. Lonny would be wise to remember that.

She'd sworn she wasn't angry with him for fixing her up with Carl Dunlap; she'd sworn that she found the evening "edifying." Yet less than half an hour after Carl had driven off with Marcy, Samantha had announced that she wanted to call it a night. She'd shut herself up in the bathroom, emerged a few minutes later without the cosmetic rainbow above her eye, wished Lonny a good-night and vanished into her room.

Had she been able to guess what was on his mind? Had she fled to her room to avoid him, or to give him a chance to set himself straight again? Was she angry with him, not for the blind date but for some other reason? Was she afraid that he was about to upset the balance of their friendship?

He wouldn't do that. He promised to himself that he wouldn't. Watching television in his room, thumbing listlessly through three issues of *Newsweek*, lying in bed and staring at the ceiling hadn't done much to distract him from his erotic thoughts of Samantha, but a few minutes alone in the cool night air would probably do the trick.

It was funny how a man's glands could play games with him. Not his glands, Lonny amended. His brain. He didn't lust after Samantha. He didn't crave her. His desire for her was born of love, a love so deep he'd practically taken it for granted.

She wasn't like the women he usually wanted. Lowering himself to sit on the floor of the deck, he rested his back against one of the upright posts supporting the railing and enumerated the differences between Samantha and all the other women he'd been attracted to. For one thing, she wasn't pretty. Sure, she was beautiful, but she wasn't cover-girl pretty like Marcy, or like Moira Davis, or like—what was the name of that russet-haired knockout Samantha had set him up with after he'd given up on Moira? Elizabeth? Lisbeth, that was it. Lisbeth Something-or-other, from Shaker Heights and the Taft School. Strange that he could remember her pedigree, but he couldn't remember her name.

It wasn't that he was attracted only to women with up-bringings like his. Far from it. If he were all that enamored of the trappings of wealth, he wouldn't be forging a career in building renovation. Instead, he'd be living in a glamorous house like his parents', and working at a job like his father's—or possibly working for his father, bucking for partner in the law offices of Reed, Jackson, Tuttle—and dating women who would eventually resemble his mother, attractive, well-bred women who worked in chic boutiques or antique shops by day and attended country club dances by night.

He had turned his back on that sort of status-conscious existence years ago. He loved his parents, and they loved him enough to forgive him for having rejected law school in favor of what they called his "bum's life." But, after having viewed their high-pressure, achievement-oriented life at close hand, he'd deliberately chosen not to emulate it.

Samantha, on the other hand, strove for that kind of success. A year and a half ago, when she'd been promoted to product manager and telephoned Lonny with her good news, he'd given her a stern lecture about Type A personalities, the importance of establishing one's priorities to place inner peace ahead of financial gain, the peril of worshipping the Golden Calf. To which she'd responded, with complete justification, "You've had a chance to reject wealth. I haven't. Get off your high horse, Lonny, and let me have my chance."

All right. She wasn't as pretty as Marcy, and her values differed from his when it came to careers and money. Lonny gave those two facts sober consideration, then discarded them. They didn't make him want Samantha any less.

She probably didn't want him. Now there was a good reason to forget about pursuing anything romantic with her. Just as Lonny had never made a secret of his negative opinion of her professional drive, so she'd let him know that, like his parents, she viewed him as something of a derelict. "You've had all the advantages people like me dream about," she often reproached him. "And you've thrown them all away. I'm happy that you're happy, Lonny, but don't expect my approval."

She didn't approve of him. She undoubtedly believed that the only men worthy of her approval were men like Stephen, men who were properly groomed and upwardly mobile, the antithesis of Lonny. If Lonny wanted to be Samantha's lover, all he had to do was remember what her previous lover was like. If she had honestly loved a martini drinker like Stephen, then the chances were pitifully slim that she could give her heart to a straight-from-the-bottle beer guzzler like Lonny.

"How's the weather out there?" a woman's voice called out to him.

He flinched and turned to the house. Samantha stood at one of the open windows of her room, dressed in a flowered cotton nightgown with white lace shoulder straps and trim. In the diffuse light from the moon, he could barely decipher her features, but her body was silhouetted enticingly beneath the loose fabric, and her hair billowed around her shoulders like a cape.

"Did I wake you up?" he asked contritely. He'd been certain that she was asleep hours ago.

She shook her head. "I've got a terminal case of insomnia. Can I come out?"

"Sure."

He rose, crossed to the window and unfastened the screen for her. Then he took her hand and helped her over the sill. She had to bunch the hem of her nightgown up to her knees to climb out, and even at that, her foot caught on the ledge. Only Lonny's steadying grip on her kept her from falling. "You made window-hopping look easy when you did it yesterday," she complained good-naturedly, sliding her arms free of his hands and letting the gown's lace edge drop down to her ankles again. "Is coordination inborn, or can it be learned?"

"It can be learned, but you have to start young. I learned it by spending the better part of my youth attending dance classes. I despised them, but look at me now."

"Able to leap tall buildings in a single bound," Samantha joked. She drifted to the railing and sat, drawing her knees to her chin beneath her gown and patting the floor beside her for Lonny to join her. "Okay, Superman," she said. "Tell me why you're still awake."

He stared at her for a long moment. The wind swept her hair back from her face. He could see it clearly now, her wide-set eyes, her broad nose, her endearingly lopsided smile. Not cover-girl pretty, but beautiful, the most beautiful woman he could imagine.

Even though he hated to keep secrets from her, he couldn't tell her why he was still awake. He couldn't tell her what thoughts had kept him restless for half the night. Not now, not yet. "You go first," he invited her, moving to the railing and settling himself on the floor next to her. "Why are you suffering from terminal insomnia?"

She combed her fingers through her hair, tucking it behind her ears, and smiled. "I've been wondering about whether Carl might still be at Marcy's house tonight."

Lonny's eyes widened as he assessed her. "Are you jealous?"

"Heavens, no," she answered. "I think they make a terrific couple."

"And you think you and he make a dreadful couple?" Lonny hazarded.

"What do you think?" she posed. "You tried to set me up with him, after all."

"You told me you weren't angry with me for arranging the date," he reminded her.

"I'm not angry. Just curious. Why him, Lonny? Why did you link me up with him?"

Lonny analyzed her light tone and concluded that there was no rancor in it. "Well, I didn't present him to you as a potential husband. I didn't expect you to go bonkers at the mere sight of him. On the other hand..."

"On the other hand, you *did* think he was my type," said Samantha.

He again paused to analyze her tone. She wasn't angry, but she seemed more than simply curious. "He's a go-getter in the business world. Rich and accomplished, and that whole trip. Isn't that what you want in a man?"

This time Samantha took her time before responding. She twirled a stray lock of hair around her index finger, studied it intently, then let it drop to her shoulder. She turned to

Lonny. "You've never tried to fix me up with anyone before."

Her remark surprised him. She sounded almost accusing. "When would I have had the opportunity?" he asked.

She smiled wistfully. "In college, maybe?"

"You already knew all my friends in college, and they knew you. You didn't need me as a go-between if you wanted to get together with Brad or Phillip or any of the others."

"No, I don't suppose I did." She exhaled. "If they had wanted to ask me out, they would have. I guess they weren't interested in me that way."

He tried frantically to interpret what she had said, searching for the underlying message she was trying to communicate. "Were you interested in them, Sammy? I never knew. If you had told me, I would have done whatever I could to turn them on to you. I mean that."

She chuckled and shook her head. "No, I wasn't interested in them. If you want to know the truth—" She turned away, apparently unable to look at him when she revealed, "*You* were the one I was interested in."

"Me? You were interested in me?" He nearly laughed, and he nearly moaned. If there hadn't been a half-moon in the sky, the bombshell Samantha had just dropped would have made him half-insane. "Sammy," he reproached her, utterly astonished that he could have known her so long, and so well, and yet never have known this about her, "why didn't you ever say so?"

"What could I have said? You were interested in Moira, and then in Tracy Aldridge—"

"Who?"

"Tracy Aldridge," Samantha repeated, her eyes twinkling with amusement. "Don't you remember? The belle of

Beaufort, North Carolina. She had a drawl that made Scarlett O'Hara sound like she came from The Bronx.''

He entertained a vague recollection of a Southern beauty from Samantha's dorm, someone very tall and thin, and hot to trot. "Oh, her," he said with a laugh as his memory clarified her. "The nympho."

"That's the one," Samantha confirmed.

"She was very good-looking," he recalled.

"They all were," Samantha said with just a touch of acid in her voice. "And I was a porker, without any class. Why should I have told you I was interested in you?"

"Oh, Samantha..." He sighed and arched his arm around her shoulders, cuddling her to him. Seducing her was the farthest thing from his mind as he urged her body closer to his. All he wanted was to comfort her, and to seek her forgiveness for his having unwittingly hurt her in college. If only she had told him, if only she had let him know how she felt...

No. She was absolutely right. He hadn't been interested in her in college, not that way. If she had told him, it only would have made him feel guilty, and it would have spoiled their friendship.

Except that now he wondered how close that friendship could have been, if she had been concealing something so important from him. He all but forgot about his desire for her. What mattered most right now was repairing their past. "You had more class than any of those other women," he remarked.

Samantha nestled her head against his shoulder and chuckled again. "I also had more flab."

"I never noticed."

"Of course you noticed," she argued calmly. "Lonny, if you put all the women you've ever dated on a stage in Atlantic City, it could pass for the Miss America Pageant. I was just Sammy, your pal, your handy-dandy matchmaker with hips as wide as the Sargasso Sea.''

"Why do you talk that way?" he asked somberly. "Why do you put yourself down?"

"I don't put myself down now," she claimed. "I know I look good these days. Back then—" she snorted "—back then it was the truth. I was a clunk, and you only thought of me as a friend. I made fun of myself so it wouldn't hurt so much."

"Oh, Sammy, Sammy." His hand slid beneath her hair and moved soothingly over her naked upper arm. He remained silent for a while, simply stroking her and meditating. "Should I say I'm sorry?"

"No," she assured him. "None of your grand affairs lasted very long, Lonny. You're much more fun as a friend. Besides," she added, twisting to peer up at him, "look how different we are. Talk about bad matches! Marcy and Carl are like twins compared to you and me."

Her eyes were round, filled with humor. And her smile was so unexpectedly bewitching that it almost took his breath away. The hell with patching up the past, he mused, his pulse accelerating slightly. He *did* want her. The way she was talking, it might be too late for him to become her lover. He might be a victim of the world's worst case of bad timing.

If she had been dishonest in their friendship ten years ago, he was being no less dishonest not to share his feelings with her now. He groped for a way to tell her, a way that would sound as sedate and unthreatening as her revelation had been. The only words that sprang to his mind were *I want you.* She was used to bluntness from him, but still... Better not to speak at all, he resolved, slipping his fingers up her arm to her chin, cupping his hand beneath her face and drawing her to him.

His lips brushed gently over hers, and she gasped. "Lonny—"

If he gave her a chance to talk, she might tell him to stop. So he pressed his mouth to hers again, more firmly this time, and tightened his grip on her chin to hold her steady.

Her fingers curled around his wrist, as if to pull his hand away. But his persistence began to affect her, and before long he felt her lips moving beneath his, softening, welcoming him. He dared to let his tongue explore the fullness of her lower lip and she sighed shakily. "What are you doing, Lonny?" she asked in a hoarse whisper.

"Kissing you."

"No kidding," she murmured, her fingers trailing across his palm, easing his hand from her face.

He wove his fingers through hers, guiding her hand safely to his lap, and used his other arm to pull her closer to himself. "Are you going to stop me?" he asked, his lips continuing to wander over hers as he spoke.

"Do you want me to?"

"No."

"Then I won't," she said, the words melting into another throaty sigh.

His tongue ventured deeper, touching hers almost shyly. She seemed to blossom around him, against him, her body shifting to fit more snugly against his, her free hand rising to touch his chest. She had touched his chest before, while poking him in humor, or shoving him off her bed, or...at some time, he was certain, she must have touched him. But never before had she touched him as a woman touching a man. Never before had she molded her palm to his naked skin, tracing his sinuous muscles with her fingertips, caressing the hard frame of his lower ribs, using her femininity to draw out his deepest, most physical responses.

"I want you," he said. Blunt, tactless, but true. His hand arched over her shoulder, skimming forward, approaching her breast. "Sammy, I want you."

"So it seems."

He drew back, nonplussed. His hand fell away, and he struggled for breath. "*So it seems?* What do you mean, *so it seems*? What kind of thing is that to say?"

She blinked, fighting to regain her composure. "What should I have said?" she asked.

"You should have said you want me, too."

Her gaze met his, and she laughed softly. He tried to look wounded, but he couldn't resist the sweet music of her laughter. He succumbed to a grudging smile. "What is this?" he asked. "Revenge? I was a blind, dense idiot in college, and now you're going to get back at me?"

"No, of course not," she said. "Of course I want you, too, Lonny. I don't..." Her laughter faded as her gaze dropped to his chest, which was still rising and falling erratically as he tried to control his breathing. "I don't respond to men I don't want," she finished faintly. Her voice emerged stronger when she added, "Maybe... maybe we ought to be rational here."

"I detest being rational," Lonny complained.

"Oh, Lonny, don't you see?" She was no longer smiling. "So many things could go wrong if we followed through on this. Marcy was right. We could ruin our friendship."

"Nothing could ruin our friendship," Lonny asserted.

"What if we didn't enjoy it? What if we felt awful afterward? What if—" She bit her lip to check herself and turned to stare out at the water.

Lonny wished he could read her mind. Obviously he wasn't much of a mindreader when it came to Samantha. He hadn't been able to read her mind ten years ago; how could he expect to know what she was thinking now?

Her back was to him. He stroked her hair. "What if what?"

"Nothing," she said curtly. When she turned to him again, he saw that her eyes were glistening with tears. "Good night, Lonny," she mumbled, rising to her feet and hurrying across the deck to the window.

He made no move to assist her as she hiked up her nightgown and climbed through the window. She wished she could have made a more graceful exit, but grace had never been one of her strong points. At least she managed to stumble back into her room without breaking her neck.

What if she fell in love with him?

She sat on the edge of the mattress in the dark room and hugged her arms around herself. Glancing out the window, she could see him, still seated by the railing, gazing off into the distance. She turned away.

She hadn't intended to confess her schoolgirl crush to him. Her mind had been occupied by far more immediate concerns when she'd called to him through her open window. She'd been lying awake for hours, thinking about the similarities between Carl Dunlap and Stephen, and wondering why she'd grown so impatient with Carl when she'd managed to convince herself that she loved Stephen for nearly four years. She'd been trying to decide whether she had changed, or whether she'd disliked Carl because she was still furious with Stephen or still in love with him. She wasn't good at baring her soul, not even to Lonny, but she'd hoped she could discuss the possibilities and get some useful feedback from him.

She hadn't expected to blurt out that once upon a time she'd been infatuated with him.

And she certainly hadn't expected him to tell her he wanted her.

It wouldn't have been so bad if she didn't find him so damnably attractive, if his kiss hadn't flooded her with such a searing warmth, if she hadn't suddenly found herself wanting him ten times as much as he wanted her. If he'd just kissed her cheek, if she'd felt nothing when he stroked her arm, if his shirt had been buttoned, if he hadn't said, "I want you, Sammy," if, if, if . . .

Her body still seethed with feverish expectation. Lying down and shutting her eyes didn't help. She relived the sensation of his hand journeying toward her breast and imagined what it would have felt like if it had reached its goal. She imagined what his lips would have felt like on her flesh, what his lean, lithe body would have felt like against her.

A low groan escaped her, and she rolled onto her side and punched her pillow in frustration. She could never make love with Lonny, because she couldn't make love with a man unless she was *in* love with him. She loved Lonny, yes, but she wasn't *in* love with him. And if she fell in love with him, and he didn't love her in the same way, she'd be devastated.

Or perhaps he'd fall madly in love with her, and then fall madly out of love with her. That was his habit with women; he himself boasted of being an expert at it. If he fell madly out of love with her, she'd wind up hating him forever.

She couldn't chance it. Even the tender passion his kiss had promised couldn't make her take a chance on destroying their friendship. They would simply have to be rational about the situation, no matter how much Lonny detested rationality. They would have to be rational and forget about following through on what they'd unthinkingly begun.

Samantha left her bedroom with some trepidation the following morning. It was only eight o'clock, too early for Lonny to have departed for work, and she dreaded the awkwardness she anticipated when she and he came face-to-face. Although she planned to spend the day at the beach, she took the precaution of dressing in a pair of white jeans and a blousy orange jersey before descending to the first floor. She didn't want Lonny to have to see her in her nightgown or in her bikini.

She could hear him in the kitchen, singing an old James Taylor song that had been popular during their college years. "'Whenever I see your smiling face, I have to smile myself, because I love you...'" his voice filtered out to her. It was a bouncy, happy song, one of her favorites. She wondered if Lonny remembered that she was a James Taylor fan, and that for her twentieth birthday he had bought her the album that contained that song.

"Good morning," she said, interrupting his singing as she entered the kitchen.

Lonny spun around from the stove where he was fussing over a pan of scrambled eggs and greeted her with a hesitant smile. He examined her face for a hint of her mood, then returned her greeting. "Good morning. How'd you sleep?"

"Poorly," she told him. "How about you?"

"Not a wink." His smile expanded. "Any chance you want to rethink this rationality stuff?"

His good humor caused her to smile as well. Bless him for being able to make light of what could have been an uncomfortable situation. Looking at him in his snug-fitting dungarees and a brown T-shirt that hugged his limber chest, she definitely did want to rethink whether she wanted to be rational and spurn the advances of such an appealing man. But her common sense won out, and she shook her head. "I think I did the right thing last night."

He peered past her, then shrugged. "At least I don't see your suitcase all packed up by the front door," he said. "You still want to spend the week under my roof."

"Only if I'm welcome."

"You're very, very welcome." He pointed to a chair by the table. "Have a seat, Sammy, and I'll scramble up some eggs for you."

"No, thanks," she declined, walking to the refrigerator and pulling out a pitcher of orange juice. "I'll just have some juice and coffee."

He stared at her as she poured herself a glass of juice and returned the pitcher to the refrigerator. "Have I made you lose your appetite?" he asked, concerned.

"No," she assured him. "I never eat much in the morning."

"No wonder you're wasting away to nothing," he commented. "You should always eat a good breakfast. It helps you stay awake and alert when you march off to confront the day."

"Confront what day?" she countered. "The only thing I'm planning to confront today is the beach."

He emptied the contents of the pan onto a plate for himself and carried it to the table. "Wouldn't you rather confront Point Pleasant?"

"What's in Point Pleasant?" she asked.

"The house Jack and I looked at yesterday. I thought you might like to see it."

Samantha eyed him curiously. "Why might I like to see it?"

"To give you an idea of what I do for a living. I want to go back and have another look at it today, and I'd love your company."

That he could resume their normal friendship so easily, despite what had happened the night before, cheered Samantha immensely. Besides, she was interested in learning more about Lonny's work. He'd seen her in her professional milieu dozens of times on his trips to New York, but the closest Samantha had ever come to seeing Lonny at work had been when she watched him prowling about his roof two days ago. "All right," she said. "I'll go to Point Pleasant with you."

As soon as they were done with breakfast, they climbed into Lonny's pickup and headed for the beach town some ten miles to the south. The houses were smaller there than in Spring Lake, and the main roads were suffering from the blight of overdevelopment. The house Lonny drove to was actually a bedraggled bungalow. Even from the cab of the truck, Samantha could see that its walls hadn't been painted in ages, and that its front porch listed dangerously to starboard. "It's a wreck," she pronounced.

"Be it ever so humble," Lonny concurred, swinging his door open and leaving the truck. He strode directly to the front walk, not bothering to open Samantha's door for her. A good sign, she decided. If he'd done something so uncharacteristically chivalrous, she'd worry that he wasn't thinking of her strictly as a pal.

She slid off the truck's high seat and jogged up the crumbling walk, catching up with him on the porch. "Can you salvage a house this far gone?" she asked as she approached one of the cracked front windows and peered through its lacy curtain of spiderwebs into the gloomy front room. "Who lives here?"

"Nobody at the moment. It's owned by a widow who's living near her kids in Virginia. She held on to the house, thinking the kids might want it as a vacation home, but they don't. Now she's desperate to sell it."

"If I owned this shack, I'd be desperate to sell it, too," Samantha muttered, wandering to another window and snooping through the glass. "It's a mess."

"Which means my partners and I can easily afford it," Lonny explained. "I know it doesn't look like much, but it's only five blocks from the beach. With a little work, we'll be able to turn it over for a hundred-percent profit."

It had never occurred to Samantha that a such a huge profit could be made from a single house. She figured that Lonny earned enough to live on, even enough to be able to own the Victorian in Spring Lake himself. But to hear him speaking like a shrewd businessman disarmed her. She backed away from the window to assess him. "Quite a lucrative enterprise you're in," she said wryly. "One-hundred-percent returns on your investments is pretty impressive."

"We don't get that kind of return on everything we buy," he remarked. "And of course, that doesn't account for the value of our labor. Hey, look out!" he shouted just before Samantha took another step backward and tumbled off the porch.

She landed on her rear end in the unmown grass. Staring up at the porch, she noticed that a few sections of the railing had fallen off. She had thought she'd been backing up to one of the sturdier sections. Obviously she hadn't.

"Are you all right?" Lonny asked, sprinting off the porch with his customary grace and kneeling down beside Samantha.

"Physically, I'm intact," she replied grimly. "Psychologically, I'm not so sure. If these pants got grass stains on them, I'll scream."

Laughing, Lonny rose, grasped Samantha's hands, and hoisted her to her feet. Then he turned her around to examine the seat of her pants. He gave her bottom a few energetic swats to dust it off. "No grass stains," he reported. "Just a little dirt. Nothing that some water therapy in a washing machine can't handle."

Samantha grunted h

"To someone as unsteady on her feet as you are, it *would* be hazardous," Lonny mocked her. She spun around, brandishing her fists, but he easily caught her wrists and pinned her arms to her sides. "Fixing old houses isn't for klutzes," he noted, grinning wickedly. "But I wouldn't worry about it if I were you. As long as you can manage to plant your butt in the chair behind your desk at LaBelle without killing yourself in the process, you're probably in the right line of work."

She scowled at his playful laughter. "In my next incarnation, remind me to take dancing lessons at an early age," she grumbled. Mustering what little dignity she had left, she marched around the house and pretended to be engrossed in the peeling shingles of the rear wall.

Lonny thoughtfully gave her a few minutes of solitude to compose herself. When he finally joined her at the back of the house, he'd regained his business demeanor. "When we consider a house like this for purchase, we make a distinction between cosmetic problems and structural problems. Now, these shingles are flaking, but under the paint they're in good shape. Parts of the porch railing are gone, but the porch itself—"

"Is at a forty-five degree angle to the ground."

"More like ten degrees," Lonny corrected her. "A relatively simple repair. The foundation is solid. The walls have integrity."

"Integrity? I wouldn't trust them with my money," she laughed.

Lonny remained straight-faced. "I would. In fact, I will. We'll have Carl bid on the house for us. I think we'll be able to buy it for next to nothing."

"_____" Samantha snorted. Deone to wax poetic about the joy of hammering nails into wood, but it was nonetheless reassuring to hear him discuss his work in the most pragmatic terms. She knew he wasn't going to become a millionaire by buying hovels like this bungalow and repainting the shingles, but at least he was practical enough to seek profitable properties to buy. He might not be interested in becoming wealthy, but he had the good sense not to lose money at what he did.

She contemplated his serious attitude as he pointed out some of the bungalow's virtues to her, and some of its drawbacks. He hadn't brought her to Point Pleasant only because he wanted her company, she recognized. He seemed exceedingly eager to teach her about his profession. Although he often discussed a particular job with her during their telephone conversations, he'd never gone into such detail with her regarding his work before, and he'd never made such a point of explaining its financial aspects.

She was impressed, yes, but also bewildered about why Lonny was trying so hard to impress her. "Is today's ture over?" she asked as he escorted her to the front of the house once more.

He measured her wry tone and shrugged. "I'm sorry if I lectured. I thought you might be interested in what I do."

"I *am* interested," she swore. "I'm interested in everything you do, Lonny."

"But...?"

"But... well, it seems like you've got a viable business going here, and you can obviously support yourself in the style to which you've grown accustomed—"

"Crude though it may be," he added with a chuckle.

"It's just... very different from what I'm used to," Samantha concluded as she let herself back into the truck. "I can't shake the notion that if a person can wear jeans to work, he can't *really* be doing work."

Lonny laughed and started the engine. They cruised down the street toward Point Pleasant's town beach. "You must be starving," he guessed. "If you're open to temptation, I think there's a store on this boardwalk that sells frozen custard cones that are half chocolate, half vanilla."

"If they keep the vanilla half to themselves, I might be tempted," said Samantha. No matter how hard she tried to watch her diet, the mention of a chocolate ice-cream cone was enough to wreak havoc with her willpower. If it were considered at all proper to eat devil's food cake for breakfast, she was sure she'd be the most enthusiastic breakfast eater in the world.

Lonny parked in a municipal lot and they strode up the ramp to the boardwalk. It was cluttered with souvenir shops, eateries, skee-ball parlors, video arcades, and booths where one could test one's skill at throwing balls through hoops or shooting at moving targets with air guns. Interspersed among the shops were tiny amusement areas filled with merry-go-rounds, bumper cars, roller coasters, and more hair-raising rides.

Wide-eyed, Samantha surveyed the panoply of diversions and the throngs of people surging along the boardwalk. It was a far cry from the tranquillity of Spring Lake.

A rowdy group of young teenagers emerged from a pizza parlor, one of them carrying a portable stereo blaring loud rock music. As they clamored around Samantha, she momentarily lost sight of Lonny. As soon as the youngsters had passed her, she raced to his side and clung to his hand. "This place is a circus," she said.

His hand tightened around hers. "Don't worry, I'm not going to lose you," he promised, leading her along the boardwalk to the ice-cream shop he had in mind. He paused at a shooting gallery next door. "Do you want me to win you a big stuffed animal?" he asked, inspecting the tiers of prizes above the cardboard bears that slid mechanically back and forth across the counter from the air guns.

"No, thanks," Samantha replied. The huge pink and purple monkeys lining the shelves didn't excite her. She'd much prefer a chocolate cone.

Lonny noticed where her attention lay and he dutifully bought her a large cone. They ambled along the boardwalk, munching on their ice cream and chuckling at some of the ridiculous souvenirs for sale: oversize sunglasses, sweatshirts with risqué slogans on them, slimy plastic spiders and lizards. "How about it?" Lonny asked, drawing to a halt before one of the souvenir shops and lifting a white sailor hat with Point Pleasant, New Jersey printed across it in bright red. "This would look perfect with some of your snooty little city dresses, don't you think?"

He plopped the hat on Samantha's head, and she checked her reflection in the mirror next to the hat stand. "I don't know," she demurred. "Do you think it's me?"

"It's as much you as that rainbow you painted over your eye yesterday," Lonny answered.

Samantha adjusted the angle of the hat and grinned. "In that case, we'd better buy it," she resolved.

Lonny handed the clerk a few dollars, slipped Samantha's hand through his elbow, and led her out of the store. "What else can I treat you to?" he asked. "A spin on the merry-go-round?"

"Just strolling is nice," Samantha declared. "Let's keep walking."

"That sounds like a wonderful idea," Lonny readily agreed, tucking her hand more firmly against his arm and adopting a leisurely pace. The wind blew his dark hair into a disheveled mess, and he didn't bother to fix it. Instead, he began to sing the same James Taylor song he'd been singing that morning in the kitchen. "'Whenever I see your smiling face, I have to smile myself...'"

Samantha's fingers curled comfortably around the bend in his arm, and she sighed happily. Late Monday morning, and there they were, savoring the last of their ice-cream cones while sauntering along a boardwalk. Most Monday mornings found her buried under a pile of papers on her blotter, with her secretary buzzing her to announce three incoming calls, an advertising representative setting up a display on an easel across the room, a cup of coffee growing cold at her side, her hair beginning to unravel from the knot in which she habitually wore it, and her feet secretly wriggling free from her confining high-heeled pumps underneath her desk. Not that she didn't love her job, not that she didn't love the hectic pace and the excitement, not that she didn't feel a whole lot safer in her office than she had been when she'd tripped off the porch of the bungalow and injured her pride, if not her body. But how nice it would be to have a job that allowed one to wear jeans and to take off for a few hours in the middle of the day in order to stroll the length of a boardwalk and nibble on an ice-cream cone.

She would never feel quite right working a job like Lonny's, with no set hours, no bosses to answer to, no regular paycheck. But how nice it would be, every once in a while, to live the life Lonny lived.

Chapter Five

At first Samantha couldn't find the T-shirt shop. She walked two blocks of Spring Lake's main street in one direction, then made a U-turn and retraced her steps. She spotted Carl's boat-sized Buick parked in front of a real estate office across the street, so she knew she couldn't be far from the store where Marcy worked. But the only shops on her side of the street were a pharmacy, a beauty parlor and a liquor store.

Then she noticed the door next to the pharmacy, with a sign reading, To a Tee—Customized T-shirts. One Flight Up. Peering through the glass in the door, she saw a flight of stairs. She closed her umbrella and stepped inside.

She was almost glad it was drizzling. Lying on the beach every day was beginning to bore her. Yet she'd needed the excuse of the dismal weather to motivate her to visit Marcy instead of returning to the beach for yet another day on the sand. She wasn't sure what she was hoping to accomplish by this visit, but Marcy seemed to be fairly knowledgeable on the subject of best friends. Any woman who could claim with a straight face that she had three best friends at one time—even if she wasn't talking to one of them—had to know more than Samantha did about best-friendship.

The situation between Samantha and Lonny was becoming downright peculiar, and she wasn't certain what to do about it. Monday, the day they'd spent inspecting a shack in Point Pleasant and sightseeing at the boardwalk arcade, had been a wonderful day. So had Tuesday. Lonny had gone off to work on a renovation in progress with his partners, leaving Samantha with a spare key to his house and a note promising to be back by suppertime. That evening, after they'd eaten a delicious meal of fresh shrimp and stir-fried vegetables, they'd retired to the veranda. They'd sipped beer and talked first about Samantha's father's latest girlfriend, and then about Lonny's brother's sterling success as a young attorney, taking up the banner Lonny had dropped after he'd graduated from college. They'd remained outdoors in the balmy night until they were ready to go to sleep. Then they'd gone inside, climbed the stairs, and bade each other good-night with a chaste kiss.

But yesterday, after dinner, something had gone terribly awry, just because Lonny innocently informed Samantha that *Blazing Saddles* was going to be broadcast by one of the cable channels on television.

Blazing Saddles was a movie with a special significance for Lonny and Samantha. They'd seen it together at the ninety-nine-cent theater in downtown Providence during their college days. In fact, Samantha had arranged the evening as Lonny's first date with Moira Davis. Theoretically, it had been a group outing: Samantha had brought along her roommate Moira, and Lonny had brought along his roommate Phillip. But the real purpose of the evening had been for Lonny to get to know Moira better.

Samantha and Lonny had loved the movie's sophomoric humor and slapstick quality, and they'd roared with laughter throughout the entire film. Moira had hated it. Her lack of enthusiasm for Mel Brooks's brand of comedy hadn't discouraged Lonny, however. At the end of the evening he'd asked her out for the following weekend, and she'd accepted.

Why hadn't Lonny been able to appreciate that Samantha's taste in movies was much closer to his than Moira's had been? It didn't matter, she'd recognized at the time. Samantha was his friend, and he undoubtedly assumed she'd share his taste. Moira didn't have to like what he liked. She had beauty and sex appeal and charm, which mattered much more when one was falling in love.

Still, *Blazing Saddles* became an inside joke with Lonny and Samantha. They memorized its theme song, and they quoted its lines ad nauseam. "Don't shoot Mongo, you'll only make him mad!" they used to shout to each other across campus. They nicknamed the stuffed black poodle Lonny gave Moira one Valentine's Day "Black Bart," after one of the characters in the movie.

When, on Wednesday evening, Lonny told Samantha that the film was going to be on television, she was as eager to see it as he was. The problem was that the television set was in his bedroom.

As soon as Samantha entered his room, she felt a tension fill the air, as real as the clammy fog that was thickening over the beach down the street from the house. Neither she nor Lonny dared to comment on it as they took their seats side by side on his comfortable double bed. Lonny propped the pillows up behind them, and they sat, rigid and stoical, staring at the screen as the movie progressed. They barely talked; they barely smiled at jokes that should have had them gasping with laughter. As soon as the final credits began to roll, Samantha bolted from the bed, mumbled a farewell and dashed out of the room.

That was definitely not the way best friends were supposed to behave.

The rain that greeted her when she arose Thursday morning suited her mood perfectly. She didn't like what was happening between her and Lonny. She didn't like the fact that she'd lain awake on her thin mattress for most of the night, her senses refusing to relinquish the sensation of warmth she'd felt emanating from him when she'd reclined beside him on his bed. She didn't like the fact that her pulse seemed out of kilter, racing whenever she thought of his lanky body next to hers and slowing to a dirgelike pace whenever she contemplated the stilted silence that had closed around them like a smothering blanket. That Lonny had apparently been as uneasy as she'd been was small consolation.

She waited until she heard him leave the house before emerging from her room. When she trudged down the stairs to the kitchen, she had absolutely no appetite, but she forced herself to pour a cup of coffee from the pot he'd left heating on the stove for her. Lowering herself glumly into a chair, she caught sight of a drawer left slightly open. She crossed the room to shut it, but saw inside it an envelope with photographs spilling out of it. Her curiosity piqued, she pulled the photographs from the drawer.

They were pictures that dated back to their college days. Several of the photographs had been taken at a rowdy birthday party one of their friends had thrown in his own honor. In two of the pictures Samantha, Lonny and several other people were dancing on a wide windowsill in a dorm room. In another picture Samantha was nestled deep inside a beanbag chair on the floor, hoisting a porcelain beer mug with the college insignia painted on it. Another series of photographs had been taken when she and a group of her friends had traveled to Roger Williams Park to tour the city zoo. There was Samantha, standing in front of a sleepy-eyed camel, and there she was again, mimicking the antics of an orangutan.

She could scarcely stand looking at the pictures. She appeared so young in them, and so...fat. Pleasantly plump, cheerfully chubby, pinchably soft—none of the euphemisms would do. She'd been a tank in those days, a tubbo, a lump of lard. It was no wonder Lonny hadn't been conscious of her as a potential lover back then. It was no wonder she'd kept her infatuation for him a secret. He looked utterly gorgeous in every photograph and she looked utterly hideous.

She knew intuitively the reason the photos had been out of their envelope and scattered in the drawer. Lonny must have been looking at them sometime between the end of *Blazing Saddles* the previous night and his departure for work that morning. He must have pulled them out to refresh his memory of who he and Samantha were, where they'd come from, what they used to mean to each other. Obviously he was as confused by the current state of their relationship as she was.

She had come to Spring Lake hoping to find resolutions, not complications. She had come to have her heart mended, not torn open. Staring at the photos, she suffered a fresh surge of the consuming love she'd felt for Lonny back then. They weren't the same people they'd been close to a decade ago, but she yearned for him just as much.

Deciding to see Marcy was an impulse Samantha couldn't explain. She wasn't even sure of the nature of Lonny's relationship with the pretty blond salesclerk. In the past, he would have gladly filled her in on his latest love affair; in the past, she wouldn't have hesitated to ask him all sorts of nosy questions about the woman—or women—in his life. But not after he'd kissed her and confessed his desire for her. Everything was changed between them now, and while they'd managed to ignore that truth for a few days, they couldn't ignore it forever.

At the top of the stairs she found a door bearing a brightly colored sign reading, To a Tee. She twisted the knob, and the door swung open.

The store was small and crammed with racks of T-shirts, sweatshirts, windbreakers and hats. Behind a long counter, the wall was decorated with more T-shirts displaying numerous slogans, appliqués and silkscreen designs. Two teenagers in yellow rain slickers stood at the counter, studying several designs printed on paper. Marcy emerged from an open door behind the counter, carrying a box. The shirt she had on read Feast Your Eyes in proud silver letters across a black background. Samantha couldn't imagine a more appropriate shirt for a woman as gorgeous as Marcy.

She set the box on the counter and glanced toward the door. Seeing Samantha, she offered a warm smile. "Hi! How's it going?"

"All right," Samantha lied.

"Are you in the market for a shirt?" Marcy asked.

Samantha shook her head. "Why don't you take care of those girls? I'll just browse."

She pretended to be fascinated by a row of sweatshirts on hangers while Marcy wrote up a sales slip for the teenagers. As soon as the girls were gone, Marcy glided around from behind the counter to Samantha. "These are neat sweatshirts," she said in an enthusiastic sales pitch. "You can get the same designs on them as on a T-shirt."

"I didn't come here to buy anything," Samantha informed her. "I came to talk."

Marcy didn't seem disappointed. "Great. I love talking. Would you like some tea?" she offered. "I've got a kettle of water boiling in back."

Ordinarily Samantha wouldn't have wanted to drink hot tea in mid-July. But the day was unseasonably cool, and the cuffs of her jeans were damp with rainwater. "Thanks," she accepted. "That would be nice."

"It's herbal tea," Marcy called over her shoulder as she strode around the counter and vanished into the other room. "I was just about to have some myself. It's great stuff." Her disembodied voice floated through the doorway to Samantha. "No caffeine. Not that I'm a health freak or anything—I mean, I like caffeine as much as the next person. But drink as much tea as I drink in a day, and you'd be bouncing off the walls." She returned, carrying two plastic mugs of steaming tea. "I hope you don't take anything in it, because I haven't got anything to put in it. I'm a purist when it comes to certain things."

"I take it straight," Samantha said, smiling privately. Marcy certainly did love talking. If only Samantha could figure out how to steer the conversation toward what she wanted to talk about. Taking a long sip from her mug and feeling it thaw her chilly bones, she tried to organize her thoughts.

"Where's your rainbow?" Marcy asked.

"My what?"

"Over your eye. Your rainbow."

"Oh, that." Samantha grinned. "I don't wear it every day," she explained. "Only on special occasions."

"I had a great time Sunday night," Marcy said. "Wasn't it fun?"

"I enjoyed it," Samantha answered honestly. "I—I take it you aren't angry that Lonny didn't drive you home."

Marcy blithely waved her hand through the air. "Not at all," she assured Samantha, leaning comfortably against the counter and sipping her tea. "It was fun driving home with Carl. We argued the whole way. I love arguing with him.

He's taking me out for dinner Saturday night. I bet we'll argue the whole time." She grew solemn for a moment. "Do you think Lonny will mind?"

"No," Samantha said, then hesitated. "I don't know. You know more about your relationship with him than I do."

"Well, it's nothing serious," Marcy remarked. "Just some good times, that's all. Nah, he won't mind." She drank her tea thoughtfully. "Does he tell you about his love life? I mean, being that you're his best friend and all."

Samantha took a minute to collect herself. She had wanted to talk to Marcy about Lonny, but now that their dialogue was focusing on him, she wasn't certain how to proceed. "He tells me some things," she mentioned, choosing her words cautiously. "I'm not sure we're still best friends, though. I mean, we are, but . . . well, you said it yourself; it's tricky being best friends with a person of the opposite sex."

"Especially someone as fantastic as Lonny. I don't know how you do it, Samantha," Marcy said admiringly. "If I were his best friend, I'd want to drag him to bed. Truth is, even if I weren't his best friend, I'd want to drag him to bed. He's so sexy, don't you think?"

Samantha decided it was best not to answer that question, even though she was tempted to shout out in the affirmative. "Tell me, Marcy," she ventured, "did you really destroy a friendship by sleeping with your best friend? How can a solid friendship be destroyed by something like that?"

Fortunately, Marcy seemed engrossed enough in her recollection of her own affair not to make a connection between Samantha's inquiry and her friendship with Lonny. "It's hard to say," she ruminated out loud. "It's hard to say exactly what destroyed the friendship. I guess if it was that solid it wouldn't have fallen apart. But you know, you start adding all sorts of baggage when you sleep with a guy. You start expecting things from him, and he starts expecting things from you, and you start making demands on each other, trying to change each other, keeping secrets from each other, and . . . well, you know how it is with guys.''

Given Samantha's rather limited experience, she didn't know how it was with guys. The only man she'd been deeply in love with had moved to Denver promising that their love would survive the distance, and then had become involved with other women and broken Samantha's heart. She and Stephen had never made demands on each other, though, nor had they tried to change each other. At least Samantha hadn't tried to change him. She'd been quite content with things as they were.

"Anyway, it's much better sleeping with guys you aren't friendly with," Marcy concluded. "Look at me and Carl. I find him a first-class prig, he pretty much hates my guts, and here we are, all set for Saturday night." She shrugged and gave Samantha a sweet dimpled smile. "If you ever start fighting with Lonny, if you ever start hating his guts, drag him to bed. You won't save the friendship, but at least you'll have some fun.''

Samantha tucked that bit of advice in the back of her skull. She would never be able to drag Lonny to bed if she hated his guts. In her scheme of things, she wouldn't start hating his guts until after they'd slept together, after he'd fallen madly in and then out of love with her. As long as they didn't sleep together, she assumed that he couldn't fall madly out of love with her. And if he didn't, she wouldn't hate him. Her entire approach to men seemed the inverse of Marcy's.

Yet there was a skewed logic lurking in Marcy's words. Friendship entailed a unique kind of love, while the decision to sleep with a man could be based on the most mundane kind of love. Sleeping with Lonny might debase the unique love she had for him. Maybe that was what Marcy was saying.

A customer entered the shop, and Samantha drained her mug of tea. "I'd better not keep you from your work," she said, grateful for the chance to leave before she revealed anything too personal about her feelings for Lonny. "I don't want you to get in trouble with your boss."

Marcy rolled her eyes. "My boss isn't the nicest person to work for," she confided. "It's a miracle he lets me drink tea on the job." She plastered a welcoming smile on her face and turned to the customer. "May I help you?" she asked, waltzing over to the nearest rack of shirts. "These sweat-shirts are neat, and we can put the same designs on them as we can on the T-shirts."

Samantha set her mug on the counter, waved discreetly and left the shop. She descended the stairs to the street and peered through the glass door. Across the street, she saw Carl escorting a couple from the realty office and unlocking his car. He wore a beige trench coat over his business suit, and even in the rain his hair remained perfectly groomed. As the couple climbed in, he lifted his eyes to the second-story shop where Marcy was working. What an odd couple, Samantha pondered, envious of Marcy's ability to take romance so lightly.

Without bothering to open her umbrella, Samantha stepped outside and ducked into the pharmacy next door. She entertained a vague notion of getting some food into her stomach, but the display of candy bars beside the cash register did nothing to inspire her. She must be in bad shape if even chocolate couldn't revive her appetite, she contemplated as she left the pharmacy.

She forced her mind to go blank and strolled to the corner. The light rain felt refreshing on her cheeks and scalp as she headed east toward the ocean. The only sign of life on the boardwalk was a dedicated jogger, his gait sluggish and his sweatsuit drenched as he plodded along the soggy planks. Samantha scaled the ramp to the boardwalk, walked as far as the gazebo and sagged against the railing underneath its protective roof.

She wasn't Marcy. She wasn't a beautiful, immensely self-confident blonde who could wear a shirt reading Feast Your Eyes. Nor was she any longer a tubby working-class girl who could hide her insecurities behind a self-deprecating sense of humor. She was a mature professional woman with an education and income that assured her a rightful place among the successful people of the world. Yet she couldn't shake her image of herself as a rotund, lovesick young lady who could dance with Lonny only on a windowsill at a rambunctious birthday party where the beer was flowing like a river, and the *real* dances, the private, sensuous, one-on-one dances, took place somewhere beyond her reach.

She wondered if she'd ever actually stopped loving Lonny. Even while she'd been involved with Stephen, he had been an active part of her life. Stephen had resented Lonny; he'd complained whenever Samantha engaged in her hour-long telephone conversations with him, and as a rule, he'd refused to join her when she met her friend for dinner during his occasional jaunts through New York. Stephen couldn't avoid Lonny completely, of course. Often Lonny wound up spending the night at Samantha's apartment—on her couch in the living room. Although Stephen had access to Samantha's bedroom and Lonny didn't, Stephen made no bones about his mixed feelings regarding the other man. "I don't ask you to love my friends, so don't ask me to love yours," Stephen justified himself. "I'm sure Lonny is a swell guy, but he's different from you and me, and I'd rather you count me out when you see him."

Lonny *was* different from Stephen and Samantha, and she could understand Stephen's reluctance to befriend him. Like her, Stephen had come from a humble background. He'd put himself through school and was busy clawing his way into a higher social stratum. At times, Samantha had found fault with his ambition. She had worried about his single-mindedness in pursuing his professional goals. It was that single-mindedness that led him to accept his current position in Denver at the expense of his relationship with Samantha.

Admittedly, her own professional ambition had foreclosed the option of her quitting her job and moving to Denver with him. He had suggested the idea, and she'd rejected it. Denver wasn't the hub of the cosmetics industry, and she had been skeptical about finding an equivalent position in another field. She'd worked as hard for her success as Stephen had, and she wasn't about to abandon everything she'd accomplished.

But maybe there was another reason she hadn't given up her job and accompanied Stephen to Denver. Maybe it had nothing to do with her work. Maybe she simply hadn't loved him enough. Maybe, just maybe, she'd wanted to remain on the East Coast so she wouldn't be too far away from Lonny.

None of which helped her in her present dilemma. That Lonny wanted her now, after years of feeling nothing more than a platonic affection for her, was flattering. But she'd listened to too many of Lonny's tales of misery concerning his love life. He was forever wanting some woman and then losing interest in her, craving someone and then falling madly out of love. Samantha knew Lonny too well to believe that his passion for her could last. She trusted his friendship, but she didn't trust his desire.

Shivering in the raw afternoon air, she decided to return to the house and warm up. Marcy's opinion might or might not prove useful to Samantha, but her offer of tea had been right on target. Samantha decided that she'd rummage through Lonny's kitchen until she found some tea—or better yet, hot chocolate. The pharmacy's candy bars hadn't stimulated her taste buds, but then, candy bars weren't warm and soothing. Cocoa was.

Halfway back to his house, she noticed a sky-blue van parked by the curb in front of her rented Chevette. Lonny's truck was in the driveway. She halted on the sidewalk, unsure of whether she wanted to see him. Then she shored up her courage and proceeded along the street. Last night had been awkward, but they couldn't avoid each other forever.

The front door was unlocked, and she entered to find Lonny, Jack Rogan and a third man seated on the floor of the parlor, huddled over a series of blueprints spread across the coffee table. Their conversation stopped at her entrance, and Jack gallantly stood up. "Hey, Sammy!" he hailed her with a wide grin. "You're a sight for sore eyes."

"I'm nothing of the kind," she responded with a modest smile. "I'm wet and bedraggled." She balanced her unused umbrella in a corner by the door and combed her sodden hair back from her face with her fingers. Her gaze came to rest on Lonny, who was watching her warily. Her eyes met his for only an instant. She could see turbulent shadows in their pale brown depths, and she winced at the comprehension that he was still as troubled by her as she was by him. She hastily averted her eyes, and her vision settled on his body. His cotton shirt was open at the collar, revealing a sliver of his bronze chest. She winced again as a memory of the feel of his skin flickered awake inside her.

"Who is this?" the third man asked, studying Samantha inquisitively. Although he was seated, she could tell that he was shorter than Lonny and Jack, with a stocky build and a bushy brown beard covering half his face.

"This," Jack boomed, sliding an arm casually around Samantha's shoulders, "is Lonny's good ol' chum, Sam. Believe it or not, Howie, Sam is—well, you can see for yourself what she is. A prime specimen of womanhood."

"So she is," the man observed. "How do you do, Sam? I'm Lonny's partner, Howie."

Samantha shook the man's extended hand, managing to extricate herself from Jack's clasp in the process. "Nice meeting you," she said politely.

"What do you think?" Jack persisted. "Is this a woman? To listen to Lonny talk about her, you'd never guess, huh?" He eyed Samantha appreciatively. "But looking at her leaves no doubt whatsoever. Tell me, pretty lady, are you having a good time with Lonny? Because if you aren't, I'm more than willing to volunteer my services."

"Cool it, Jack," Lonny snapped. "We've got work to do here, if you don't mind."

His sharp tone surprised Samantha. She'd never seen Lonny lose his temper before. A quick glimpse of his scowl informed her that he was seething with anger.

She didn't know whether she was the source of his anger, or whether it had arisen from the work with which they were occupied. In either case, she resolved to make herself scarce. "I didn't mean to interrupt anything," she mumbled, moving directly to the stairs. "Please, get back to whatever you were doing."

"Honey, you can interrupt me anytime," Jack called after her. "Or maybe I should say, *almost* anytime," he added, his voice heavy with blatant sexual innuendo.

When she'd first met Jack, his flirting had amused her. Now it rankled. She didn't blame him; he couldn't possibly know about the tension simmering between her and Lonny.

Still, she raced up the stairs, trying to blot out the sound of Lonny's harsh retort to his lusty colleague about keeping his libido under control. She dashed into her room, slammed the door and sank onto the mattress with a sigh.

She almost didn't hear the timid knocking on the door. Over an hour had elapsed, an hour she'd spent motionless on the mattress, her arms hugging her knees and her eyes closed as she tried in vain to clarify her thoughts. If Lonny had been reduced to snarling at his partners because of her, she probably ought to leave Spring Lake. Her visit wasn't serving its purpose anymore, and she didn't think she could bear another tense night like last night.

"Sammy?" Lonny whispered through the closed door. "Can I come in?"

She opened her eyes and lifted her head from her arms. "All right."

He opened the door, but remained standing in the doorway, as if afraid to enter. "I'm sorry." He drew in a long breath. "I already said I was sorry to Jack, and now I'm saying I'm sorry to you."

"*I'm* sorry," Samantha countered. "I shouldn't have barged in on you while you were busy with work."

"How could you not have barged in?" Lonny asked. "You're staying here at my house, and it was raining out. You had every right to march in on our powwow. I..." He inhaled again and shoved a thick black clump of hair out of his eyes. "I was rude. I should have introduced you to Howie, and I should have told you about what we were working on, if you were interested. But...I couldn't stand watching Jack come on to you the way he did. I acted like a jerk, and I'm sorry."

"Oh, Lonny, he doesn't mean anything by all that nonsense," she said with a laugh. "Can't you tell that? He's just reciting his lines for practice. He's harmless. He doesn't mean half of what he says."

Lonny crossed the threshold and approached the bed. "I don't care whether he meant what he said or not," he confessed, lowering himself to sit beside her. "It still made me see red." He stretched out his legs before him and stared down them at his bare feet. "It's not like me to blow my stack over something so ridiculous, Sammy. I don't know— maybe my personality's mutating or something."

"Have you been celibate that long?" Samantha asked, wondering whether Lonny's professed desire for her was merely the result of a temporary lack of sexual activity in his life.

He didn't answer immediately. "At the moment," he muttered, "I feel like a novitiate with serious misgivings about my vows." He reached out and touched the wavy honey-colored tress that fell across her shoulder. "Your hair's still wet. Why didn't you use your umbrella?"

"I was hoping a cold shower would knock some sense into me," she told him.

He chuckled and shook his head. "They don't work. I tried one this morning, in the bathroom. So much for water therapy." His smile waned, and he cursed softly. "It was bad enough that neither of us laughed at Black Bart's Gucci saddlebag," he said, alluding to the movie they'd watched last night. "But when you've got to apologize for walking into my house, things have reached a pretty pass."

"What do you think we ought to do about it?" she asked, not daring to look directly at him. The question was risky enough without having to see his deep-set eyes, his sharply chiseled nose and chin, the sensuous mouth that had taken hers once and undermined her equilibrium. She almost hoped he would ask her to leave, but even more than that, she hoped he would beg her to stay with him, to work out whatever was boggling their friendship, to make them both whole again.

He slid his hand beneath her chin and turned her face to him. "I think we ought to say: to hell with being rational," he replied before brushing her lips with his.

She felt something flare to life inside her at his gentle kiss, something hot and hungry that defied rationality. Clinging to a shred of sanity, she nudged him away. "I don't know, Lonny. This scares me."

"It scares me, too," he admitted, touching his lips to the velvety skin of her brow when her mouth was no longer available to him. "I love you, Sammy."

"I love you, too, Lonny, but—"

"No." He cupped his hands over her cheeks and held her head motionless before him. "I'm not talking about friendship, and I'm not talking about ten years ago. This is now, and we're two adults. I love you. Do you understand what I'm saying?"

Her eyes locked onto his. Downstairs, she'd seen roiling fury and confusion in them. But now they were clear and steadfast, a shimmering amber-tinged brown that affected her even more strongly than his words. He was no longer discussing his wants. He wasn't even discussing being in love with her. He was discussing *love*.

She responded not as a dewy-eyed eighteen-year-old with an incurable crush on a handsome upperclassman, but as an adult in the thrall of a love that transcended friendship. Praying that she wasn't about to make the biggest mistake of her life, she leaned toward him, seeking more than the comfort and reassurance she had always found in his embrace. Her mind wasn't certain, but her heart told her that she wanted all the love Lonny had to give her.

Their lips found each other, opened to each other. His hands dug deep into her hair as his tongue overtook hers.

Her body trembled slightly when she recognized the sheer force of his love in his kiss. Her arms circled his torso, holding him to her, and he eased her back onto the mattress, covering her body with his.

He felt amazingly right in her arms, amazingly natural, as if he'd belonged there all along. She reveled in his weight upon her, in the length of his legs weaving through hers, in the lean firmness of his chest against the pliant flesh of her breasts. One of her hands rose to his silky black mane, her fingers twisting through the long locks and tensing into a fist as his tongue continued to probe her mouth. He even tasted right, a clean, minty flavor far more satisfying than chocolate or ice-cream sundaes, far more delicious than anything she'd ever tasted before. She felt strangely deprived when he lifted his face from her, breaking the contact of their mouths.

His breath was ragged, and his eyes were half closed but glittering, still unwavering as he gazed down at her. "I want to undress you," he said.

She nodded, unable to look anywhere but at him as his hands moved to the front of her blouse and opened the buttons. He tugged the shirttails free of her jeans and spread apart the fabric. His fingers trailed across her midriff, up to her throat, and then around her back to unfasten the clasp of her bra. Her breathing quickened as the lace cups of the bra went slack and he pulled off the garments and tossed them to the floor. He bowed to kiss her collarbone. "You're so beautiful," he murmured against her skin, his voice unrecognizably husky.

"Didn't you say something about my being underweight?" she teased, her breathlessness making her sound just as unrecognizable to herself.

"I was wrong. You're perfect," Lonny decided, nibbling a path to her breast. His tongue flicked over her nipple, and he and Samantha gasped in unison. He pressed his mouth to the soft, pale skin above it, and he moaned quietly. "I can't believe this, Sammy," he whispered. "I can't believe we're doing this."

"Do you want to stop?" she asked, her voice shaking slightly. If he did want to stop, she'd respect him for his wisdom, but she probably wouldn't forgive him.

"Never," he assured her, sliding his hand upward to caress her other breast. "I want to be like this with you forever."

She had known that Lonny had a sentimental streak in him—only a truly sentimental man could fall in love as often as he did. But to hear him express such a tender thought in reference to her was as exciting to Samantha as the friction of his lips on her, and his fingers dancing in light circles over her full flesh and then centering on the swollen red crest.

For a long moment she only lay beneath him, luxuriating in the shimmering sensations he was creating within her. But gradually her selfish pleasure was overcome by a need to learn his body as he was learning hers. She wedged her hands between their bodies, forcing him back from her so she could unbutton his shirt. He impatiently wriggled free of the sleeves and flung the shirt away, then lowered himself back into her arms.

Her hands journeyed the length of his back, delighting in the smooth texture of his skin and the supple flexing of the muscles beneath it. His back was graceful, as were his arms, his shoulders, his streamlined, hairless chest. Everything about Lonny, from the way he moved to the way he loved, was graceful.

"Sammy," he groaned, leaning away only so she could reach the flat stretch of his abdomen with her questing fingers. "Talk to me. Tell me what you're thinking."

"I'm thinking about how graceful you are," she candidly told him.

"Four years of dancing lessons had to be good for something," he mused, his voice dissolving to another groan as she traced the edge of his jeans with her thumb.

"Is this what they taught you in dancing school?" Samantha asked incredulously. Her hand drifted lower, feeling his hardness through the thick denim.

"I wish," he rasped, peeling her fingers away and struggling for control. He reached for the zipper of her slacks, and Samantha's breath caught in her throat. Merely anticipating his touch aroused her incredibly, yet she was more than aroused. She was happy. She felt enormously relaxed with Lonny, inexplicably friendly toward him. The only tension she felt with him now was the physical tension building inside her body, pulling at her nerve endings and stretching them taut.

As soon as he had her jeans off, he shed his own. Samantha's hands grasped his hips and clung to him. She felt him shuddering, fighting against her grip. "Don't rush me, Sammy," he pleaded.

Her eyes widened. She hadn't intended to rush him. But her own body was rushing her, eager to know Lonny completely, and it was her body, not her mind, that was governing her actions now.

He propped himself up on his elbows and peered into her face. "This is so special," he murmured, leaning down to nip her exposed ear. "I want it to be magic for you. I want it to be like—like rainbows in your eyes. Magic."

"It already is," she said with a sigh. When his hand roamed down her body to stroke her, he found her damp and waiting, her body ready to welcome him. Closing her eyes, she arched against his hand and cried out softly. "Lonny..."

"I love you, Sammy." His voice was less than a whisper, but his lips were so close to her ear that she could easily hear him.

Or perhaps she felt the words more than heard them. She felt his love above her, against her, coursing through her body in fiery waves. "I love you," she echoed, speaking the words she'd stifled so long ago, refusing to embarrass herself by revealing her secret love even to her best friend, the one person she might have trusted, yet, paradoxically, the one person she could never have told. Now the truth burst free, liberating her. She pulled his body fully onto hers and buried her lips in the warm crook of his neck. "I love you, Lonny," she declared, savoring each word before she uttered it.

Her statement spurred him on. His hips settled between her thighs, and he entered her. She shifted her face from his shoulder as he raised his head, and their eyes met. Although her hands could detect the clenching of his muscles as he wrestled against his body's imperative hunger, his expression was serene. She felt serene, too. She knew now that making love with Lonny was the right thing to do.

Her legs wrapped around his, urging him deeper. He slid one hand to her hips and pressed her against himself. His other hand raveled into her hair, delighting in its long, loose waves and golden highlights. His lips grazed her cheeks, her nose, her brow, her chin, and finally her mouth.

Samantha felt conquered, if not by Lonny then by her body's powerful response to him. She surrendered to the compelling force of his thrusts, letting them carry her to a shattering peak. A choked sob escaped her. Within an instant, Lonny followed her into the blissful oblivion of his own climax.

He remained on top of her as their bodies unwound, his heart thudding against her breast, his breath shallow and rapid. After several minutes he stirred, his hands drifting through her hair and his legs sliding out from between hers. He rolled onto his side next to her and hugged her tightly to himself. "Are we still friends?" he asked.

"I think so." Samantha cushioned her head against his shoulder and kissed the underside of his jaw.

"You aren't mad at me?"

She shook her head. She was madly in love, perhaps. But not mad. Definitely not mad.

He stroked her hair back from her cheek. "*I'm* mad at me," he said.

She bit her lip, unsure of what he was getting at, and almost afraid to find out. Yet she had to know. "Why?" she asked, bracing herself for whatever answer he would provide.

"I'm mad at me for wasting time with your friends in college, when you were there all along."

"There was too much of me there," she reminded him. "I wasn't the person I am now, Lonny."

"You were beautiful then," he insisted. He kissed the crown of her head and sighed. "Beauty has nothing to do with how much a woman weighs, Sammy. I could kill myself for taking so long to figure that out."

"Don't kill yourself," she consoled him, grinning. "It would be silly for you to have to die so soon after making such a big discovery."

"You're right." He propped himself up on his elbow and gazed down at her. His fingers wove through her hair again, wandering behind her ear in a gentle pattern. "What a discovery you are. I should probably thank Jack Rogan for making me jealous."

"He made you jealous?"

Lonny nodded.

"But, Lonny, all those phony lines of his . . . that was all they were."

"Maybe he didn't intend to follow through on any of them," Lonny allowed. "But he had the good sense to realize what a magnificent woman you were before I did."

"Stephen realized what a magnificent woman I was," she pointed out. "Are you jealous of him, too?"

"He's in Denver," Lonny said with a confident shrug. "And you're all through with him." He smiled mischievously. "Didn't I promise you I'd help you to get over him if you came to Spring Lake?"

"True to your word, Lonny," Samantha praised him, not bothering to add that she had probably gotten over Stephen long ago. What Lonny had done was to make her recognize that she didn't love Stephen. Even when she and Stephen were together, she'd never felt anything for him like the profound all-consuming love she felt for Lonny. She and Stephen may have been lovers; they may have been *in* love. But they'd never been friends, and that made all the difference.

"This mattress is awful," Lonny muttered, pushing himself up to sit and frowning at the skimpy pad. "It's like lying on a bed of nails. Why didn't you say something?"

"I'm not a complainer," Samantha claimed.

"I am." Lonny's frown intensified, though he succumbed to a laugh. "So allow me to complain on your behalf. This mattress is awful."

"As I recall," Samantha reminisced with a teasing smile, "you gave me a choice between comfort and safety. I opted for safety."

He laughed. "And look what good that did. Come on," he said, standing and pulling her to her feet. "Let's be comfortable."

Leaving their clothing strewn about the floor, they hurried down the hall to Lonny's bedroom. Although Samantha had been in it the previous night to watch television, she'd been so anxious at the time that she had hardly absorbed her surroundings. Now she took a moment to examine the room.

It was larger than the "royal suite," the side windows offering a better view of the ocean and the front windows overlooking the street. The furniture was eclectic: the bed was apparently new, but the desk and bureau were both old and scratched, the former finished with a pine stain and the latter made of a darker wood. Neither piece matched the two maple night tables. A faded brown area rug covered most of the floor. Samantha understood that Lonny couldn't afford a matching bedroom set on his income, as she herself could, and the irony of an erstwhile rich kid living in a room furnished with Salvation Army castoffs, while she lived in an apartment that looked professionally decorated, caused her to chuckle.

Lonny beckoned her toward the bed. She paused at the foot of it, staring up at the wall above the pillows. A poster print of an impressionist landscape was tacked to the wall. "Monet!" she exclaimed, recognizing the poster. "I gave you that print, didn't I?"

"It was your graduation present to me," he refreshed her memory.

"That's right." She remembered that he'd hung the poster in the rat-trap apartment he'd lived in after he graduated from college, when he decided to stay on in Providence to audit an architecture course at the Rhode Island School of Design and apprentice himself to an electrician. The poster had looked appropriate in that dreary apartment, but now that Samantha could afford nicer things, she thought the print looked shabby and cheap.

"I ought to buy you a better one," she mused, joining him on the bed. "A framed print on canvas."

"Hey, with what you earn, you could buy me the original," Lonny joked.

"Not quite." She rested her head on one of the pillows and gazed upward at the poster. "Should I attach some special meaning to the fact that you've got it hanging over your bed?"

He twisted to peer at the poster. "I wonder," he mused. "Maybe I was under the influence of some subconscious impulse when I hung it there."

"Probably not," Samantha decided with equanimity. "Admit it, Lonny—until very recently, you thought of me only as your best friend."

"Hmm." He ran his hand along the narrow curve of her waist, then arched his fingers enticingly over her breast. "Maybe it's time to start thinking of you as my bosom buddy."

"Don't be fresh," Samantha chided him with a laugh.

He eased her onto her back and blanketed her body with his. His devouring kiss silenced her laughter, and she accepted that, however he thought of her—best friend or bosom buddy—love was the most important part of it.

Chapter Six

The piercing blare of an automobile horn outside the window jolted Lonny awake. He tried to sit up, then fell back to the pillow, pinned down by Samantha's slumbering body, which lay half across his. His movement roused her, and she sighed.

Smiling, he closed his arms around her shoulders. Her hair was splayed across his chest, and its silky strands tickled him in a delightful way. If she ever again dared to wear it in a bun when he saw her, he'd attack her with a hairbrush. Or better yet, with a powerful magnet, which would suck all the offending hairpins out of her locks. Shutting his eyes, he tried to picture her standing in front of LaBelle Cosmetics' Manhattan headquarters in one of her prissy business dresses, her bobby pins flying and her hair unraveling as Lonny came at her with an outlandishly huge horseshoe magnet. He chuckled at the image.

"What's so funny?" Samantha asked drowsily.

"Nothing," he said, wondering whether she would find the idea as comical as he did. Samantha had the best sense of humor of any woman he knew, but she did tend to take her professional demeanor very seriously. Too seriously, perhaps. She ought to arrive at her office with a rainbow painted above her eye someday, he thought.

She started to roll off him, and he tightened his hold on her. "Don't move," he whispered. "I like having your weight on top of me."

Lifting her head, Samantha opened her eyes and gazed down at him. Although she was still sleepy, her eyes were bright beneath her lowered lids, their dark irises radiant with sparks of life. "Maybe I ought to get fat again," she suggested playfully.

"I'd still like it." He wedged his knee between her thighs, and her muscles tensed around him. "What a wonderful way to get crushed. I'd die with a smile on my face." He kissed her cheek. "I ought to start plying you with chocolate-covered ants."

She snorted. "That's one way to guarantee that I'll stay thin."

"I'll bear it in mind." He used his thumbs to angle her face to his, and their lips met. Just one kiss from her, one kiss from this wonderful naked woman, and his entire body hardened with readiness for her.

He couldn't believe that Samantha—his good ol' chum Sammy—could do what she was doing to him with her hair spilling across his skin, with her soft, warm flesh blanketing him, with her womanly fragrance filling his nostrils, with her tongue probing the recesses of his mouth. He couldn't believe it, but he accepted the truth of it. The night they'd spent together was proof enough that she could bewitch him, that she could arouse him in ways he could scarcely comprehend.

Why had it taken them so long to figure it out? Why hadn't they realized sooner what could exist between them? Why had she been wasting her time with that twerp Stephen? Why had Lonny refused to think of her as anything other than his pal?

The whys didn't matter, he resolved, molding his hand over the curve of her bottom and flexing his thigh against her. She moaned helplessly, her fingers digging into his shoulders and her body arching in rhythm with his. This was all that mattered—that they had finally found each other, that they had finally plunged fully into the love that had always bound them together.

He shifted onto his side, urging her down to the mattress and then following onto her. "Lonny," she murmured, welcoming him with her eager motions. She had spoken his name countless times in the years they'd known each other, but he'd never perceived the sweet music of her voice until now. "Lonny..."

And then the horn again, honking insistently in the street below. Lonny cursed. A hazy memory struggled to take shape, something about a promise he'd made....

The sound of Jack's voice bellowing through the window brought it home to him. "I know you're in there, Lonny! Come on out with your hands over your head!"

Samantha's eyes widened in shock. Lonny cursed again and sprang from the bed. He raced to the window and stared down at his partner. "Cool it, Jack," he called through the screen, squinting as the morning sun bounced off the soaked pavement and glared into his eyes. "I'd like to remain on speaking terms with my neighbors, if you don't mind."

"Your neighbors have probably been awake for hours," Jack shouted up to him. He was leaning against the hood of his car, his hands shoved into the pockets of his baggy overalls and his blond hair ruffled by the constant ocean breeze. "I told you I'd be here at eight. We've got things to do, man. Why didn't you set your alarm clock?"

I had other things on my mind, Lonny answered beneath his breath. He shrugged sheepishly at his colleague. "Go buy yourself a cup of coffee. I'll be ready when you get back."

"If you were any kind of friend, you'd make me a cup of coffee yourself," Jack retorted. "Don't tell me you're turning into a cheapskate in your old age."

"Buy yourself a cup of coffee, and I'll reimburse you," Lonny offered.

"Forget it," Jack growled, though he was grinning. "Put some clothes on and act like a human being. I'll meet you at the front door."

Exhaling, Lonny turned from the window. Samantha had sat up, and the blanket was bunched around her waist. He stared longingly at the alluring slope of her shoulders and the full flesh of her breasts. "This hurts me more than it hurts you," he mumbled disconsolately as he approached the bed.

"Can't you call in sick?" she asked.

He lowered himself onto the bed beside her. "One of the drawbacks of being your own boss is that you can't cheat yourself out of a day's work," he pointed out. He kissed her brow, then stood and walked to the closet. "You can stay put if you want, but I've got a living to earn."

"No, I'll get up, too," Samantha said, pushing back the blanket and swinging her feet over the side of the bed. Lonny's vision settled on her legs for a minute. She really wasn't tall; her head barely reached his shoulder when they stood side by side. But her legs were wonderfully long, long enough to envelop him, to hold him to her, inside her...

He cursed one final time and deliberately turned his back on her. "I *am* sick," he confessed, rummaging through his closet for a shirt. "Heartsick. Lovesick. Especially sick of the deadline we're facing on this job. But such is life, Sammy," he summarized with a dramatic sigh.

"Are you going to work on that deathtrap hovel in Point Pleasant?" she asked.

Her innocent question thrilled him. Not that he considered the house in Point Pleasant a hovel or a deathtrap. What pleased him was that Samantha was showing a genuine interest in his work. Ever since he'd realized the depth of his feelings for her, he had understood that it was vitally important for her to come to terms with what he did for a living. She didn't have to like it, and she didn't have to view it as refined or proper or appropriate to someone of his background. But she had to respect it, because it was what he'd chosen to do with his life.

"No, it's another place," he answered, tossing a pale blue work shirt onto the bed. He pulled some underwear, a clean red bandanna, and a fresh pair of jeans from his bureau and dropped them onto the bed on his way to the bathroom. "The owner contracted us to fix the place up. That's what we were working on yesterday with the blueprints," he informed her. "This sort of job is money in the bank, not like the speculation we do on places like the Point Pleasant bungalow. The downside of a job like this is that the man who commissioned us wants to move his family into the house on September first, so we've got to hustle to meet his deadline."

"Such is life, Lonny," Samantha echoed with a chuckle before leaving his room.

A touch of masochism compelled him to follow her to the doorway and watch her stride down the hall to her own room. Her body was as beautiful when seen from behind as it was when she was facing him. Particularly her legs, though her firm, round derriere also had much to recommend it. And her delicate waist... He tried to recall the way she'd looked in her former chubby incarnation and came up blank. If she had ever appeared less than incredibly sexy, the night they'd just spent together had erased the memory from his mind.

By the time he'd showered and left his room, she was emerging from the guest bathroom, dressed in a pair of cotton shorts and the gaudy blouse she'd worn the day she arrived in Spring Lake. Lonny wished she'd donned slacks instead. A lecher like Jack Rogan didn't deserve to see her legs, even if he'd already seen much more than her legs the day he and Lonny had met her on the beach. But Lonny didn't want to sound like a fanatically jealous lover, so he didn't comment on her outfit as they descended the stairs together.

Jack was pacing on the veranda when Lonny opened the front door. "It's about time, lazybones," he reproached Lonny. "A man could die out here, waiting for a lousy cup of coffee."

"Maybe I should have made you wait a little longer, then," Lonny grumbled none too graciously. "Come on in."

Jack's eyes shifted to Samantha and began to sparkle. "Now *this* is definitely worth the wait," he boomed, bee-lining to her side. "Good morning, darling. You certainly are looking chipper this morning."

"Heaven knows why," Samantha said ingenuously. "I hardly got any sleep." Lonny shot her a quick look and found her grinning mischievously at him.

Damn her for teasing him, he groused silently as he stalked ahead of her and Jack to the kitchen. Damn her for even daring to insinuate—in front of Jack—that Lonny had been the reason she'd hardly gotten any sleep. He couldn't deny that their night had been less than restful, but she was as much to blame for that as he was. More, he decided self-righteously. She'd better behave herself, or he'd point the accusing finger at her.

His indignation was short-lived. He might have gotten less sleep than he needed, but he could think of no better way to spend a night than the way he'd spent the previous one. His unvoiced offer to give Samantha all the blame—all the *credit*, he amended—was actually quite benevolent.

He hummed absently as he prepared a pot of coffee. "James Taylor," Samantha murmured, sitting on a chair by the table and swinging her bare feet in tempo. "You gave me that record, remember?"

"Of course I remember," Lonny replied. "Why do you think I'm singing it?"

Samantha smiled. Jack's eyes shuttled from her to Lonny and back again. "Lonny sounds like a bullfrog in heat when he sings," he pointed out to her. "Don't tell me you enjoy listening to that."

"Bullfrogs in heat sound wonderful to other bullfrogs," Samantha commented lightly. "I think I'll have some toast. Does anybody else want any?"

Both men quickly answered in the affirmative. Lonny extended one of his arms and gave her a squeeze. "I heartily approve," he praised her. "Get some good food into your stomach."

"If I'm going to get fat, I'd rather go with toast than chocolate-covered ants," she informed him, pulling several slices of whole-wheat bread from the bread drawer and popping them into the toaster.

"You don't want to get fat, do you?" Jack asked, appraising her from across the room. "I think you're gorgeous the way you are. Don't you think she's gorgeous, Lonny?"

"Yes," Lonny concurred. "I think she's gorgeous."

"Keep it up, guys," Samantha encouraged them, her smile expanding. "This is turning into one of the better mornings of my life."

"That's because I'm here, sweetheart," Jack boasted. "Don't forget, I noticed you were a girl long before Lonny did."

"She's not a girl," Lonny corrected Jack. "She's a woman."

"Oh, so you *have* noticed," Jack taunted him. "You ought to thank me for having pointed it out to you."

"You're right, Jack," Lonny agreed good-naturedly. "Thank you very much." Jack didn't have to know how sincerely Lonny intended his expression of gratitude. He probably would have noticed Samantha's feminine assets eventually without Jack's assistance, but Jack had helped to speed things along. If it hadn't been for Jack, Lonny wouldn't have had to rescue Samantha, wouldn't have had to lift her into his arms and carry her off and hold her to himself above the surging ocean. Lonny owed Jack a debt far greater than he'd ever admit to.

"I wonder if the old geezer's going to be there today," Jack said to Lonny as Samantha carried butter and jam to the table.

"Who's the old geezer?" she asked.

"Bill Tucker. The man who commissioned us to renovate his house," Lonny told her. He poured the coffee and took a seat with the others at the table. "I wish you wouldn't call him an old geezer," he scolded Jack. "For one thing, he's middle-aged. For another, he's a nice guy."

"Right," Jack snorted sarcastically. "Signs us on, and *then* he throws his impossible deadline at us."

"We could have torn up the contract when he mentioned September first, but we didn't," Lonny argued. "We agreed to his deadline. The man's paying us a good dollar." He buttered his toast and shrugged. "He's not such a bad guy. He reminds me of my father."

"Since when do you like your father?" Jack inquired.

"I've always liked my father. We've had our ups and downs, but I've always liked him."

"You told me he was a prime candidate for ulcers."

Lonny nodded. "If I didn't like him, I wouldn't care about the condition of his stomach lining. He works too hard and worries too much, but that's the way he is. I chose not to follow in his footsteps. But that doesn't mean I can't enjoy his company."

"Have you ever met his father?" Jack asked Samantha.

"A few times. I like him, too."

"I've never met him, but he sounds like a stuffed shirt to me," Jack opined. "I like a guy you can sit down and have a beer with. Like my old man. You can sit down with him, open a couple of Buds, and talk politics. That's my kind of guy."

"You can talk politics with my father, too," Lonny maintained. "You might disagree with him, but he comes up with challenging arguments. He makes you think." Sipping his coffee, Lonny decided that he'd have to visit his father again soon. He hadn't seen his parents since the day last March when he'd swooped through New York, meeting Samantha for lunch and sensing subliminally that her emotions were not in the best of shape. Now that her love life was exactly what Lonny wanted it to be, he planned to go to New York much more often. Maybe on his next sojourn north, he'd pick her up and take her with him to see his parents. It was no wonder she liked them; she had more in common with them than Lonny did.

"How about your folks?" Jack was asking Samantha. "Can you talk politics with them?"

"My mother died sixteen years ago," she said emotion-lessly. "My father...sometimes I can talk to him. Sort of."

"Do you think yesterday's rain is going to slow things down today?" Lonny asked Jack, deliberately changing the subject. He knew that Samantha didn't like discussing her family. She confided in Lonny about her distant, difficult relationship with her father, about his tendency to overlook his children, his having arbitrarily assigned her to the role of housekeeper simply because she was the only female in the house, his negative attitude toward her achievements. He expressed pride in her schooling and her prestigious job, but Samantha had told Lonny she suspected that her father secretly condemned her for having overstepped her rank, for having risen high above the socioeconomic constraints that had limited him. Lonny had only met Mr. Janek once, at Samantha's graduation from college, but that one meeting had convinced Lonny that Samantha's suspicions were well founded.

Jack's comments on the dry weather being forecasted for the next few days brought Lonny's attention back to the breakfast table. "Most of it's interior work, anyway," Jack remarked. "By tomorrow, everything should be dried out, so there's no point starting on any of the exterior stuff today."

"Are you going to have to climb on the roof for this job?" Samantha asked.

"There isn't too much roof work on this one," Lonny assured her, then grinned wickedly. "But if I really feel like risking my neck, I may just walk backward on the porch." Samantha's cheeks turned a dark crimson at his reference to her clumsiness. Jack seemed puzzled, but before he could question them, Lonny emptied his cup. "Well, I guess we'd better get in gear," he said, pushing back his chair and standing. "Howie said he'd meet us there at nine."

"And if we're late, it's your fault," Jack reminded him, rising from the table as well. He glanced at Samantha. "Are you going to be doing your beach-bunny routine today, Sammy?"

"I'm going to the beach, if that's what you're asking," she replied coolly.

"I'll close my eyes and dream of you in your bikini," he promised.

"That's just what we need—you trying to work with your eyes closed," Lonny muttered. "Put a lid on it, Jack. She isn't interested."

Samantha cast Lonny a measuring look. He was angry with himself for uttering what was a patently jealous remark ... and then he noticed her shy smile and the glimmer of pleasure in her lucid brown eyes. She seemed to be touched by his jealousy. In that case, he mused, mirroring her smile, he didn't mind being jealous. If it made her happy, he didn't mind it at all.

He bade her goodbye with a light kiss on the cheek and left the house with Jack. He would have greatly preferred a more passionate farewell with Samantha. For that matter, he would have greatly preferred more passion and no farewell. But he let discretion dictate his behavior with her in front of Jack. Even if half of what Jack said was meaningless, as Samantha contended, Lonny would rather not have to listen to his partner making lascivious comments about the reason Lonny overslept.

He didn't want to think about Jack's attraction to Samantha. It was more than jealousy that made him resent Jack's behavior with her; it was that she was so special to Lonny, so precious that he couldn't bear the idea that anyone could think of her in such physical terms. Sure, the physical aspect of his relationship with Samantha was splendid, and the joy of waking up with her glorious body next to him was indescribable. But beyond the physical pleasure they shared their friendship. Sammy was still Lonny's best friend—only now she was that and more.

Marcy didn't know what she was talking about, he contemplated as he unlocked the passenger door of his truck for Jack and then climbed in behind the wheel. Marcy was all wrong. Sex didn't have to spoil a friendship. In his and Samantha's case, it had enhanced their friendship. It had magnified it, glorified it, exalted it.

No question about it: He was madly in love. Driving through town, he began to sing the James Taylor song again. " 'I thought I was in love a couple of times before—' "

"Spare me!" Jack cut him off, then addressed the air around them. "Forgive me, bullfrogs of the world. Comparing Lonny's voice to yours was an insult to you." Lonny only laughed.

Howie was already at the Tucker house when Lonny and Jack arrived. The back doors of Howie's van were open, and he was lugging a heavy toolbox up the walk. "It's about time you guys showed up," he griped.

Jack spread his arms in a pose of innocence. "Don't look at me, Howie. I got to Lonny's place on time, and he was half-asleep and running around bare-assed. My guess is, he had one too many last night."

"One too many what?" Lonny asked in a level voice.

"Now, that's an interesting question," Jack mused, winking broadly. "You and Sammy all alone in that big house with the rain pouring down on the roof... The possibilities are endless."

"Your stupidity is endless," Lonny said brusquely, heaving a canvas drop cloth from the back of the van and following Howie toward the house.

"Hey, I'm just ribbing you," Jack said, lifting another drop cloth and chasing Lonny along the sidewalk. "Hey, Lonny, I know she's your friend. I'm just kidding you. Actually," he added, stepping aside so Lonny could precede him into the house, "I was thinking, maybe after work, I'd take her out for a drink or something. What do you think?" At Lonny's stony stare, he added, "Come on, I'm not going to maul her. I just want to spend an evening with her. She's a big girl; she can handle me. All right? I just thought I ought to check with you first, given that she's your houseguest and all."

Lonny bit back the words that sprang to his lips. He almost said that Jack didn't have a prayer with Samantha, that Jack wasn't her type, that she was far more than Lonny's friend and that Jack would be wise to cross her off his list here and now. But while Samantha might be flattered by Lonny's jealousy, he had no good reason to let Jack see any evidence of it.

He quirked an eyebrow nonchalantly. "If you want to ask her out, be my guest," he said, practically choking on the words. "As you said, she's a big girl. She can decide for herself how she wants to spend her evenings."

Even though he was certain Samantha would refuse Jack's invitation, the idea of Jack's asking her out continued to haunt Lonny while he stripped the faded wallpaper from the kitchen walls. He wasn't the first man to love Samantha; for all he knew, neither was Stephen. Just because Lonny had noticed her beauty belatedly didn't mean that other men failed to be impressed by her. New York City was filled with men. Lonny wondered how many of them made passes at her, and how she handled it.

It was odd for him to consider Samantha in such terms. He knew that she had gone out on dates in college, but she had done so only rarely, and those dates had never led to anything serious. Lonny had been too shortsighted to give much speculation to her sluggish social life back then. He'd assumed that she was a fine person, and that if she wasn't dating much it was by her own choice. It had never occurred to him that she didn't date much because she was overweight—or because she was carrying a torch for him.

Now she was no longer overweight, and she was too mature and sensible to carry a torch for anyone. She had obviously recovered completely from her affair with Stephen. Who knew what she would do once she returned to Manhattan and was surrounded by all those red-blooded men?

New York was only an hour and a half's drive from Spring Lake, he consoled himself. It wasn't as if they would be fifteen hundred miles apart, and it wasn't as if Lonny would be courting oil barons' daughters in Samantha's absence. He loved her, after all. He would have to have faith that she loved him, too. And if they really loved each other, the distance between them wouldn't matter.

"Tucker's here," Jack announced, emerging from the powder room where he and Howie had been working. "I just saw him parking his car outside. It seems like the right time to break for lunch. We're heading out to Burger King. Wanna join us?"

Lonny pulled his bandanna from his hip pocket. He mopped the perspiration from his brow, then rolled the bandanna into a narrow strip and tied it around his head to hold back his floppy hair. "I'll pass," he said. "I want to finish this wall. Bring me back a Whopper, would you?"

"Showing off for the boss-man," Jack mocked, shrugging his broad shoulders amiably. "All right. One Whopper to go. Howie?"

Howie stepped out of the bathroom in time to greet Bill Tucker, who entered the house through the open kitchen door. A tall, trim man whose striking silver hair was belied by his youthful face, he wore a LaCoste polo shirt of kelly green and cotton slacks cinched at the waist with a canvas belt. It was the sort of attire Lonny's father favored on his days off: crisp and dapper, in impeccable good taste. "Hello, boys," he said cheerfully, picking his way around the plaster dust on the kitchen floor. "Working hard, I see."

"With one eye on the calendar, Mr. Tucker," Howie assured him, offering an artificial smile. "We're just about to take off for lunch."

"Go right ahead." Bill waved generously toward the door. "I'll have a look around."

"Watch your step in the powder room," Howie warned him. "There's a mess of tools on the floor."

"Will do," Bill promised. He started directly to the powder room as Jack and Howie left the house. Peering into the bathroom, he shook his head. "This room will look marvelous with those new fixtures in it," he predicted. "I wonder what possessed the former owners to install a purple commode."

"There's no accounting for taste, Mr. Tucker," Lonny observed, yanking off a sagging strip of wallpaper.

Bill turned back to Lonny. "Don't you want to go for lunch with the others?" he asked.

"They're going to bring something back for me," Lonny assured him, standing and taking a step back to assess what he'd accomplished so far that morning. The plasterboard behind the wallpaper was in excellent condition. After some sanding it would take fresh paint without any trouble.

Bill leaned against one of the counters and folded his arms. "I hope you boys don't mind if I drop in from time to time and see how you're coming along," he commented. "It's not that I don't trust you; it's just that I'm very excited about the house. And things are quiet on campus at the moment, so I've got plenty of time on my hands."

Bill had already told Lonny and his partners that he was an administrator at Princeton University. "Driving down here every now and then will get you used to the commute," Lonny noted.

"It isn't a bad trip," said Bill. "Thirty, forty minutes. Princeton's a nice town to live in, but my family would rather live near the ocean."

"When my dad was at Princeton," Lonny remarked, "he and his friends used to make the drive all the time. Maybe that's why I love living by the shore now."

"Your dad's a Princeton man?" Bill asked, evidently surprised. At Lonny's nod, Bill narrowed his eyes on the grubby-looking young man across the room from him. "Was he disappointed that you didn't follow in his footsteps?"

"And how," Lonny recalled. "When I decided to go to Brown, he threatened to string me up with his official orange-and-black Princeton Tigers necktie."

Bill's astonishment increased noticeably. "You went to Brown? Brown University?"

"That's the place," Lonny said, dragging over his stepladder and mounting it, ready to attack another strip of wallpaper.

Bill rubbed his jaw thoughtfully. "If I'm not being too presumptuous, how did you end up doing...this?" He pointed vaguely at the wall where Lonny was working.

Lonny chuckled. "I enjoy it," he explained. "Sitting at a desk and wearing a three-piece suit isn't for everybody, even among those of us with Ivy League degrees."

"You mean, you really find this sort of mindless labor fulfilling?"

"It isn't mindless," Lonny objected as he scraped off a stubborn piece of paper with a razor blade. Actually, yanking wallpaper from walls was about as mindless a task as

Lonny could imagine. But it didn't seem quite so mindless when he could exercise his brain by talking to Bill Tucker while he worked.

Samantha undoubtedly considered his work mindless. So many people seemed to think that you weren't doing something worthwhile unless you were ensconced in a grand office somewhere, making supposedly portentous decisions and scribbling meaningful notes on memo pads with your name embossed across the top. Yet people lived in houses; their very lives depended on the condition of their homes. Ask a street person, Lonny mused silently. Ask a bag lady if she wished she could live in a house that had been painstakingly renovated, made safe and beautiful by "mindless" laborers like Lonny and his partners.

He was probably overreacting to Bill Tucker's comment. The man spoke from ignorance, that was all. Lonny had endured enough heated disputes with his father concerning his choice of a vocation to be able to accept Bill's observations without becoming hot and bothered. Lonny knew why he was overreacting, though: He was thinking of Samantha, of how much her approval meant to him, now that he was in love with her.

"Here's what I think, Mr. Tucker," he said, climbing down from the stepladder and moving it out of his way. "You don't really consider this mindless labor. If you did, you wouldn't have hired three smart guys like my partners and me to do it for you." Lonny wished he could hear Samantha express a similar sentiment. She ought to be impressed by more than the fact that sometimes he and his partners were able to turn a one-hundred-percent profit on a particular property bought on speculation.

"I guess I did hire you because I liked the way you thought," Bill granted. "Then again, you boys put in the lowest bid for the job. That had something to do with it, too.''

"We're smart, and we're also hungry for work," Lonny conceded. He almost added that he, Jack, and Howie were men, not boys. But there was no point in getting on a soap-box with Bill Tucker. The man had contracted his services, not adopted him. Lonny didn't have to convert Bill. He just had to fix the man's house and get paid for it.

At least Samantha didn't think of Lonny as a boy. Or so he hoped.

HEARING THE TRUCK COAST up the driveway, Samantha spun back to the kitchen table and surveyed it carefully. She couldn't do much about the chipped dishes Lonny owned, but the additions she'd purchased that afternoon made the table look festive. She'd bought cloth place mats and matching linen napkins, two ornate brass napkin rings, and, as a centerpiece, a polished brass candlestick with a red ta-per rising from it. She listened to the sound of the engine shutting down and lit the candle.

Her white dress was a mass of wrinkles, thanks to her romp through the ocean the last time she'd worn it. But the dress she had on, featuring an aquamarine print and a complex lacing of straps across the back, was equally be-coming. She'd adorned her eyelids with a complementary green shadow, more for the fun of it than because she thought it improved her appearance. The perfume she'd dabbed behind her ears wasn't for fun, however. It subtly musky scent implied that she was more interested in pas-sion than in playing.

She would have liked to turn on some romantic music, but the only functioning radio in the house was Lonny's alarm-clock radio in his bedroom. His stereo components were still sitting in the basement of the house, stored in boxes until he completed his refurbishing of the living room.

Shrugging blithely, she decided that they didn't need background music. If necessary, Lonny could always serenade her with some old James Taylor songs. She didn't know what a bullfrog in heat sounded like, but she was certain Lonny sounded nothing like one.

The clomp of his footsteps on the veranda alerted her to his arrival. Fluffing out her hair with her fingers, she hurried to the front door and swung it wide. Seeing Jack instead of Lonny standing before her startled her so much that she lost her balance and stubbed her toe on the threshold. She howled a string of oaths.

Jack waited patiently until she simmered down. "Have you crippled yourself, darling?" he asked compassionately.

"Hardly," she muttered, rubbing her aching toe through the opening in her sandals. "Where's Lonny?"

"He's doing something in the truck," Jack answered. Peeking past him at the driveway, she spotted Lonny in the driver's seat, apparently engrossed in his keys. "So," Jack continued, drawing her attention back to him, "now seems as a good a time as any to ask you out."

"Ask me out where?" she mumbled. She was annoyed with Jack for inadvertently having caused her to injure her toe, and she didn't do much to hide her foul temper.

"Wherever your little heart desires," he said. "You look fantastic, Sammy. You smell fantastic, too. I've got to shower, but I could pick you up in a half hour."

Her vexation ebbed, replaced by bewilderment. Staring past Jack at the truck again, she spotted Lonny watching her intently. It dawned on her that he was remaining in the truck to give Jack a moment of privacy with her, to give him the opportunity to ask her out.

What on earth was Lonny up to? Did he *want* Jack to ask her out? Was he idiotic enough to think, as Stephen did, that she should spend an evening with Jack to enrich her relationship with Lonny? Or was he simply testing her, trying to determine the extent of her fidelity to him?

If he was, he had one hell of a nerve. She didn't like being tested that way.

Her gaze traveled back to Jack. "I'm really a nice guy," he pressed his case, misreading her hesitation. "Maybe I've come on a little strong with you, but I was only kidding. I mean, I figured we could have some dinner and few drinks and see what happened. No harm in that, is there, Sammy?"

"I'm sorry," she said, her anger tensing her voice. "I've got other plans for tonight."

"You mean you didn't get all duded up for me?" Jack asked with pretended disbelief. "I guess it was too good to be true."

She shook her head, determined not to take out her anger on Jack, even if he had caused her to stub her toe. "I appreciate the invitation, Jack, but no. I'm sorry."

"Well, you can't blame a guy for trying," he said, offering her a grudging smile. "All right. I'll go get Lonny."

He pivoted and jogged down the steps to the walk. His final words convinced Samantha that Lonny had been in collusion with him. By the time Jack had gotten into his own car and Lonny had left the truck, she was seething again.

"You look wonderful," Lonny declared as he bounded energetically up the steps to the veranda.

"Jack thought I looked fantastic," she snapped. "Did you two little boys practice your lines before you got here?"

Lonny frowned. He grabbed her arm and held her in the doorway as she was about to return to the kitchen. "Don't call me a little boy, Sammy," he muttered. "I'm a man, damn it."

She had expected that her anger would irk him, but she was surprised that he had chosen instead to react to her choice of words. "I called you a little boy because you're playing games, you and Jack both. What the hell was that all about?"

"He wanted to ask you out to dinner," Lonny explained, his grip on her arm relenting as he entered the house behind her. "So I let him."

"And aren't you feeling just swell, now that I turned him down," she muttered.

"Well, sure," Lonny admitted. "Sure, I'm glad you turned him down."

"I passed the test, then." She stalked into the kitchen, fuming.

Lonny chased her, perplexed. "What test?"

"You were testing me, weren't you? You sicced Jack on me to test me. Lonny, you know how I feel about you. Why in God's name did you send Jack here to court me? Does it do your ego good to hear me rejecting other men?"

Lonny sorted his thoughts carefully before speaking. "My ego, Samantha, is very gratified to know that you aren't interested in other men. But I'm in no position to speak for you. Jack told me he wanted to ask you out for dinner, and I wasn't going to stop him. Saying no is your job, not mine." He gazed at the table, and a shy smile crept across his face. "You did all this for me?"

"For us," Samantha told him, her voice muted. "Lonny, you could have spared Jack the trip up the front walk. You could have told him that we're...that we're..."

"Lovers," he supplied, his hands now gentle on her arms as he turned her to face him. "I could have told him, but it's none of his business. For all I know, if we weren't lovers, maybe you would have said yes to him. It was your decision to make."

"Do you think I would say yes to Jack if you and I weren't lovers?" she asked, curious. "Do you think he's my type?"

"I don't know what your type is anymore," Lonny replied. "I thought Carl Dunlap was your type."

Samantha peered up into his gentle eyes. "You're my type, Lonny," she confessed.

His smile expanded, and he kissed the tip of her nose. "I'm not sure what that means," he pondered. "Your type is now a seedy day laborer with a fancy diploma collecting dust in his parents' attic, is that what you're saying?"

"If that's what you are, that's my type," Samantha confirmed, her good spirits returning.

He eyed the table again, and then the pots on the stove. "This is an awfully domestic scene, Sammy. Seedy day laborer comes home to find the little lady slaving over a hot stove. What did you make?"

"Nothing too exciting," she cautioned him. "Chicken, rice and string beans. Store-bought chocolate cake for dessert. I'm not a great cook, but I tried to compensate with atmosphere."

"It's a very nice atmosphere," he whispered, nuzzling her neck. "I think the seedy day laborer had better shower and change his clothes or he won't be fit to sit at such a lovely table."

"Fine," Samantha agreed, ushering him to the stairs. "Can I watch?"

"Watch?"

"Watch you shower," she said, grinning seductively. "I may be little, but I'm not such a lady."

"Bless you for that," Lonny murmured, hooking his arm around her shoulders and walking up the stairs with her.

"I'll make a deal with you, Sammy: I'll never call you 'little lady,' and you'll never call me 'boy.'"

She scowled, still unable to fathom why he had latched on to that word when she'd used it. "Why does it bother you so much?"

He paused halfway up the stairs and turned her fully to him. "The guy we're working for on this latest project calls us boys," he revealed.

Samantha's scowl intensified. "So what?" she asked. "Jack calls him the old geezer."

Lonny's lips twitched as he tried to explain himself. "Bill Tucker calls us boys because he thinks we're below him." A line of consternation formed above his eyebrows as he added, "He was really shocked today when I told him I was an Ivy League graduate."

Samantha tried unsuccessfully to interpret what Lonny was saying. "Is that so surprising?" she asked. "Most Ivy League graduates don't do what you do."

"What difference does that make? I don't belittle most Ivy League graduates for doing what they do. Why should people belittle me?"

"Oh, you don't belittle them, is that so?" she grunted in disbelief. "You only give them holier-than-thou lectures on the subject of Type A personalities and worshipping the Golden Calf."

"I—" He pressed his lips together, then shook his head contritely. "If I ever did that, Sammy, I'm sorry. I don't look down on you. And I don't want you to look down on me."

He seemed so somber that she felt the need to joke. The evening she'd dreamed of spending with Lonny—a romantic dinner by candlelight, followed by a heavenly night of making love—was failing to materialize. It was time to bring some levity into the atmosphere. "How can I look down at you?'' she teased. "You're at least six inches taller than me."

He accepted her good-humored initiative by grasping her waist and lifting her onto the riser above the one he stood on. "There," he said, his face on a level with hers. "Now we can see eye-to-eye on things."

"Fair enough." She wrapped her arms around his neck and planted a warm kiss on his mouth. "I sure hope you'll see eye-to-eye with me on how I plan to spend this evening with you."

"Hmm." He grinned seductively. "Come on up and watch me shower, and we'll take it from there."

She happily raced him up the stairs, not caring one bit if the chicken overcooked and the candle burned out.

Chapter Seven

"It looks repulsive," Samantha said adamantly.

"I think it looks daring," argued Paul. "If we handle this right, we can create a big sensation with it."

Samantha shook her head. "The only way to handle blue lipstick is to take the entire concept and toss it into the circular file."

"It's not blue," Paul protested. "It's lilac."

"It's the bluest-looking lilac I've ever seen," Samantha said with a sniff. She stared at the photos displayed on one wall of the conference room. They featured models with a variety of facial types, all sporting the weird-colored lipsticks Paul and his people at Research and Development had concocted for the Artist's Eyes line of cosmetics at LaBelle. "If you ask me, those poor women look anemic."

"Samantha." Lynette Magnusson was LaBelle's vice president in charge of new product development, and when she spoke, everyone listened. "What we're looking for is something as novel and exciting as the eye products. If we can sell women on orange eye shadow and green eyeliner, then don't you think we can sell them on lilac lipstick?"

"Lilac, maybe," Samantha conceded grudgingly. "But that—" she pointed at a photograph on the wall "—is blue." She turned to John, the West Coast sales manager, who had flown in from Los Angeles to attend the meeting. "Help me out, John," she implored him. "You don't like it, either."

He shrugged uncomfortably. "Personally, no, I don't like it. The eye products have a certain whimsical appeal. But lip colors...well, you run the risk of giving the consumer a sickly appearance. Not necessarily anemic, mind you. Hypothermic seems closer to the mark."

"Whatever," Samantha hastily agreed, happy to have someone on her side in the debate.

"We're not interested in your personal opinion, John," Lynette reminded him, her voice soft but imperious. "All we want to know is, will it sell out West?"

"Well, my target market is a bit more adventurous than the East and Midwest markets," he granted. "You know me, Lynette. If you put a gun to my head, I can sell anything."

Samantha cringed inwardly at his capitulation to the powerful middle-aged woman at the head of the conference table. But she refused to surrender. "Read between the lines, Lynette," she suggested. "What John is actually saying is that blue lipstick is homicidal."

The entire group of market strategists erupted in laughter. Samantha smiled slightly, relieved to have injected some humor into the meeting. But she didn't feel victorious. Her impromptu jokes often helped her to win company disputes, but not always. The fact that Lynette was chuckling didn't mean she was ready to scrap the idea.

"Besides," Samantha pressed her case, "blue—pardon me, lilac—is one of the tamer colors Paul and his witch doctors at the New Jersey lab have come up with. Now this made here..." She pulled another illustration from the file of pictures each of the meeting's participants had been given. "It's gray."

"It's mauve," Paul asserted.

"It's gray. I can buy the orange, and I can buy this purplish one—I think it looks appalling, but I'll go along with it. But when you start discussing gray and blue, no way. John said it best: our customers want to look playful. They don't want to look deathly ill. Healthy lips are naturally red-toned. Lipstick ought to reflect that—pinks, reds, oranges."

"Lilac has red in it," Paul maintained.

"Lilac *might*," Samantha snapped. "Unfortunately, *that*—" she pointed at the photograph of the model again "—is blue."

"I'd love to straddle the fence here," Jill Stockton, the head of Midwestern sales, chipped in. "But I've got to admit, lilac and mauve are going to be awfully hard to promote in my region. What with the miserable winter weather in places like Chicago and Minneapolis, women's lips are blue for half the year. They're looking for warm colors."

"Like the orange," Paul said, indicating another photo on the wall.

"Sure. The orange is great. Kind of tarty, but fun. But Samantha has a valid point regarding these blue and gray hues. They're bloodless, and one thing people in my region don't need every winter is to be reminded that their blood has turned to ice."

"On the contrary," Rex McCaulley, the Southern sales rep, drawled, "we do very well with the dusty-musty colors down in my area. Our women are much too hot-blooded to begin with. I think lilac and mauve will go over wonderfully down there."

"We're selling to a nation united," Jill remarked. "The Civil War is history, Rex—and by the way, it was won by the North."

"Ah, now there's a marketing angle," Samantha quipped dryly. "Blue and gray lipsticks, just like the blue and gray armies."

"Something tells me we're not going to reach any resolutions today," Lynette wisely noted. "I think it's time we adjourned. We should all go off on our own and meditate overnight on Paul's concepts. We'll reconvene tomorrow with some fresh insights."

"R and D is hosting a luncheon and presentation for the regional reps tomorrow," Paul reminded her.

Lynette nodded. "What time will you be done?"

"Around three," he told her. "We can be back in the city by four. Probably not much earlier, I'm afraid."

"Four o'clock it is," Lynette decided.

Samantha stifled a groan. Tomorrow was Friday. By four o'clock on Friday, she had planned to be cruising to Spring Lake on the Garden State Parkway for a weekend with Lonny. "Tomorrow afternoon isn't good for me," she said meekly.

"We've got to do it sometime tomorrow," John observed. "I've already got my flight home booked for Saturday morning."

Lynette favored Samantha with a piercing stare. "Is tomorrow afternoon simply not good, dear, or is it impossible?"

Samantha wilted in her seat. Although she did a creditable job in her position, she was attuned enough to the upper levels of management of LaBelle Cosmetics to know that she was still viewed by her superiors as a mere youngster who had to prove herself again and again. Missing an important meeting simply to visit her lover would be impolitic, to say the least. "I'll... I'll be here," she acquiesced, hoping she didn't appear too glum.

"Fine." Lynette released Samantha from her paralyzing gaze. "Tomorrow at four, then. Let's get this subject resolved before our regional people have to leave for the airport. We can send out for sandwiches, if need be." Closing her folder with a flourish, she rose and strode regally from the conference room.

Samantha swore beneath her breath. This wasn't the first time a last-minute meeting had been called for a Friday afternoon. She was used to devoting more than the standard forty-hour work week to her company; she recognized the demands of a high-power, high-pressure job, and she accepted them. Or at least, she had always accepted them in the past. She had even liked the demands. They enhanced her sense of importance, her image of herself as an indispensable cog in the corporate machine.

But working late and attending last-minute meetings had never been a problem when she was dating Stephen. For one thing, he had lived only minutes from her, so they could be more flexible about seeing each other. For another, he understood her desire to excel at LaBelle Cosmetics, since he, too, was riding on the fast track in his company. He could empathize with her when she told him she had to break a date because of her work.

And for another, she realized in retrospect, spending an evening at her desk was frequently more fulfilling than spending an evening with Stephen. She hadn't loved him anywhere near as much as she loved Lonny.

It was bad enough that she wouldn't be able to see Lonny until Saturday. Even worse was that he wanted to take her to a party Friday night. He hadn't explained much about the party, only told her that he wanted to bring her with him. Would he be as forgiving as Stephen had always been when she canceled an engagement with him? Or would Lonny subject her to one of his lectures about how she was too committed to her job and was running the risk of developing into a Type A personality?

Returning to her office with her folder wedged under her arm, she felt her bun sagging low on the back of her neck. Despite the building's air-conditioning, she felt sticky and droopy. What she needed to cool her off wasn't a climate-controlled ventilation system but the balmy shore breezes that gusted through the windows of Lonny's house.

She reached her office and checked her wristwatch. Four-thirty. Slumping into the chair behind her desk, she punched her intercom button to signal her secretary. "Any calls while I was at the meeting?" she asked.

"Nothing," her secretary replied.

"Good. I'm heading for home, then. We're going to be burning the midnight oil here tomorrow, so I'm taking off early today."

"May as well," her secretary agreed.

Samantha slid the folder of offensive lipstick colors into her briefcase and loosened the bow at the neck of her flowered shirtwaist dress. She pulled a dollar's worth of change from her purse before snapping the briefcase shut. Although her apartment was only a twenty-minute walk from her office, she was going to splurge on a bus ride home. She suspected that she would need all her energy for her telephone call to Lonny that evening.

As soon as she got to her apartment, she kicked off her shoes and wiggled her toes. Even though she wore well-made leather pumps with modest heels, by the end of a muggy summer day her feet were cramped and aching. In the past few years, the city's streets had started to swarm with professional women who wore jogging shoes with their business suits and dresses. Samantha didn't blame those women for choosing comfort over style in their footwear, but she thought they looked rather silly, and she couldn't bring herself to imitate them.

Actually, she mused as she tossed her briefcase onto the coffee table in the living room and then went to her bedroom to change her clothes, if women could create a new fashion by wearing jogging shoes with business dresses, who was to say they wouldn't also be willing to wear blue lipstick?

She decided not to phone Lonny until after dinner. She picked listlessly at the salad she fixed for herself, rehearsing in her mind exactly what she'd say to him. The more she thought about it, the more she recognized that she wasn't really worried about his possible resentment concerning her job, or his anger over her having to beg off his invitation for the party Friday night. What was truly bothering her was that she missed him terribly. She didn't want to have to wait until Saturday to see him. The four days since she'd kissed him goodbye and left Spring Lake had dragged torturously. She wanted to be with him, and she didn't want to have to wait an extra day.

What little appetite she'd had vanished when she thought about how wonderful her week with him had been, and how lonely she'd felt since leaving him. She hadn't felt so lonely when Stephen had moved to Denver. But then, it hadn't been him she'd missed as much as their life together. She didn't really have a "life" with Lonny, not in the same way. What they had was each other, a deep trust and a deep love.

Shoving her plate away, she rose from the table and walked to her bedroom. She lifted the phone from her night table and dialed his number. It rang six times on his end before he answered. "Hello!" he panted.

Simply hearing his voice elated her. She stretched out on her bed and smiled. "Did I interrupt your shower, or something more compromising?" she asked impishly.

"Sammy!" He sounded equally delighted to be talking to her. "Hello! What you interrupted, if you really want to know, is that I was up on my roof. I was checking the seals around the chimney." He took a minute to catch his breath, then chuckled. "Thank God it was you on the phone, and not some salesman trying to talk me into a new telephone service or something. You're worth risking my life for by running over the roof at breakneck speed. Telephone salesmen aren't."

"Next time, don't run," Samantha scolded him affectionately. "I never hang up before the tenth ring, and I'd rather you didn't risk your life for me, even if I'm worth it."

"Ten rings," Lonny echoed. "I'll remember that."

"Why were you up on your roof at this late hour?" she asked. "It's nearly seven o'clock."

"The sun hasn't set yet," he explained. "With that September first deadline on the Tucker house, I've been hard-pressed to find time for my own house. I want to make sure the roof's tight and well insulated before the summer's over, so I've got to take advantage of whatever daylight I've got." He exhaled. "I'm beat," he said wearily. "I'm working too hard, Sammy. I thought the only people who worked too hard were people with jobs like yours."

"Funny you should mention that," she muttered. "Lonny, I've got—"

"I'm glad you called, though," he cut her off. "I was going to call you later tonight to remind you to bring something fancy to wear to the party tomorrow. I can't remember if I told you, but it's going to be a dressy affair."

She indulged in a brief speculation of what Lonny would wear to a dressy party. His madras jacket, perhaps? Her lips arched in a wistful smile as she recalled his oddly appealing getup the night they'd gone on their double date. Dwelling on a memory of that night only made it more difficult to break her bad news to him, but she had no choice. "Lonny, I can't come to the party."

"What do you mean, you can't come?"

"I've got to go to a business meeting tomorrow," she informed him. "It's scheduled to start at four o'clock, and I can't miss it."

He didn't speak for a minute. "How come you can't miss it?" he asked finally.

Please, she prayed silently. *Please don't give me a hard time.* "It's for my product line," she said. "LaBelle wants to introduce a line of lipsticks to go along with Artist's Eyes."

"What are they going to call them?" he asked sardonically. "Artist's Mouths?"

"They ought to call them Diseased Mouths," she grumbled. "They've cooked up some hideous colors, and I seem to be the sole voice of reason on the subject. If I'm not there to talk some sense into everyone, they're going to wind up trying to market blue lipstick."

Lonny again lapsed into a brief silence. "Did it ever occur to you, Sammy," he asked, "that discussing the merits of blue lipstick is a pretty stupid way to make a living?"

Samantha suffered a sharp spasm of rage. It was one thing for Lonny to express disappointment at her having to break their date. It was quite another thing for him to disparage her entire career. Stupid, indeed! "Did it ever occur to you," she countered in a gritty voice, "that not everyone can derive satisfaction from such intellectually stimulating tasks as tightening the screws on doorknobs?"

"Now, Sammy, I didn't mean—"

"Like hell you didn't," she snapped. "But then, I suppose that you don't have to make sacrifices for your work. If you ever decided that you didn't want to hang doorknobs on a Friday afternoon—because it interfered with your social life, for instance—you could always just quit working and live off your rich relatives for a while."

"I've never taken a dime from my relatives!" he objected.

"No, of course not. We won't count your school tuition or your vacations in the Bahamas."

"Sammy, Sammy, what are we fighting for?" He took a deep breath. "I didn't mean to belittle your work," he apologized. "I'm just teed off that it's spoiling our plans for tomorrow night."

"I'm angry about that, too," she concurred quietly, more than willing to forgive him. "I tried to get the meeting rescheduled, but I struck out. I'm sorry."

"So am I," Lonny said. "I really wanted you with me."

"A dressy affair," she reflected, wondering how Lonny had gotten roped into attending such a party. The parties he enjoyed most were the bashes he and she used to go to in college, where lots of beer was served and people danced on the windowsills. "Who's hosting it?"

"A couple whose house we worked on last spring. They've just finished furnishing it, and they're throwing a housewarming. They invited dozens of friends to see the place, and they invited my partners and me so we'll be able to reap the credit. We felt we ought to go."

"Well," Samantha said, "you can go with Jack and Howie."

"Jack and his date and Howie and his wife?" Lonny snorted. "Talk about being a fifth wheel."

"I guess you could always ask someone else to go with you." The words slipped out of their own volition; Samantha was so used to talking to Lonny about his social life, she'd temporarily forgotten that *she* was his social life now.

Realizing what she'd said, she felt her hands grow clammy. She held her breath and waited for his response.

"I don't want to," he said slowly, carefully. "Do you think I should?"

"No." Relief was evident in her voice. "Of course I don't want you to take anyone else. But it's your decision, you know."

There was another pause before he spoke again. "I'm really sorry about what I said before, Sammy, about your work. I just—I wish you didn't live in New York. I wish you were here. I miss you."

She allowed herself a moment to savor his compliment. "I miss you, too," she murmured. "We'll have the rest of the weekend together, at least. I can leave here at the crack of dawn on Saturday and get to your place in time for breakfast."

"In time to kiss me goodbye on my way out the door," he predicted morosely. "We're planning to work on the Tucker house over the weekend. We've got barely a month to get the job done."

"Oh." Samantha fidgeted with the telephone cord and tried to keep her tone calm when she asked, "Would it be better if I didn't come down to see you, then?"

"Are you kidding? Sammy, if you don't come down, I'll be driven to drastic measures. I might become so despondent I'll hurl myself off a porch."

"If suicide is your goal," Samantha grunted, not exactly pleased to be reminded of her own clumsiness, "take it from someone with experience. Porch falls aren't fatal."

"As long as I'm going to see you at some point this weekend, suicide isn't my goal," Lonny assured her. "Do get here early on Saturday, though. Jack is going to call for me at around eight, and I don't want you to get here and find an empty house. Nor do I want to give Jack the opportunity to humiliate me the way he did the last time he called for me at eight."

"I'll leave here at six," Samantha promised. "I should arrive at your place around seven-thirty. That gives us a half hour of leeway."

"Not nearly enough for what I have in mind," Lonny said devilishly. "But better than nothing. I'll see you bright and early Saturday morning."

"Don't drink too much at the party," Samantha warned him. "I don't want you to have a hangover when I see you."

"Yes, ma'am."

"Goodbye, Lonny."

"Goodbye."

Samantha lowered the receiver to its cradle and returned the telephone to the night table. Then she lay down, resting her head on the pillow and closing her eyes. She reran the entire conversation through her head and tried to sort out her thoughts.

His comment about the stupidity of blue lipstick hadn't warranted her furious outburst. The truth was, blue lipstick *was* stupid, and Samantha knew that as well as Lonny did. She'd blown up at him not because she disagreed with what he'd said, but because his words had struck a nerve. He'd given voice to something she herself hadn't had the courage to admit.

It wasn't that she considered her job worthless. It wasn't that she was ready to resign. But if she had any say in the matter, any choice at all, she would certainly have chosen to go to a party with Lonny instead of a meeting with Lynette, Paul, and the regional reps.

And that cut to the heart of it. Samantha *did* have a say in the matter. She *did* have a choice. She wasn't about to quit her job in order to go to a party, but still... For the first time in her life, she questioned whether her career was as important as spending time with the man she loved. By breaking her date with Lonny, she had sensibly chosen to preserve her career, and making that sensible choice meant that she would spend Friday evening gnawing on tasteless sandwiches with her colleagues in a conference room while Lonny went to a party without her.

Without her, and possibly with someone else. He had said he didn't want to bring anyone else to the party, but he hadn't said he *wouldn't*. For all Samantha knew, he might be on the phone with Marcy right now, begging her to fill in for Samantha on Friday night. Marcy would probably do it, too. Or if not Marcy, perhaps some oil baron's daughter, some woman who was born wealthy and beautiful, who had never been fat in her life and who never worried about getting grass stains on her butt because she was graceful as a gazelle. Lonny knew enough women like that. Until last week, such women had definitely been his type.

Samantha didn't think that Lonny could fall madly out of love with her so soon. However, she also didn't think he'd care to attend the party stag tomorrow night. If she could choose her work over him, then surely he might feel justified in asking another woman to accompany him to the party. Maybe he would even see taking another woman to the party as a way of enriching his relationship with Samantha.

Damn long-distance romances, she thought disconsolately. And damn Lonny for making her wonder whether she'd made the right decision about Friday night.

LONNY SMILED THROUGH HIS PAIN. Four hours after he'd smashed his thumb while trying to install a new vanity in the powder room of Bill Tucker's house, the finger still throbbed.

He rarely injured himself while working. But he'd been distracted while he worked that day. He'd been troubled by thoughts of Samantha, angry with her for deciding not to come to the party with him, and angry with himself for having made snide references to her work when they'd talked the previous night. And as a result, he hadn't paid close enough attention to what he was doing, and he'd gotten his thumb caught between the cherry-wood vanity and the wall. Now the top joint of his finger was three shades of purple, with a rim of scabbing blood around his nail. About as pleasant to look at as blue lipstick, he thought caustically. He hid his hand in his trousers pocket and wove through the crowd to the bar for a beer.

He shouldn't have argued with her on the phone last night. He'd had no right to condemn her for getting stuck with a business meeting. It wasn't her fault, any more than it was his fault that he'd be spending the better part of the weekend at Tucker's house instead of with her. She'd be renting a car and driving all the way to Spring Lake, and in all likelihood he'd be able to visit with her for a grand total of one night.

"I understand you're the fellow responsible for resuscitating this joint."

Lonny accepted the bottle of beer from the hired bartender and turned to greet the man who had addressed him. A dark-haired man in a pale blue summer suit, apparently not much older than Lonny, he appeared to be well-heeled. "My partners are at least as responsible as I am," Lonny said generously.

"Well, I've got to say, you did a swell job of it," the man praised him, extending his hand. "Harvey Bolton," he introduced himself as Lonny set down the beer bottle and shook his hand. "And you're Ronny something, is that right?"

"Lonny Reed," Lonny introduced himself. "Nice to meet you."

"My wife and I own a house just up the road in Belmar," Harvey told him. "We bought it new, and it set us back a pretty penny. I've got the feeling, after seeing this place, that we did things the wrong way. Buy one of these rattletraps, hire a crew like yours to rehab it, and you come out way ahead."

"Sometimes," Lonny allowed. "It depends on how rattly the trap is to begin with."

Harvey surveyed the spacious sunroom, with its buffed parquet floor, its rugged natural wood paneling along an inner wall, and the broad picture windows Lonny and his colleagues had installed along the outer wall. "When Roy first bought this place, I told him he must have gone off the deep end, sinking good money into a dive like this. But he obviously had some prescience when he chose this house. He must have known that a few talented folks like you and your partners could transform it into something grand. I've got to hand it to you, Ronny. You did quite a job here, quite a job. I'll have a martini," he told the bartender.

Lonny considered correcting Harvey about his name, then thought better of it. Why bother? They'd never see each other again after tonight. "How do you happen to know Roy?" he asked politely.

"Olive, not onion," Harvey instructed the bartender, then turned his attention back to Lonny. "Roy and I go way back," he said. "We were at Andover together."

Preppies, Lonny grunted to himself. *A preppy martini drinker. Sammy's type.*

That wasn't true, not anymore, he amended himself. Lonny was her type, even if his hair was too long and the suit he was wearing had been purchased ages ago. And if preppies *were* her type, well, Lonny himself had graduated from prep school before entering college. He had no right to view people like Harvey Bolton with disdain. Despite the outward trappings, Harvey might well have a great deal in common with Lonny.

"So, how come your wife isn't here?" Harvey asked him.

"My wife?" Lonny scowled. "You must have me mixed up with my partner, Howie. He's the married one."

"Forgive me." Harvey chuckled knowingly. "I assumed you were married because you seem to be alone, and you've got your left hand jammed into your pocket. Hiding your ring in order to check out the ladies, I figured."

Lonny pulled his hand out and exhibited his gauze-swaddled thumb. "What I was hiding was my war wound," he explained. "I'm not married."

"In that case..." Harvey moved closer to him and pointed out an attractive woman in a revealing dress of raw silk. "That's my wife's sister. She's staying with us these days, recuperating from a messy divorce. Very, very available, if you'd like to meet her."

Lonny gave the woman an objective perusal. She was strikingly tall and slim, with lush auburn hair and delicate features. "She's a beautiful woman," he granted. "But no, thanks. I'm already taken."

"You just said you weren't married," Harvey reminded him.

"I'm not, but I'm attached," Lonny said. "My girlfriend couldn't make it tonight. Business obligations." He was surprised to hear himself confiding so easily to Harvey, a man he'd never met before, a man who couldn't even get his name right. Yet Lonny *did* have certain things in common with Harvey, their differing preferences in liquor notwithstanding. Lonny had grown up with men like Harvey. He'd gone to school with them, and to college, and he'd socialized with them. Lonny couldn't deny a certain kinship with the man at his side.

"What business is your girlfriend in?" Harvey asked.

"Cosmetics," Lonny told him, adding almost proudly, "She's a product manager at LaBelle." Yes, he *was* proud of Samantha. Even if her job had cost him her company at this party tonight, even if he thought she risked turning herself into a money-grubbing corporate zombie, he was proud of her accomplishments, and he didn't mind boasting about them to a snobby, urbane man like Harvey.

"LaBelle Cosmetics," Harvey said with a chuckle. "My wife's a walking advertisement for that outfit. Our bathroom looks like a veritable artist's studio, with all her arty eye paints lined up at the sink."

"No kidding," Lonny exclaimed. "Samantha would be thrilled to hear it. That's her product—Artist's Eyes."

"That's the stuff," Harvey confirmed. "Costs a fortune, but my wife swears by it."

"How about you?" Lonny asked. "What line are you in?"

"Corporate finance. Nothing as macho as building houses, Ronny, but I'm happy to say that the only war I wound myself in is the ongoing war between my chin and my razor." He took a sip of his cocktail and smiled complacently. "Fact is, Ronny, corporate finance is as creative in its way as house-building. I spend my days looking for money, looking for investors, figuring out ways to make very big ends meet. Playing with zeroes. I love it."

"I can tell," Lonny commented. He wished he felt as enthusiastic about his own work as Harvey seemed to be about his. Corporate finance sounded incredibly dull to Lonny, but perhaps that was only a matter of reverse snobbism on his part.

"Oh, now here's somebody you ought to meet," Harvey declared, waving to an older gentleman who had approached the bar. "Pete, come on over here and meet Ronny—I'm sorry, what was it?"

"Lonny Reed," he said, shaking the man's hand.

"How do you do, Lonny?" Pete had a crushing grip; Lonny wondered whether he'd require some bandages on his right hand, too, by the time the man was through with him. "Pete LaFarge, here."

"Pete's in the market for a house," Harvey said, explaining his eagerness to introduce the two men. "He's getting sick and tired of the condo scene. Why don't you tell him about the joy of buying a fixer-upper and hiring someone like you and your friends to do all the work?"

"Are you looking into purchasing an old house?" Lonny asked, warming up to the older man. "My partners and I did all the renovation work on this house."

"In that case," Pete said robustly, "you're definitely the man I should be talking to."

Harvey discreetly made his exit, leaving the two men to discuss Lonny's trade. Lonny described his abilities directly and honestly. If he were to think about it, he might well be surprised to hear himself selling his services so effectively. Not that he had any doubts about his talent, or any qualms about promoting himself to prospective customers.

What would have surprised him was that, in a sense, he was as much a businessman as the men he was talking to, as much a professional as Samantha. The clothing he wore to work, the odd hours he put in, the externals of the job were as irrelevant as the age of the suit he was wearing, or the length of his hair.

Long after he had written down his phone number for Pete LaFarge, as well as for several other guests who had been impressed by the transformation the host's house had undergone, long after Lonny had left the party and driven home, that revelation continued to haunt him. Unable to sleep, he slipped on a pair of jeans and climbed through his bedroom window onto the deck. To the east, the ocean whispered its tidal lullaby to him, and to the south the ripening moon cast a silver sheen over the neighborhood. Lonny rested against the railing, letting the warm wind rustle through his hair, and mulled over his discovery about himself. He was a businessman.

Just like Samantha, he had to support himself. He had to earn his keep. He had to bend to the demands of his work. He had to dress in a certain way, and while he greatly preferred wearing jeans to wearing the corporate uniform men like his father wore, who was to say that Samantha didn't prefer wearing her dowdy dresses and her classic shoes? Was wielding a hammer more virtuous than wielding a pen? Did scaling roofs constitute a more valid existence than vending eye paints that made women feel pretty? Was it acceptable to work all weekend while one's lover was visiting, and yet find it contemptible for one's lover to miss a Friday night party to meet the obligations of her work?

And if Samantha's work seemed so uninspiring to Lonny, why was it that she had the most beautiful, gentle, soft hands he had ever seen, while his left thumb was currently battered and aching like the dickens?

The bottom line, he contemplated as he stared out at the black water, was that no job could be all that wonderful to him if it meant he had to spend less time with the woman he loved. Samantha would come to Spring Lake tomorrow, and he would see painfully little of her because some silver-haired college administrator who called Lonny a "boy" wanted to move his family into his house by September first.

Lonny had always delighted in his work. He'd considered it romantic, a craft bordering on art. But after spending an evening at a party, behaving like a high-class huckster as he drummed up new customers, he viewed his career in a different light. What he did was no better or worse than what anyone else did to make money. Just like everyone else,

Lonny worked, he put in his time and energy, and he took home his pay.

The key to happiness wasn't a career. The key to happiness was love, being in love, being with the woman you loved. Sitting in solitude on his deck, Lonny understood that his work no longer mattered to him the way it once had. All that mattered was that he was in Spring Lake and Samantha was in New York, and they would both be much happier if they were together.

It was the sort of epiphany he longed to share with his best friend. Tomorrow—tomorrow night, after he'd spent another long, tiring day banging nails with a hammer instead of being with Samantha—he would tell her.

Chapter Eight

Samantha closed her eyes, relishing the sweet lassitude that washed through her body. Lonny's room smelled of the ocean, fresh and salty, cleansing her lungs of the city's soot and grime. She cuddled closer to him, using his shoulder as a pillow. "What time is it?" she mumbled.

She felt him shift beside her as he glanced at his clock radio. "A quarter to eight." He delicately lifted a strand of her hair away from her face. "You must be exhausted."

"Tooting your own horn, aren't you?" she teased him, laughing airily.

He stroked his hand through her hair to her shoulder and traced a lazy pattern across her skin. "What I meant was that you must have had to wake up in the middle of the night to get here so early this morning."

She shrugged languorously. "I picked up the car last night after my meeting," she told him. "The rental place doesn't open until eight-thirty on the weekends."

"Your meeting," Lonny said, half to himself. "Sammy, we've got to talk."

"I know," she concurred pleasantly. Opening her eyes, she smiled at Lonny. His hair was disheveled, and his angular features were set in a solemn cast. She lowered her gaze to his long, naked body next to hers and grinned.

"We've behaved like animals, Lonny. We barely said hello to each other, and suddenly there you were, tearing off my clothes—"

"I had plenty of enthusiastic assistance from you," he reminded her, sharing her smile. "Don't forget, we were racing against the clock. Jack is going to be here soon."

"I know," she conceded. "But still, Lonny...we used to enjoy talking as much as we enjoy this, didn't we?"

"You're mixing apples and oranges," he chided her. "Talking and making love are two very different things."

"Are they?"

Lonny mulled over her question and nodded. "I have no objection to talking to you in front of Jack," he said. "But as for making love...no, I definitely wouldn't want to do that in front of him."

"Good point." Samantha closed her eyes and rested her head against his shoulder again.

He bowed to kiss her forehead. "I've got to get dressed," he told her. "Why don't you stay in bed and catch up on your sleep? We'll talk later."

"We're talking now," she observed.

He eased out from under her and sat up. "And we'll talk some more when I get home from work," he promised as he stood.

Samantha propped her head against a pillow and watched him dress. "How was the party?"

"I'll tell you about it tonight," he said, stepping into his jeans and pulling them up.

She studied his face, trying to discern from his expression whether he'd taken her up on her suggestion and escorted another woman to the party. He appeared somber, almost grim, and she wasn't sure why.

If he had been with another woman last night, Samantha didn't think he'd try to conceal the news from her. After all, their friendship left no room for deception. Yet how common was it for a man to tell his lover about another woman? Now that she and Lonny were more than simply friends, would they start hiding the truth from each other?

She tried to recall what Marcy had said about the perils of sleeping with one's best friend. Marcy had pointed out that lovers kept secrets and made demands on each other. Samantha would never make demands on Lonny—at least, she hoped she wouldn't. If he had been with another woman last night, she would try not to hold it against him. She would try not to succumb to jealousy.

But still, she had to know. She couldn't spend the entire day in ignorance. "Tell me," she said softly, realizing at once that she was making a demand on him, yet unable to stop herself. "Tell me now."

"Tell you what?" he asked innocently.

No. She wouldn't let him see how anxious she was about what might have happened last night. "Tell me what happened to your finger," she substituted for her original question.

He flexed his bandaged thumb and grinned. "Nothing much," he assured her. "I pinched it while installing a bathroom vanity yesterday. I'll live."

She sighed, feeling like a coward for her failure to question him about what she really wanted to know. Taking a deep breath, she asked, "Lonny, did you—" She swallowed and started again. "Did you take another woman to the party?"

A curious smile tickled his lips. He turned from her and reached for his shirt. "What makes you ask that?"

"Well, we did discuss the possibility over the phone," she refreshed his memory. Her stomach began to knot with dread as he continued dressing in silence. Lord help her, she didn't want to be jealous, but she couldn't seem to help it.

He spent an inordinate amount of time buttoning his shirt, with his back to her. "I take it you'd be furious with me if I did," he guessed.

"Of course not," she lied, her voice high with tension. "It's just that, well, if you spent all night with another woman and then raced back home ten minutes before I got here, and then succeeded in ravaging me with so much energy, you might deserve a place in the *Guinness Book of World Records*."

He laughed and turned to her. "I hate to disappoint you—to say nothing of Mr. Guinness and Mr. Book—but no, I didn't spend all night with another woman."

The knot inside her began to unravel, but only slightly. "You dropped her off after the party and came home alone, is that what happened?"

"I didn't take anyone with me," he said quietly, stuffing his bandanna into his back pocket and crossing the room to the bed. "Someone tried to set me up with his sister-in-law there, and I told him I was already taken. Okay?"

Samantha tried not to look as relieved as she felt. "I don't like that phrasing—that you're already taken. It makes it sound as if I owned you or something."

He sat on the edge of the bed and caressed her cheek. "Sammy," he said solemnly, "I love you. You ought to have a little trust in me."

"I do trust you," she insisted, averting her eyes. His hand felt so warm on her, so soothing. She turned her face and kissed his palm. "It's just—I've learned from experience that it's very hard to live far away from someone you love. Especially for men. They mutate and all."

"After two weeks," Lonny reminded her. "This has only been five days."

She raised her eyes to his and saw the glint of mischievous humor in them. "Then how come you acted like an animal when I walked through the door?'' she challenged him.

"It takes one to know one," he parried her. The sound of a car horn blasted through the open window, and he stood. "I've got to go. I'll see you later."

"Be careful," she called after him as he strode out of the bedroom. "Don't hurt any more of your fingers."

"Yes, Mother," he shouted back to her before descending on the stairs to meet Jack.

Samantha flopped back down onto the mattress and stared at the ceiling. She was irked at having questioned him about other women, and she was irked at having to be irked. Worrying about whether the man you loved had spent an evening with another woman was normal. She shouldn't feel so guilty about suffering from such a typical worry regarding Lonny.

Yet it troubled her. They were friends first: that ought to elevate their love and make it immune to typical worries. She was troubled by her jealousy, and by the fact that she'd misinterpreted his casual remark that he would tell her about the party later. She had thought he was being evasive, and he had probably thought she was being nosy.

Before last week, she could have asked Lonny anything and everything about his love life—and she usually did. She had never hesitated to grill him about his female friends, about his party companions, about whether he was madly in love with this or that woman. He used to welcome her questions. He had loved discussing the condition of his heart with her.

But now that was changed between them. Now, for the first time, she felt guilty asking him such questions. And now, for the first time, he felt obliged to request that she trust him. Now, when he said he loved her, he meant something quite different from what he used to mean. Marcy was correct: becoming lovers *did* involve making demands on each other. Samantha didn't like it, but she couldn't deny it. Things had changed.

She listened to Lonny's and Jack's voices in the parlor below her, a muffled jumble of words she couldn't decipher. Then came the click of the front door, two heavy sets of footsteps on the veranda, the slams of the truck doors being shut, the roar of the engine revving. She waited until the truck had driven away before climbing out of the bed, then donned her shorts and T-shirt and went downstairs.

She fixed herself a pot of coffee, and investigated the contents of Lonny's refrigerator while it brewed. She didn't have an appetite for much other than a glass of juice, but a bakery box of brownies on a lower shelf caught her eye, and her resistance crumbled. She pulled a brownie out of the box, shoved it to the back of the shelf, and then surrendered to temptation and pulled it out again for a second one.

By the time she'd wolfed down both brownies and several cups of coffee, she felt bloated and more than a little disgusted with herself. She'd consumed the brownies not because she was hungry but because she was angry and depressed. She had been an idiot to suggest to Lonny that he invite another woman to the party, and then she'd compounded her idiocy by being so inquisitive this morning.

She wanted to trust Lonny as much as she always had, and he deserved her trust. Yet, despite her achievements, despite her attractiveness, she still harbored too many insecurities. She couldn't quell her memory of herself as she had been years ago: the plump impoverished student mooning over a man who hadn't even been conscious of her as a woman.

If she hadn't already been disgusted with herself for making such a pig of herself with the brownies, her indulgence in self-pity would have done the trick. Shoving away from the table, she stood and rinsed out her coffee cup and the pot. Then she pocketed the spare key Lonny had left for her and exited the house. A brisk walk might burn off some calories, undoing the damage of her gluttonous breakfast.

She marched down the street to the boardwalk and headed south. The beach, while not jam-packed with bathers, was moderately crowded. If Lonny hadn't had to work that day, Samantha would have liked to spend the day at the beach with him. But after her sinful breakfast, she wouldn't have had the nerve to don a bathing suit and expose herself to the world.

Eventually she reached the southern tip of Spring Lake, where the boardwalk ended at a picturesque inlet. Turning around, she retraced her steps, her pace slackening as fatigue crept over her. By the time she reached Lonny's block, she was sweaty and yawning. Entering his house, she decided to forgo lunch. She went directly up the stairs to his room, collapsed on his bed and shut her eyes.

It was after four o'clock when she awoke. She felt grubby, and her reflection in his mirror disgruntled her. Maybe it was only her imagination, but her stomach seemed to bulge above the waistband of her shorts. She could almost visualize the brownies protruding through the skin of her abdomen.

Grimacing, she undressed and stepped into the shower. The bathroom connected to Lonny's bedroom was in much better shape than the guest bathroom, its fixtures fairly new and sparkling from regular cleaning, its walls freshly painted. She stood directly underneath the powerful spray of the shower tap and let the lukewarm water pound down around her head.

It was more than a lack of trust that had made her question Lonny about other women, she realized. It was that when she'd asked him about the party, he'd answered,

"We'll talk about it later." What kind of answer was that? she wondered edgily. He could have simply said, "The party was great," or "The party was a dud."

But he hadn't. He'd said, "We'll talk about it later," as if what he had to say about the party was so significant that he needed lots of time and the proper setting in order to discuss it. No wonder her suspicions had been aroused.

She wouldn't ask him any more about it, though. She wouldn't let him see that she was suspicious. She wouldn't give him the opportunity to accuse her of not trusting him.

She shut off the water and wrung out her hair. Drawing back the shower curtain, she was startled to find Lonny lounging in the open doorway and watching her with unabashed delight. "Not bad," he appraised her, his eyes twinkling with an amber glow as they wandered the length of her glistening body.

Inexplicably embarrassed, she reached for the towel and wrapped it modestly about her. "I look like I'm six months pregnant," she muttered.

His eybrows arched and his smile faded. "What?" he exclaimed, blanching. "You're pregnant?"

"Yeah," she grunted, drying herself vigorously. "I'm carrying twin brownies. Why did you have to leave a box of brownies in your kitchen, Lonny? Are you trying to test my willpower?"

"I take it you failed the test," he taunted, prying the towel from her hands and applying it to her back with gentle strokes. "I bought those brownies just for you, Sammy, so I'm glad you helped yourself to a few of them."

"Will you still be glad when I devour the whole box of them and resemble the Goodyear blimp?" she asked grumpily. "Look at me, Lonny. I look like—"

"A vision out of a dream," he murmured, tossing the towel aside and gathering her in his arms. "If the Goodyear blimp looked as sexy as you, nobody would bother watching the football games." He nuzzled her neck with his lips. "I shouldn't be doing this," he whispered, his mouth hot against her neck. "You're clean, and I've got a century's worth of crud caked all over me."

"Then maybe you ought to wash up," Samantha advised him, though her voice was too low and husky to be persuasive. She moaned as his teeth caught the tip of her earlobe and his hands curved over the roundness of her bottom.

"I'll get to it," he mumbled, browsing along her hairline. Her fingers attacked the buttons of his shirt, and he stopped breathing for a second. "I'll get to it later," he resolved, stepping back from her only to remove his shirt and then urging her ahead of himself into the bedroom.

He paused at the edge of the bed to pull off his jeans, then joined her on the mattress. His lips fused with hers, as hungrily as if they'd been apart for days—for years—even though they'd made love just that morning. As his tongue conquered the recesses of her mouth, his hands toured her body, teasing her breasts, tickling her belly, sliding along the inner skin of her thighs and then upward, arousing her fully with his tender motions.

Although she had been exaggerating when she'd called him an animal that morning, there was something so basic about his lovemaking, so primal, that it almost transcended the limits of human behavior. He acted naturally, instinctively, knowing where to touch her, how to touch her, never having to ask. His hands moved with miraculous precision, sensing intuitively where she most wanted him to caress her, where her nerves were singing out for him. By the time he took complete possession of her body, she had been reduced to that same basic level, a creature distilled to her own womanly essence, all joyous reflex, all ecstatic response.

They strove together for the ultimate moment, and it swept through them in blissful waves of fulfillment. Lonny didn't withdraw from her until the final pulses had ebbed away, leaving them both replete with satisfaction.

He lay on his side next to her, his hand wandering aimlessly over her cooling body. "How was your day?" he asked her.

"The past fifteen minutes have been spectacular," she told him in a deliciously drowsy voice. "How was yours?"

He smiled almost shyly at her compliment. "It was all right, I guess. At least I emerged unscathed today." He fluttered his healthy right hand before her eyes, then lowered it to rest on the swell of her hip. His smile faded as he contemplated her. "Sammy, we've really got to talk."

She cringed slightly. "I wish you wouldn't keep saying that," she said, resolving to be honest. "You sound like the voice of doom when you do."

"No," he reassured her. "There's no doom about it." He lapsed into silent meditation for a minute. He appeared to be struggling with himself, on the verge of saying something profound, but he checked himself. "I tell you what," he proposed, pulling away from her and sitting up. "Let me take a shower, and we'll put on some clothes so we won't keep acting like animals, and then we can talk."

Before Samantha could stop him, he had broken free of her embrace and was on his way to the bathroom. She stared after him for a long while, gaping at the closed bathroom door, listening absently to the rush of the water as he showered.

She was unnerved by his inablility to say what was on his mind while they'd been lying in bed. They had never had trouble talking before, no matter where they were or what they were doing.

Trying to still her apprehension, she got up to put on some clothes. She pulled a blouse and a pair of slim-fitting khaki slacks from her overnight bag and donned them. Buckling her belt, she noted with satisfaction that the buckle fastened at its usual hole. Apparently, her vigorous walk and her decision to skip lunch had been penance enough to overcome the sin of eating the brownies.

She was brushing the tangles from her hair when Lonny emerged from the bathroom, a towel wrapped discreetly around his waist. He offered her a quick smile before busying himself with the contents of his bureau. Samantha had to bite her tongue to prevent herself from ordering him to speak. His prolonged silence fed her tension, but she wouldn't make demands on him. She wouldn't.

When he was dressed, she waited for a cue from him. His gaze circled the room, alighting briefly on the door to the hall and then settling on the window. "Why don't we go outside on the deck?" he proposed, crossing to the window and lifting it open.

Anything Samantha might have said would have come out wrong. She only nodded and let him assist her through the window. He followed her out and led her to the railing. They both sat. "It's a beautiful evening," he declared, taking a deep breath of the mild, briny air.

"Much nicer than summer evenings in Manhattan," Samantha concurred, wondering how long they were going to have to chat about the weather before they could get down to business.

"Summer evenings in Manhattan can be lovely," Lonny remarked, though he didn't sound convinced of it. He looped his arm around Samantha's shoulders and took another deep breath of the bracing sea-tinged air. "How was your meeting yesterday?" he asked.

That was the last topic she'd expected him to bring up. But why not? Perhaps, when he'd said they had to talk, he'd meant that they had to resume their usual relationship, gabbing about all the inconsequential goings-on that cluttered their daily lives. If so, his decision that they should get dressed first made some sense. Not much sense, but some.

"It was a meeting like most," she said blandly, still wondering whether there was something more important that Lonny wanted to talk about. "We batted ideas around, we politely begged to differ with each other, we ate cold roast beef sandwiches on rye, and we decided that the people at R and D would add some more red to the blue lipstick and see how it looked before we put it into production."

"How reasonable," Lonny said, sounding less facetious than Samantha would have predicted.

"It *was* reasonable," she admitted. "But I would rather have been at the party with you." She bravely decided to press ahead with that subject. He'd practically balked when she'd mentioned it that morning, and she was anxious to delve into what was behind his uncharacteristic reserve. "What was the party like?"

"It was very nice."

"Be serious, Lonny," she prodded him. "You hate elegant affairs like that."

He didn't respond immediately. His eyes flitted toward the dark water to the east, and then back to her. He shrugged. "I used to hate them," he conceded. "But I enjoyed this one."

"Even without a gorgeous woman at your side?" Samantha needled him, already feeling more comfortable. She could almost forget that just minutes ago they'd been wrapped up in passionate unity on his bed. Sitting with him on the deck at dusk, both of them clean and dressed and behaving like friends again, eased her tension enough that she could joke with him.

He eyed her with spurious dismay, then chuckled. "There was only one gorgeous woman I wanted at my side, and she was in New York eating a roast beef sandwich on rye," he said. "What am I supposed to think, Sammy, when you tell me you'd rather be eating a sandwich than hanging off my arm at a party?"

"They were awful sandwiches," she muttered. "Roast beef sandwiches should be hot, not cold. With lots of gravy slathered over them."

"At least you were eating real food," Lonny pointed out. "At the party, they served those cutesy little canapés—you know, bread cut into tiny squares, with a microscopic dab of liver pâté on top. It was all a healthy man could do to keep body and soul together."

"But you enjoyed it," she countered.

"Yes, I did." He stared past her for a moment, reminiscing. "The people I met there, Sammy... they reminded me of people we used to go to school with, people like Brad and Phillip. I *like* Brad and Phillip, Sammy."

"Of course you do," Samantha agreed.

"I don't keep in constant touch with them, but they're good people. Maybe their priorities aren't the same as mine...but maybe they aren't so different from mine, either. I walked into that party with a chip on my shoulder, thinking I was superior to all the other guests, just because they'd spent real money on their clothes and had their names painted on their office doors. But damn it, I enjoyed talking to them. I had a good time."

Samantha took a minute to absorb Lonny's statement. After waiting all day to hear what Lonny had to say about the party, she'd been expecting some great revelation. Not a simple claim that he'd had a good time.

Yet what he was telling her *was* a revelation. At least, he seemed to think it was. "Why is it so strange that you enjoyed the company of those people?" she asked. "A person's worth shouldn't be measured by how personalized his office is."

"Or even if he has an office at all," Lonny added. His jaw flexed as he considered his words. "I was wrong the other night when I ridiculed your work, Sammy. That was unfair of me. I know that what you do is worthwhile. Particularly given the size of your office," he concluded with a self-mocking grin.

"My office," she grumbled sourly. Listening to him describe the party to her made her wish all over again that she'd been with him. "You don't have to take back what you said," she claimed. "There was more than a grain of truth in it. You were right—blue lipstick is a pretty inane thing to be wasting my life with."

"Is that what you think?" he asked, leaping on her words. "That by working at LaBelle you're wasting your life?"

Samantha pressed her lips together and puzzled through her thoughts. Of course she didn't think she was wasting her life with her work. Why had she just said that she was?

She peered at Lonny. He was watching her carefully, not a trace of teasing in his eyes, not a hint of condemnation in the gentle arch of his lips. She knew she wasn't going to receive a lecture from him on the folly of corporate climbing. She wouldn't have to defend herself to him, given that he seemed rather generously disposed toward business executives at the moment. So she was free to answer him frankly. "I like my job, Lonny," she began haltingly. "But there are times when I don't like it, or at least I don't like what it does to me."

"What does it do to you?" Lonny asked.

She covered his hand with hers and played her fingers over the hard surfaces of his palm as she mulled over her answer. "It prevents me from going to parties with you whenever I want to."

"The value of life isn't measured by how many parties you go to," he consoled her. "Keeping your job is important, too, Sammy. And if you want to keep your job, you sometimes have to go to meetings and miss parties."

"It's not just missing the party," Samantha emphasized. "It's missing you."

"That's not the fault of your job, either," Lonny maintained. "It's simple geography. You live there and I live here."

Samantha struggled to pinpoint what had been bothering her all week. "I don't just mean I missed *you*, Lonny. I missed . . . I missed your style."

"My style?" he hooted. "Don't tell me you think I'm stylish. Did that madras jacket of mine really turn you on?"

Samantha allowed herself a brief smile. "Not the jacket, but . . . You have the courage to wear a jacket like that. You wear jeans and grow your hair long and set your own hours. You're your own man, Lonny. That's what I mean by your style. You're your own man. All those people you enjoyed at the party—they're working for other people, traveling to their bosses' beats instead of their own."

Lonny laughed caustically. "Sure. That's why I spent all day today at Bill Tucker's house instead of with you. I work for other people too, Sammy. I'm at their beck and call just as much as you are. The only difference is that you've got a company paying for your health insurance. I've got to pay for my own."

"There are other differences, too," Samantha insisted. "You can take off a weekday morning and walk around the arcade on the Point Pleasant boardwalk, if you feel like it."

"Yes, and I can also get stuck having to work weekends to meet a deadline," Lonny pointed out. "Don't glorify my work, Samantha. It's no better than what you do."

Samantha shifted against the railing in order to study Lonny more closely. He met her gaze resolutely. She gave him the chance to retract what he'd said, or to elaborate on it, clarifying that while his work didn't make him superior to people like her, what he did was more purifying for the spirit, because one couldn't be corrupted by power or money by hammering nails into shingles.

But he didn't say anything of the sort. That alone was a revelation. "What brought on this change of heart?" she asked, curious and a bit concerned. She was used to thinking of Lonny as a rebel, an iconoclast who held fast to his own sometimes unrealistic principles. She was totally unprepared for the possibility that he'd altered his views.

He twisted his hand to capture her fingers. The light pressure of her wrist against his injured thumb caused him to flinch and suck in his breath. "Maybe battering my thumb had something to do with it," he said.

"No, Lonny," Samantha corrected him with a grin. "*I'm* the clumsy oaf, remember? You're the graceful one."

"I've got one big, fat bandage here that says otherwise," Lonny countered.

"That was an accident. An anomaly. Please don't tell me you're as inept as I am. I don't think I could stand it."

He laughed, then settled more comfortably against the railing and drew Samantha's head onto his shoulder. "It's good talking to you, Sammy," he murmured.

She listened to the constant rush of the water against the sand behind them. Yes, it was good when they talked. As good as when they made love. No matter what became of their love affair, she hoped they'd never lose their ability to confide in each other.

"You know, I haven't been up to visit my parents since last spring," he remarked. "God knows how long my weekends are going to be tied up with the Tucker house, but I sure would like to see my folks."

Anyone else might have questioned Lonny on his abrupt change in subject. Samantha didn't. She knew he'd make the connection for her sooner or later. "If you're planning a trip north, you've got a place to stay in New York," she told him.

"I have a better idea," he said. "I could pick you up on my way, and bring you with me to Tarrytown. How does that sound?"

Samantha knew better than to read too much into Lonny's invitation. She had visited his parents a few times as his friend. It wasn't as if he were bringing her home like a girlfriend to meet his relatives and win their approval. "Are you anticipating a battle with your father?" she asked with a smile. "Are you going to expect me to referee?" She'd served in that capacity on previous visits, when Lonny and his father engaged in heated debates about what Mr. Reed considered to be Lonny's disreputable existence and what Lonny considered to be Mr. Reed's ulcer-producing pursuits.

"I think it's going to be a peaceful visit," Lonny predicted hopefully. "But I'd like you along because, as things now stand, you and I aren't going to be seeing much of each other except on the weekends."

"And we won't be seeing much of each other then either," Samantha commented. "Not as long as you're facing that September first deadline." She examined the large, callused hand that clasped hers. "Maybe you ought to wait until your thumb heals before seeing your father. I can just imagine what he'd say if he found out you hurt yourself."

"He'd say I had it coming," Lonny imagined. "My mother would fuss over me as if I were an invalid."

"I wonder what they'd do if they found out you spent half your life prancing about on the rooftops," Samantha mused.

"They'd die," Lonny told her in a deadpan voice. "They'd keel over and die."

"Then we'll keep that our secret," Samantha promised. "Definitely."

They fell silent, watching the progression of the sky's color from pink to lavender to a darkening blue. Sooner or later, they would have to get up and do something about dinner, but Lonny didn't want to move. He wanted to remain outdoors on the deck, with Samantha's body snuggled cozily to his.

There was still a great deal to talk about, but it could wait. He'd said enough for now.

He wondered why he'd become tongue-tied with Samantha when they were in bed together. He had wanted to tell her about the party then, and about his acceptance of the life she'd chosen for herself, about his respect for her. Yet having her beside him, so warm and alluring, her dark eyes glittering with the exhilaration of their lovemaking... He hadn't been able to speak then. All he could think of was how wonderful a woman she was, and how much pleasure she had brought him.

He didn't want to think of her as two separate people, yet that was the way it was panning out. In bed, she couldn't be Sammy, his chum, his good ol' pal. She could only be Samantha, a beautiful woman, all flesh and sensation and honey-colored hair. Compartmentalizing her that way struck him as abominably sexist, but it was the truth. He couldn't deny his feelings.

He wanted both Sammys, the pal and the lover. No woman had ever satisfied all his needs as a man the way Samantha could. He had never been able to talk to Moira Davis the way he could talk to Samantha. Or Lisbeth Whatever, or that Southern belle Tracy, or Marcy, or any of the others. Sex was terrific, but sharing one's body wasn't the same as sharing one's soul.

He wanted Samantha with him when he visited his parents. Not merely because he didn't want to spend a weekend without her, but because he would need her with him for moral support. Explaining to Samantha what he'd learned about himself last night at the party had been extremely difficult—and he wasn't certain he'd done an adequate job of it—but explaining it to his father would be next to impossible. And asking his father for help would be, if anything, even harder.

But with Samantha at his side, he might be able to do it.

Chapter Nine

After giving her hair a final touch-up, Samantha tossed her brush and comb into her overnight bag and zipped it shut. She pivoted in front of the full length mirror hanging on her bedroom door and gave her reflection a critical assessment. The dress she had on was a classically simple design of beige cotton, with short sleeves and an open neckline. Although her flat sandals were more comfortable, she wore a pair with cork wedge heels. She wanted to look right for Lonny's parents—not too dressy and not too casual.

She wasn't nervous about visiting the Reeds, even though she hadn't seen them in years, and even though the nature of her relationship with their son had changed drastically since that last meeting. Toting her overnight bag into the living room to wait for Lonny, Samantha was too weary to be nervous. All she wanted was to escape from the oppressively muggy city, if only for a short weekend, and to clear her mind of thoughts about work.

And to see Lonny. Spring Lake might not be as far from New York as Denver was, yet given the difficulties she and Lonny were experiencing in getting to spend time together, they might as well have been living fifteen hundred miles apart.

Samantha hadn't been able to see Lonny the previous weekend, due to a last-minute round of meetings on the Artist's Eyes lipstick line. The weekend before that had been when they'd first planned to visit Lonny's parents, but then the fiberglass tub that had been on order for the Tucker house had arrived ahead of schedule, and Lonny had canceled the trip to Tarrytown in order to remain in New Jersey and install the tub with Jack and Howie. Samantha had been unable to rent a car on such short notice, so she'd taken the train to Spring Lake. The train ride had dragged on for what felt like an eon, and Lonny had been long gone from his house by the time an overpriced cab dropped her off there. She'd gotten to spend the night with him, but the following day he'd had to return to the Tucker house to complete the work on the bathroom, and she'd caught an early train back to New York City.

They talked frequently on the telephone, but that wasn't the same as seeing each other. There was a time, only a few short weeks ago, when telephone conversations would have sufficed, but not anymore. Samantha missed Lonny's smile, his defiantly long hair, the pleasure of sleeping in the shelter of his body. Chatting on the telephone with him wasn't nearly enough to satisfy her.

She heard the buzz of the intercom in the entry hall of her apartment. When she lifted the receiver, the doorman announced Lonny's arrival. "I'll be right down," she said before hanging up and returning to the living room to fetch her bag.

Lonny was leaning against a decorative pillar in the building's lobby when she emerged from the elevator. As soon as he saw her, he straightened up and started toward her. He was dressed more conservatively than Samantha had expected. Whenever Lonny had brought her to visit his parents in the past, he had deliberately chosen to wear clothing he knew would tweak their sense of propriety: jeans that contained more patch than original cloth, flannel shirts with frayed collars and cuffs, old running shoes or mud-caked work boots.

His attire today was the epitome of good taste. The sleeves of his white oxford shirt were rolled up to his elbows, but the shirt was clean and crisp, despite the humid August heat. His tan slacks appeared brand new. His hair was neatly parted above one ear and combed back from his face. On closer inspection, Samantha realized that he'd had it trimmed.

He enveloped her in a warm embrace and touched his lips lightly to hers. His hug and kiss, no matter how innocent, had a wild impact on Samantha. Suddenly all she wanted to do was to stand necking with him in the very public environment of her apartment building's lobby. But discretion won out, and she pulled back from his arms and took a steadying breath. "Hello," she managed, her cheeks flushed and her gaze lowered as she fought for self-control.

His eyes were radiant with delight as he comprehended Samantha's slightly flustered state, her visible yearning. "You missed me?" he goaded her.

"Don't let it go to your head," she grumbled, though she was chuckling. "With men, it takes two weeks before they begin to mutate. With women, only a few days."

Lonny threw back his head and laughed boisterously. "Come on, mutant," he ordered her, gripping her overnight bag with one hand and her elbow with the other. "I'm parked illegally, so we'd better get to the truck before New York's finest do."

He escorted her from the building to his pick-up, which he'd left standing in front of a fire hydrant down the street. The fierce summer heat seared Samantha's skin as she left the haven of the air-conditioned lobby, but she didn't complain. She didn't even complain when she remembered that Lonny's truck wasn't air-conditioned. She would gladly tolerate riding to Tarrytown inside a blast-furnace, as long as she was in Lonny's company.

He helped her onto the seat, then wiggled her suitcase into the narrow space behind it. After shutting her door, he strolled around the truck, climbed in beside her and gunned the engine to life. They both rolled down their windows and he pulled away from the curb.

He didn't speak as he maneuvered the truck through the dense traffic to the West Side Highway. Samantha pondered his silence. He seemed happy to see her, yet she sensed an undefinable remoteness about him. He wasn't smiling. He didn't hum as he navigated past double-parked cars and around sluggish buses. His gaze remained riveted to the road before him, and his hands were tight on the wheel.

"I like your haircut," she said, shattering the stillness between them.

"Do you?" She noticed the glimmer of a smile on his lips. "Thanks."

"What made you decide to cut it?"

His smile increased. "Sammy, I *do* go to a barber every now and then. If I didn't, my hair would be as long as yours."

"I like your clothing, too. You're all spruced up, Lonny. What's the occasion?"

"No occasion," Lonny said impassively.

She noticed a tautness at the corners of his mouth, giving his grin a forced look. "Are you trying to make an impression on your parents?" she asked.

"I always make an impression on my parents."

"Usually a negative one," she commented. He shot her a quick look, then directed his attention back to the road.

The West Side Highway was clogged with bumper-to-bumper traffic. Despite the open windows, the air inside the truck soon grew uncomfortably hot as they inched along the crowded roadway. Samantha shifted in her seat, trying to prevent her back from perspiring and sticking to the vinyl upholstery.

Lonny's peculiar mood discomfited her. He seemed tense about visiting his parents, though she couldn't think of any reason why. His uncommunicativeness, combined with the smothering heat, made her irritable. She had looked forward to seeing Lonny, yet now that they were together, his presence was only contributing to her foul mood.

No, she wasn't going to blame his unusual quietness for her dissatisfaction. Nor would she blame the weather, although she knew that August was a far more pleasant time of year in Spring Lake than in New York. Her work was the reason for her uneasy state of mind. She ought to put aside all thoughts about it, and try to be charming.

Yet she couldn't help herself. The long lane of motionless cars in front of the truck vexed her. Their red brake lights glared annoyingly, and their hoods seemed to ripple in the heat. "God, I hate this city," she muttered.

Lonny cast her another swift look. "What are you talking about?" he asked. "You love New York."

"Not at the moment," she stewed. "Look at this traffic. New York stinks look how many people are trying to escape it."

The truck crept several feet forward. "New York City isn't the best place to drive a car," he granted. "That's why smart New Yorkers like you don't own cars."

"Sure," she scoffed. "Instead, I've got to pay an arm and a leg to rent a car whenever I want to visit you."

"Is it that expensive?" he asked. "Maybe we ought to split the cost."

"No," she hastily refuted him. She knew she earned much more money than he did. She didn't want him to have to shoulder that additional financial burden.

"You could take the train again," he pointed out. "It wasn't so bad last weekend."

"It was awful," she griped. "It was slow and stuffy. The train was so crowded, there weren't any seats in the no-smoking cars, and I wound up sitting next to a chain-smoker."

"You didn't complain about that last week," Lonny noted.

Samantha shrugged. "I'm not much of a complainer," she reminded him.

"Then why are you complaining now?"

"Because—" She took a calming breath. "I'm sorry, Lonny."

"Don't be sorry," he consoled her. "I'm a firm believer in the therapeutic benefits of complaining."

She laughed in spite of herself. "Oh, Lonny, it's been a rough week, that's all."

"Tell me about it."

She didn't want to go into the whole sorry situation with him on the way to his parents' house. However, given their crawling pace, it could be hours before they reached the genteel town on the Hudson River north of the city. And if she couldn't talk to Lonny about what was troubling her, whom could she talk to?

"I'm thinking about quitting my job," she announced.

Lonny's mouth fell open. "What?"

"We had a meeting yesterday," she related in as emotionless a voice as she could manage. "We teleconferenced with the regional reps. It was decided that the new lipstick shades R and D came up with weren't as unique and exciting as the blue and gray shades they proposed a few weeks ago. Artist's Eyes is supposed to be adventurous. So we're going with the unique and exciting colors."

Lonny mulled over what Samantha had told him. "All right," he summarized. "You lost a round."

"I lost the war," Samantha corrected him.

"So? It's not the first war you've ever lost. It's certainly not worth quitting over."

Samantha eyed Lonny quizzically. Was this the same man who, just weeks ago, had made a snide remark about the inanity of allowing one's life to revolve around blue lipstick? Admittedly, he'd referred to her work in more kindly terms since then, but that had only been his way of making amends after their argument. She had expected him to cheer over her decision to resign from her job.

Perhaps he was downplaying her problems at work because he didn't want her to be all fired up with rage when they arrived at his parents' house. But she knew he'd support her decision when he heard the rest of the story. "It gets worse," she continued. "When I expressed my feelings about the lipstick colors, and my concerns about marketing such grotesque lipsticks, Lynette Magnusson—a woman nobody in her right mind wants to cross—called me in for a private session in her office. She told me that if I wasn't willing to be a team player, I ought to give serious thought to whether I belonged on the team."

"She asked you to quit?" Lonny translated, clearly appalled.

"Not exactly. It was more like 'Shape up or else.'" Samantha scowled. "I used to look up to Lynette. She's done so well for herself in the company, climbed so high, attained so much power. I used to think of her as a role model. But honest to God, Lonny—how can I invest all my energies into something as ludicrous as blue lipstick?"

Lonny reached across the seat to squeeze her hand. "It's just one product," he remarked. "It's not worth rearranging your whole life over."

She tried to make sense of his words and of his pensive smile. She wanted to tell him that it wasn't just the lipstick that inspired her to rearrange her life, but the fact that she was Lonny's lover. She was tired of living so far from him; New York lost its attraction to her as long as he was in Spring Lake. But more than that, she had begun to view Lonny as someone much more worthy of her admiration than the likes of Lynette Magnusson. Lonny might work for other people, but if he didn't like a job, he didn't have to take it. He didn't feel pressured into doing something utterly foolish in order to keep his career alive. No matter how much he denied it, he was still his own man. Surely that was more important than earning a big salary and living in a nicely decorated apartment.

They had reached the outer limits of the city, and the traffic dissolved into a trickle of northbound cars. Lonny shifted into fourth gear for the first time since they had left her block, and the air began to stir inside the cab. It was too hot to be refreshing, but Samantha appreciated it, anyway.

"Do me a favor, Sammy," Lonny requested. "Don't do anything rash about your job, okay?"

"I wasn't planning to do anything rash," she countered. "I've been thinking about leaving LaBelle ever since—" *Ever since I realized I'd rather be with you,* she almost said. But that would come out sounding too forward, as if she were demanding some sort of a commitment from him. And she didn't want to be demanding. So she concluded, "Ever since this lipstick nonsense began."

"Still, it's the sort of decision you've got to give very careful consideration," he instructed her. "You've built your entire life around getting to where you are now. You shouldn't throw it all away.''

Again she was surprised by his positive opinion about her career. She had expected him to congratulate her on her wisdom in quitting. ''I wasn't thinking of throwing away anything,'' she mused. ''Frankly, selling blue lipstick *is* throwing away something: my common sense.''

Lonny shook his head. ''Give it time, Sammy. You'll probably feel different about it after you cool off.'' He glanced at her, then added, ''Another favor—please don't discuss this in front of my father.''

''I hadn't planned to,'' Samantha assured him. Lonny was the only person she felt comfortable with when it came to talking about such personal matters. The fact that Lonny would think it necessary to say such a thing puzzled her. ''Any particular reason?''

Lonny's lips twitched a few times as he shaped his reply. ''He thinks very highly of you. He thinks you've done very well for yourself.''

''And you don't want me to disillusion him?''

''I don't want you to get into a fight with him,'' Lonny said. ''I want this to be a peaceful visit. I'm not going to fight with him—if I can help it—and I don't want you to, either.''

So that was why Lonny had gotten his hair cut. So that was why he was dressed so spiffily. He was going out of his way to avoid any conflict with his father. She wondered why this visit in particular meant so much to him. ''Lonny, you aren't going to pull any surprises at your parents' house, are you?''

''Surprises?'' he asked ingenuously. ''What sort of surprises?''

"I mean..." She inhaled deeply. "You aren't going to announce that we're getting married or something, are you?"

He smiled broadly. "Why, Samantha Janek! Is this a proposal?"

"No," she said, trying to ignore the unbidden sadness that settled over her. Until she'd voiced the idea, she hadn't been aware of it lurking in the back of her mind. But once she'd spoken it, he didn't have to joke about it. She didn't think it was such a farfetched idea.

Obviously, he did. His smile gave way to full-bodied laughter. "Sammy, if I wanted to ask you to marry me, do you think I'd do it in front of my parents?" he asked.

If, she comprehended. *If* he wanted to. His phrasing implied, all too clearly, that he *didn't* want to.

She longed to turn on him, to pummel him with her fists and scream. She hadn't imagined that he was going to ask her to marry him, but he didn't have to go berserk with laughter at the mere possibility. He supposedly loved her, after all.

If they were simply friends, she would confront him. She would tell him that his uncontrolled mirth was totally uncalled for, that he had a hell of a nerve laughing at what she had considered a very reasonable question. When she and Lonny were friends, they could be blunt and candid with each other. They could speak their minds without flinching.

But they were lovers, and Samantha bit her lip to stifle herself. No way could she reveal to him that his reaction to her remark had hurt her feelings. She shaped an artifically bright smile and shrugged. "All I meant, Lonny, was that if you intend to spring anything on your parents, I'd like to know in advance."

His laughter waned. "I'm not planning to spring any- thing on them," he claimed. "I've got to talk some things over with my father, and I hope it goes smoothly."

"What things?" Samantha asked, finding his statement rather mysterious.

"Some business matters," Lonny said curtly, then ob- served, "You can really feel the difference in temperature between here and the city, can't you? Just a few miles north, and it's a good five degrees cooler."

Samantha contemplated pointing out that the city was always hotter because of its polluted air. But that might set her off on another streak of complaints about her current situation. After he'd laughed so unmercifully at her men- tion of marriage, she wouldn't give him the satisfaction of hearing her say that she wanted to live nearer to him.

Besides, she was too intrigued by Lonny's abrupt change of subject when she'd questioned him about what he wanted to discuss with his father. Why wouldn't he go into detail with her? What kind of business matters did he want his fa- ther's counsel on? Was he in need of a lawyer for some rea- son?

Following his lead, she kept their conversation on safe topics for the remainder of the trip. After discussing the weather, Lonny began an intriguing discourse on some of the massive old houses they spotted from the parkway. "It's amazing to think that some of these mansions date back to pre-Colonial times," he remarked. "I may work on a house that's all of fifty years old, and it's falling to pieces. Then you look at a house that was built up here by a Dutch set- tler three hundred years ago, and it's just as sturdy now as it was then. Craftsmanship," he murmured wistfully. "There's no substitute for good craftsmanship."

He fell silent, driving off the parkway at the Tarrytown exit. Samantha noticed his fingers tightening on the steering wheel again. Whatever business Lonny had to discuss with his father, she prayed that it wouldn't lead to a major verbal brawl between them. Lonny was evidently tense but hopeful about it. She wouldn't allow herself to share his tension, but she did share his hope.

Within a few minutes, they arrived at the Reeds' stately brick Colonial house, which was set on a well-tended acre lot in a residential neighborhood. Mature trees cast cool shadows over much of the lawn, and the front yard was decorated with colorful flowerbeds and trimmed with thriving shrubs. Lonny coasted up the long driveway and parked his car beside a shiny brown Mercedes-Benz sedan with a vanity license plate reading ESQ. "Your father bought a new car," Samantha observed.

Lonny chuckled. "Two years ago," he informed her. "He's probably itching to buy another one now."

She resisted the temptation to remind Lonny that if he was already ridiculing his father's acquisitiveness when it came to expensive automobiles, the visit was doomed to disaster. Whether or not Lonny and his father were going to fight today was up to them, not her.

By the time Lonny had their overnight bags out of the truck, the front door of the house was open, and his parents were bounding down the walk to the driveway. Lonny's father had a distinguished appearance that matched his ritzy car. His slate-gray hair had thinned considerably since the last time Samantha had seen him, but what was left of it was impeccably groomed. His clothing seemed personally tailored to his tall body. His beige trousers looked a good deal like Lonny's, Samantha noticed with a small grin.

Although he'd inherited his father's lanky build, Lonny's face resembled his mother's. Like him, she had sharp, striking features, straight black hair that she wore held back from her face by an ornate abalone comb, a dark complexion, and deep-set light brown eyes. She wrapped Lonny in an effusive hug, then released him before he could become too embarrassed by her maternal display. "Lonny! It's about time you got here!"

"We hit some bad traffic on the way," he explained.

"I was referring to your canceling out on us two weeks ago," she clarified herself before turning to Samantha. "I'm so glad you came, Samantha," she said with genuine warmth. "It's been too long since you paid us a call. And look at you! You've lost weight, haven't you?"

"A little, yes," Samantha said modestly.

"You look wonderful. Doesn't she look wonderful, Lonny?"

He shared a private smile with Samantha. "Now that you mention it, yes, she does." He shook his father's hand. "Hello, Dad."

"Good to see you, Lonny. You're looking well yourself," he added, scrutinizing Lonny's neat attire. "You could use a haircut, though."

"I just got a haircut," Lonny retorted, then brightened. "You could use a toupee."

"Not funny," Mr. Reed muttered, but he grinned at Lonny's good-natured kidding and slung his arm over Lonny's shoulders. "You still drinking beer?"

"Always and forever," Lonny said, lifting the suitcases and strolling up the walk to the house with his father.

Samantha and Mrs. Reed followed them to the house. "I can't get over how terrific you look," Mrs. Reed enthused. "Not that you looked bad before, of course."

"I *did* look bad before," Samantha admitted with a laugh.

"You'll have to share your secret with me," Mrs. Reed confided, holding the screen door open for Samantha. "I've tried every diet from Scarsdale to Beverly Hills, but nothing works."

Samantha eyed Mrs. Reed's slim figure and cringed inwardly. Mrs. Reed was beautiful in a way Samantha would never be—she had the beauty that evolved from a lifetime of utter self-confidence. And she certainly didn't need to lose any weight.

"Lonny, why don't you take the bags upstairs?" Mrs. Reed suggested, gesturing toward the wide center-hall stairway. "I've got the guest room set up for Samantha."

Samantha accompanied Lonny up the stairs to the second floor and down the hall to the guest bedroom. The room was decorated in cheerful shades of sunshine yellow, the sofa bed made up with fresh linens and the furniture giving off a lemony fragrance from a recent polishing. Lonny put down her suitcase inside the doorway and indicated another door down the hall with his index finger. "That's my room," he whispered. "Think you can find it in the dark?"

She gave his chest a playful poke. "This is your parents' house," she reminded him unnecessarily. "We've got to behave."

"What a depressing thought." He closed his arms around her and kissed her soundly. "It's my mother's fault for pointing out how terrific you look," he murmured, his lips dancing over her mouth and chin. "Maybe we could cut out after dinner and return to the city for the night."

"You promised your parents the weekend," she said. His kisses kindled a deep longing inside her, and she shared his frustration at the knowledge that they'd have to spend yet another night apart.

"I rue the day I did," he confessed, then released her and crossed to the air-conditioning unit in the window. "Do you want me to turn this on?"

"No," she answered, moving to his side and opening the adjacent window. "I'd prefer some fresh air. It smells so good here." Gazing out the window, she saw the Reeds standing on the backyard patio, engrossed in a conversation. "I guess we ought to go downstairs," she said.

"Before they send a search party in after us," Lonny quipped, giving her cheek a final kiss before he steered her from the room. He stopped only to toss his own bag into his room, and then they descended to the main floor and through the living room's sliding glass door to the patio.

Lonny's parents turned to greet them. "How about that beer now, Lonny?" Mr. Reed offered. "Samantha, what can I get you to drink?"

"Nothing at the moment, thank you," she declined.

"Then why don't you keep me company while I pick some vegetables for a salad?" Mrs. Reed invited her, lifting a broad wicker basket from the patio and hooking its arching handle over her arm. "Our garden has really come through for us this summer. Remind me to send you home with a 'CARE package' of fresh vegetables tomorrow." She took Samantha's hand and ushered her from the patio to the garden planted at the southern end of the spacious yard.

Samantha did her best to feign interest in Mrs. Reed's chatter about the garden's bounty, making what she hoped were appropriate comments as Mrs. Reed exclaimed over the unexpectedly large yield of her tomato plants and described the various preparations she was planning for her bumper crop of zucchini. Ordinarily, Samantha would have been fascinated by the garden. Having grown up in one of Pittsburgh's seedier inner-city neighborhoods, and now living in Manhattan, she had never cultivated a garden of her own, but she'd love to have one. If she could quit her job and find work outside the city, if she could live in a place like Spring Lake, she would definitely grow her own vegetables.

But she was unable to give her full attention to Mrs. Reed, not while Lonny and his father were seated on the patio, immersed in their own dialogue. Mr. Reed was drinking something from a tall crystal tumbler, and Lonny held his beer bottle between his knees. Lonny's face was inscrutable, and Mr. Reed seemed to be doing most of the talking. She wondered whether Lonny had raised the business matters he wished to discuss with his father. She wondered what those business matters were, and what his father had to say about them. She wondered, with some concern, why Lonny had been unable to tell her—his best friend—what it was he needed his father's advice on.

Whatever it was, their discussion seemed to be going pleasantly. They were both smiling, both relaxed in their cushioned lawn chairs. Lonny stretched his legs out in front of him as he leaned back in his seat, and Samantha felt an immediate response to his limber physique, a longing as strong as what she'd felt when he'd kissed her upstairs. Her body's intense reaction to him reminded her that perhaps they weren't best friends anymore.

"Not that I don't like flowers," Mrs. Reed was prattling as she plucked a ripe green cucumber from a vine. "I adore flowers. But why spend all that time and effort tending a flower garden, when you can grow something edible instead? You can't eat roses."

"Some people make rose-hip tea," Samantha remarked, forcing herself to focus on her hostess.

"And a vile concoction it is, too," Mrs. Reed said with a sniff. She surveyed the contents of her basket and stood up. "I've got enough to feed an army here," she boasted. "Don't let me forget to stock you up with some of these goodies tomorrow morning."

They strolled across the lawn to the patio, and Samantha's attention returned to Lonny. When she drew near enough to eavesdrop on the conversation, she was disappointed to hear that the men were talking politics. Disagreeing as usual, but it was evidently a very friendly argument. "An economic boom doesn't equate to a sound economy," Lonny was asserting. "People with cancer have days when they feel fine. It doesn't mean they're in good health."

"You're quick with metaphors," his father objected. "But not with logic. I know you, Lonny. You hate being rational."

Samantha recalled the night Lonny confessed to her, in a much different context, that he hated being rational. They had almost made love then, but she'd come to her senses and stopped him. Seeing his warm, gentle smile as he debated economics with his father, she knew that she wouldn't have been able to prevent their love from progressing into a full-fledged affair, no matter how rational she might have been. Her attraction to him defied rationality, and sooner or later she would have given in.

Yet if she hadn't, if they'd remained rational about each other, Lonny might have been able to open up to her on their drive that morning. Something had been gained when they fell in love, but something had also been lost.

Mrs. Reed departed for the kitchen to wash the vegetables, and Samantha accepted the chair Lonny's father pulled over for her in order to join in their conversation. "Now here's someone who knows what she's talking about," Mr. Reed complimented her. "A comer in the business world. How are things at—I forget, Samantha, which company do you work for?"

"LaBelle Cosmetics," she told him. "And frankly, things are—" Lonny shot her a swift look, and she smiled. "Middling," she concluded.

"Really?" Mr. Reed gave her a sharp perusal. "People aren't buying so much makeup these days?"

"No, the industry is in good shape," she said. "Some folks think that the cosmetics industry is recession-proof. When the economy is good, women have money to spend on cosmetic products. And when the economy is bad, women buy cosmetics to cheer themselves up."

"Then you've chosen the right field," Mr. Reed summarized.

Samantha shook her head. "Some people buy that theory, but I'm not sure it's true. Women will probably buy cosmetics no matter what, but during slumps they tend to buy more carefully. Which leaves me to believe that if we're heading into a slump, my product line may be in trouble."

"Oh? Why is that?"

She noticed another cautioning look from Lonny but ignored him. She was sure that nothing she could tell Mr. Reed about marketing lipstick would start an argument with him. "Artist's Eyes aren't exactly conservative products," she explained. "What we do is try to convince women that they should be spending an exorbitant sum of money on frivolous items—weird colors of eyeshadow and lipstick. Basically, I'm in the business of getting women to buy something they really don't need."

"But they *think* they need it," Mr. Reed supposed.

"Nobody needs blue lipstick," Samantha maintained.

"Yes, but people do need rainbows over their eyes every now and then," Lonny interjected. "Especially when they're down. A rainbow over one's eye can give one an entirely new perspective on life, don't you think?" His knowing smile provoked a grin from Samantha. Yes, painting a rainbow on her eyelid had made a difference in her perspective. She ought to wear it more often. Perhaps she'd wear one when she marched into Lynette Magnusson's office with her resignation in her hand.

They stayed outdoors, enjoying the mild afternoon, while Mrs. Reed completed her dinner preparations. Lonny and his father didn't fight at all, nor did Lonny broach the subject of business advice from his father. Samantha's curiosity built with each passing minute, but she remained outwardly serene.

So did Lonny. She observed that he was fidgeting with his beer bottle more than usual, and that his attention occasionally drifted as Mr. Reed embarked on a description of the corporate merger that currently occupied him at work. Westchester County was flourishing as a business center, he boasted, and no matter what Lonny thought of the economy, corporate lawyers like Mr. Reed and his partners had more than enough to keep them busy.

Mrs. Reed's face appeared in the open kitchen window. "Ben?" she hollered. "I could use some assistance with the dining room table."

Mr. Reed lifted his empty glass and smiled. "If you two will excuse me," he said as he stood. "I hear my master's voice." He strode into the house, leaving Samantha and Lonny alone.

She turned expectantly to Lonny, eager to learn whether he'd discussed his business with his father. Lonny fingered his beer bottle thoughtfully, but said nothing.

"It sure sounds as if your father's got his hands full at work," she noted. "For a man approaching retirement age, he isn't showing any signs of slowing down."

"To say nothing of his budding ulcer," Lonny added. "I wish he took care of himself as well as he does his clients." He eyed Samantha enigmatically. "Doesn't it sound boring to you, all that paper pushing and negotiating?"

"Oh, I don't know," Samantha said with a shrug. "Maybe it's intellectually challenging, getting all those divergent interests to come to terms. Sort of like playing chess."

"You're right." Lonny sounded oddly anxious to agree. "It must be intellectually challenging. Not like installing a fiberglass bathtub."

"That must be challenging, too," Samantha mused. "I bet trying to get a bathtub fixture into place is like moving chessmen into checkmate."

"Hardly." He downed the last of his beer and sighed. "I suppose I could learn to like it."

"After all this time, I would think you like redoing bathrooms just fine."

He frowned. "I wasn't talking about bathrooms."

She tried to make sense of his cryptic statement, but came up empty. "What were you talking about?"

He twisted to look at her. His eyes churned with shadows, and his lips were set in a grim line. "Can you imagine me being a lawyer?" he asked, with not a trace of humor in his tone.

"You?" In spite of his somber expression, Samantha laughed. "You, a lawyer? No, I can't imagine it. I like your father, Lonny, but you and he are two completely different breeds. I can't imagine you talking nonstop for ten minutes about the joys of facilitating a corporate merger."

Lonny didn't seem pleased by her answer. "Corporate law isn't the only kind of law there is," he pointed out. "Don't forget, I was accepted to a few law schools my senior year in college. They didn't turn me down. I turned them down."

"With good reason," said Samantha, scrambling to figure out what he was getting at. "You turned them down because you realized you weren't cut out for that kind of life."

"I was a kid then," he said. "I was an immature kid who spent all my energy chasing after superficial women instead of falling in love with you. I'd like to think I've grown up."

"Your taste in women has improved," Samantha confirmed, disguising her bewilderment with a joke. "What does that have to do with law school?"

"I'm only saying that maybe I've changed. Maybe—maybe you can also get a new perspective on life by seeing a woman with a rainbow over her eye. Maybe I'm seeing things differently now."

"Because of me?"

"Lonny! Samantha!" Mrs. Reed's voice blasted through the open window, sparing Lonny the obligation of answering Samantha. "We're just about ready with dinner, if you'd like to come in."

It was close to three o'clock, and since Samantha hadn't eaten anything for breakfast, she ought to have been famished. But she was too perplexed by Lonny's remarks to want to eat. She wished that she and Lonny could run off somewhere and finish their conversation before they had to go inside and make courteous small talk with the Reeds.

However, Lonny obediently stood and extended his hand to Samantha, and she had no choice but to enter the house with him. They walked through the living room to the formal dining room. The table was set with a lace cloth, china and crystal stemware. Samantha suspected that Lonny's parents didn't go to such an effort every time their son visited them, and the elegant table had been set in her honor. She wanted to feel appreciative, but she was too distracted by Lonny to care about the Royal Doulton plates and the Oneida flatware.

Mrs. Reed served a dinner of prime ribs, potatoes au gratin, fresh salad and warm rolls. Not a meal for someone trying to watch her figure, Samantha pondered as Mrs. Reed settled her slender frame into a chair at one end of the table. Mr. Reed took his place at the other end, and Lonny and Samantha sat facing each other across the table. "You see?" Mrs. Reed teased Lonny as she graciously passed the platters of food around. "You missed a meal like this to hook up a toilet two weeks ago."

"It was a bathtub, not a toilet," Lonny said. "Anyway, in the business, toilets are called commodes."

"How is the 'business,' Lonny?" Mr. Reed asked. The way he emphasized the word "business" implied that he didn't consider Lonny's work a legitimate business at all.

Samantha smoothed her napkin in her lap and waited for Lonny to erupt. The visit may have been peaceful thus far, but whenever Mr. Reed became condescending about Lonny's work, Lonny reacted reflexively, defending with vehemence his choice of a career.

She watched him lift his glass of Beaujolais, take a sip and set down the goblet. "The 'business' is fine," he said quietly.

Samantha sensed the restraint in his voice. Her eyes met his for a moment, and then he looked away. She knew instantly that something wasn't at all "fine" about his business, but she had no idea what.

Lonny's parents weren't fooled, either. "Financial problems?" his father guessed.

"No." He sliced a piece of meat with deliberation, then lowered his fork without eating. "We're doing well," he said, his tone still subdued. "We just put a binder on a new property. And the house we're working on is progressing. I probably should have stayed in Spring Lake this weekend to work on it, since we're facing a deadline, but Jack and Howie generously gave me a couple of days off."

"Those partners of yours," Mr. Reed scoffed. "I don't know how you can work with them. You're so obviously superior to them."

"I am not," Lonny snapped. Samantha felt a small rush of relief at Lonny's show of anger. It was much more typical than the evasiveness with which he'd greeted his father's earlier questions. "Jack and Howie are the best partners a man could hope for. They're hard workers, and they've got good heads on their shoulders."

"They aren't educated the way you are," Mr. Reed disputed him.

"So what? Do you think private schools and Ivy League colleges make such a difference?"

"Not when it comes to fixing up old houses," Mr. Reed allowed. "But you're better than that, Lonny. I don't know what possible satisfaction you can derive from construction work."

"It isn't construction work," Lonny argued. "It's *re*construction work. And as far as the satisfaction I derive from it . . ." He faltered, then fell silent. His eyes met Samantha's again, and he hastily looked away. "I'm thinking that maybe it's time for a change."

All activity at the table ceased. Samantha's hand clenched around the napkin on her knees. What was Lonny talking about? Why in the world did he want to make a change when he adored his work so much? Why hadn't he said anything to her about it before now?

Mrs. Reed studied her son, her face etched with gentle concern. "What sort of change, Lonny?" she asked.

"I was thinking . . ." He addressed his plate. "I've been thinking I might want to go to law school, after all. Given my background, and my experience, I could probably do well in real estate law. I know my timing is off. I wouldn't be able to start applying to law schools until the fall, so attending law school—assuming I get accepted—would be a year away.''

"There's no question that you'd be accepted," Mrs. Reed declared, exuding maternal pride.

"There *is* a question, Mom," Lonny asserted, then shrugged. "But assuming I got in and could start in a year...in the meantime, it would be nice to work in the real estate department of a law firm."

"Like mine?" Mr. Reed asked.

"Yes."

Samantha scarcely heard Mr. Reed's analysis of Lonny's proposal. Although he was clearly thrilled by it, he kept his voice level as he discussed potential paralegal positions in his firm, and his worry about charges of nepotism. He described the pace of Lonny's brother's ascent in the firm, and the risks and benefits of allowing another son into the firm. "I have colleagues at other firms, of course," he continued. "I can make inquiries for you, Lonny. I have favors I can call in."

She scarcely heard Mr. Reed because her attention was riveted to Lonny. He stared resolutely at his plate, his dinner untouched, his head moving in barely perceptible nods as his father rambled on about the field of real estate law. His hands clutched the edge of the table. She could feel almost viscerally the tension emanating from him.

He didn't want to go into real estate law, and she knew it. He didn't want to leave the work he loved. By the time Mr. Reed wound down, she couldn't contain herself. "Lonny, this is the craziest idea you've ever come up with."

"What makes you say that?" he asked.

She saw a hint of light in the recesses of his eyes and clung to it as a cause for optimism. "You don't want to give up your work, Lonny. You're good at it. And it's been good to you."

"I don't deny that, Sammy, but—"

"But nothing. Anyone who's as happy doing what they do as you are—"

"I'm not happy," he countered, speaking to Samantha as if he were unaware of his parents' presence in the room. "If I was happy, do you think I'd be looking for a change?"

"Is it your job you want changed or something else?" she asked, and like him, she was oblivious of his parents. She didn't give herself a chance to think that it might be his love life he wanted changed. She was responding to him only as a friend, a friend who cared about him and didn't want to see him abandoning something that brought him such joy.

"Damn it, Sammy, I want—" He lifted his eyes to hers, and this time there was nothing evasive in his steady gaze. "I feel isolated in Spring Lake," he whispered. "I want to be closer to the people I love. Not just geographically, but—but spiritually, physically, in the day-in-day-out of it. It used to be easy to reject what you do, but not anymore."

"What *I* do? What do I have to do with it?"

"Everything," he said softly.

His eyes remained constant on her, communicating what his words had failed to express. He wanted to have a "respectable" job like hers because he loved her. When they were just friends, they could live disparate lives and mock each other relentlessly about it. He could call her a materialistic corporate grind, and she could call him a bum. But now that they were lovers, he wanted to close the distance between them. Not just the geographical distance, as he'd said, but the spiritual distance.

Maybe he wasn't ready to propose marriage to her, but he was expressing a commitment far deeper than a simple marriage proposal. Her eyes brimmed with tears as she acknowledged his reason for deciding that he wanted to change careers. The reason was beautiful. But the action wasn't necessary.

"I wouldn't love you as much if you gave up the things that meant the most to you," she said.

"I'm not giving up the things that mean the most to me," he explained, his voice hushed. "I'm trying to get closer to the things that mean the most to me."

"Um—Ben?" Mrs. Reed cleared her throat. "I need your help in the kitchen."

"My help?" Mr. Reed asked, scowling. "What help?"

"Just come with me," Mrs. Reed ordered her husband, rising from the table and practically shoving him ahead of her out of the dining room.

Samantha watched their departure and smiled bashfully. "Your mother's pretty perceptive," she murmured. "At least she's discreet. Does she know what's going on between us?"

"She's probably figured it out by now," Lonny said. He reached across the table and captured Samantha's hand. "I haven't gotten around to telling her about us, Sammy, because I usually don't discuss my personal life with them."

"Just your business life. Lonny, why didn't you tell me this plan of yours? Why did you have to spring it on me in front of your parents?"

"I wanted to," he confessed. "I wanted to talk to you about it, Sammy, and I tried to, but..." He squeezed her hand. "When I'm with you, all I want to do is love you. I don't mean what you're thinking," he reproached her as he glimpsed her wicked smile. "I mean, I just want to be in love with you. It's hard to talk to you when I'm so busy being in love with you." He stroked her wrist with his thumb as he mulled over his words. "I want everything to be just the way you want it, Sammy. You want a nice, traditional man who goes to work in the morning and comes home at night, and wears a proper suit, and makes as much money as you do, and shares your goals in life. I'm willing to do that for you."

The tender caress of his thumb against her skin lulled her, preventing her from becoming as indignant as she ought to have been. "You were blind about me back in college," she said. "And you're still blind about me. I'm not looking for a man like Stephen. That's not my type. *You're* my type, Lonny, and that means *you*, running on the rooftops, with your messy hair and your faded jeans. I don't want you to change."

"But if I don't change... Sammy, we've got something good here, but it isn't all it should be. Our work gets in our way, and then we fight about it, and then—when I see you— I fall madly in love all over again. I feel like we're living two very different lives. I want things right between us."

"Okay," Samantha offered. "Let *me* quit *my* job."

"No. I won't have you changing for me, either," he insisted. "Everything you've worked so hard for, Sammy—"

"I wasn't going to quit my job for your sake," she claimed. "I was going to do it for mine."

"You aren't going to do it at all," he resolved. "It's too good a job, and you'll have a tough time trying to find another one like it. As for me, I can repair buildings anywhere. Maybe if we line up some projects closer to New York... I don't know. I just want us to be close."

"As close as best friends," said Samantha.

"Yes," Lonny confirmed. "That close."

Chapter Ten

Lonny felt peculiar entering Samantha's bedroom. He'd been in the room before, and it hadn't meant anything more to him than her dorm room had in college. How many times had he lain on her bed with his mind fixed on some other woman? How many times had he stretched out on Samantha's sheets and been unaware of the faint, sweet scent of her on them? How many times had he rested his head on her pillow without giving a thought to the way her lustrous hair would look upon it, or her face, her dark eyes, her enchanting smile?

The last time he'd been in the bedroom of her apartment had been the previous winter, when she'd asked him to keep her company while she packed her bags for her trip to Denver to see Stephen. Crossing the threshold into the room, Lonny experienced a rush of memory about that afternoon. He'd spent the entire time taunting her about her prim and proper wardrobe, her matching leather-trimmed canvas suitcases, her habit of stuffing her prissy high-heeled shoes with tissue paper and wrapping them in plastic, exactly as his mother did, before she placed them into the suitcase. He had sprawled out on her bed, making disparaging remarks about her designer-label sheets and pillowcases, and groaning when she scolded him for standing his beer bottle directly on the night table where its condensation could mar the veneer.

He had told her about the New Year's Eve party invitation he'd received from Courtney Drummond, a hometown friend who was currently legally separated from her husband. "She's a real knockout," he'd told Samantha. "If she's really serious about breaking up with her husband, I could fall madly in love with her."

"You could fall madly in love with anyone whose waist measures less than twenty-five inches," Samantha had muttered. As for herself, she hadn't said a word about being madly in love with Stephen. All she'd said was, "I hope I'll have a good time with him."

Lonny scanned the room as she carried her overnight bag to the closet and put it down. She had been right to harangue him about his thoughtlessness with the beer bottle last winter. Her furniture was obviously expensive, and she was wise to treat it with the care it deserved. One advantage of having no money to spend on fancy furniture, as far as Lonny was concerned, was that you didn't have to worry about making water rings on the night table. Invariably, the night table's previous owners—all three or four or ten of them—had already damaged the piece beyond redemption.

Lonny didn't dislike nice furniture. He found the bed's patterned blue sheets pretty, despite Hanae Mori's signature on them. He conceded that the way everything matched gave Samantha's room a unified, tasteful appearance.

It was the sort of appearance one associated with the homes of product managers. Or lawyers.

Maybe she was correct. Maybe he should forget about law school and stick with what he'd been doing. He wouldn't be any happier wearing a necktie and having to shave every day than he was now, even if Bill Tucker referred to him and his partners as "boys."

Samantha came to him and rested her hands on his shoulders. "Do you think your folks are angry because we left so early this morning?" she asked.

"We stayed for breakfast. What more can they ask for?" He gathered her into his arms and kissed her. Her mouth welcomed him, her tongue seeking, her breath merging with his. His meditations on furniture and linens melted away in the heat of her kiss. All he could think of was having her, loving her.

His fingers curled around the hem of her blouse and slid it upward. "We're acting like animals again," she said with an airy laugh, which dissolved into a moan as he opened the hooks of her bra. "Shouldn't we be talking?"

"Not now." He couldn't talk when she was so close to him, so soft, when her skin felt like velvet against his fingertips, when her breasts were so warm and full as he arched his hands beneath them.

He wanted to touch her everywhere, in every way. He wanted her throaty sighs of delight to wash over him. He wanted to forget that he was anything but Samantha's lover.

She undressed him as he undressed her, and they tumbled onto the bed. Her hands moved from his shoulders to the smooth contoured muscles of his chest, down to his hips and around to his back. She seemed no more interested in talking than he was: she seemed barely capable of anything as coherent as speech. It wasn't their minds that were communicating now, but their bodies, their souls. Words weren't necessary.

He groaned at the stunning sensation of her fingers on his buttocks, her lips on the underside of his jaw, her teeth gently nipping the firm ridge of his shoulder. He was still awed by the realization that Samantha, his Sammy, could do such things to him.

He was awed and also inspired. He slid down on the bed and closed his lips over the swollen red tip of her breast. One of her broken, blissful sighs reached his ears, exciting him as much as the pressure of her hands on his ribs and her knees against his thighs. He shifted his mouth to the other breast. She moaned something that sounded vaguely like "Lonny" or maybe "love."

Her hands wandered across the taut stretch of his abdomen, searching. He drew back, knowing that he wouldn't be able to resist the friction of her fingers on him. It was insane for them to spend so much time apart that the minute they found themselves alone he lost all sense of himself, all the patience and willpower that making love was supposed to entail. Maybe if they saw each other more frequently, if they lived closer to each other... No, it would always be like this with Samantha. No matter how often he saw her, he would always want her this intensely.

He stroked his fingers up between her thighs, and she sighed again as her hips arched against his hand. He listened to her plaintive moans as he continued to caress her. Every sound she made was like a love song to him. Every motion of her body was like a dance. He wondered if she knew how indescribably beautiful she was in the grip of passion that bound them together.

Her hand groped for him again, and when she found him, he groaned in agony. "Sammy—" he breathed unevenly, trying to pull back again.

She stifled him with a kiss. He was helpless against the powerful yearning she created in him, yet paradoxically strengthened by it. He rose onto her, moving in forceful surges as he strove to find her essence, to claim it, to absorb it until he became, for one perfect instant, a part of her. He felt her body opening to him, taking him, tensing around him.

She shuddered, then cried out softly. Her hands clutched his back as the waves swept through her. And suddenly he was with her, buffeted by the same waves, torn from the world he understood. For an immeasurable moment he was utterly lost, and then he felt her arms around him, holding him tight, comforting him as she took comfort from him, and he knew who he was once more.

He closed his eyes and sank wearily onto her, letting his head come to rest on her shoulder. She raveled her fingers through his hair and traced the edge of his earlobe. "I like your haircut," she murmured.

He chuckled softly. Samantha's comment struck him as utterly unromantic, even though it was a compliment. He rolled onto his side and opened his eyes again. She looked absolutely radiant to him, her eyes glowing, her lips curved in a contented smile as she snuggled up to him. "Do you?" he asked.

She twirled her fingers through his hair again, then toyed with the clipped ends. "It looks neater this way."

"Who says neater is better?" he challenged. "I think it's too short."

"No, Lonny, it isn't. It makes you look . . . civilized. Mature. Like a grown-up."

"It makes me look like a lawyer," he grumbled. Merely saying the word caused something to tighten up inside him.

He eased onto his back, drawing Samantha closer to himself, and stared at the ceiling. A lawyer. The term conjured up images of his father, the fathers of his friends, his friends themselves. Neat, civilized, mature people who lived their lives the way they'd been programmed to live them, who resided in classic brick Colonial houses in the suburbs or well-appointed apartments in the city, who joined country clubs and served liver pâté canapés at parties, who developed ulcers and knew better than to put damp bottles directly on tables.

He knew the image wasn't accurate. Lawyers could also work in store-front clinics or public defenders' offices or in government service; when they didn't have to appear in court, they could dress more casually. Real estate lawyers could examine houses for sale, or pore over leases and mortgage agreements. They could help their clients to find and buy the ideal homes. That wasn't so terribly different from what Lonny was doing now—except that real estate lawyers didn't batter their thumbs on bathroom vanities, and they earned a great deal more than Lonny did.

At his parents' house yesterday, Samantha had sworn that she didn't want him to change for her. Yet before they'd become lovers, when they'd only been friends, she had criticized his life-style constantly. She'd been voluble about his lack of ambition, his failure to capitalize on his education, his hypocrisy in condemning wealth after having been surrounded by it all his life. That was what she'd said when she was his friend.

Last night, she had been telling him exactly what he wanted to hear. Lovers did that. But not friends. Friends stepped on each other's feelings. They were honest, even if what they said hurt. They spoke their minds.

In his parents' dining room, Samantha had said that she loved his messy hair. Today she said that she liked his haircut. Which was the truth? Which time had she been speaking as his lover? Which time as his friend?

"Are you hungry?" she asked, breaking into his ruminations. "You hardly ate anything for breakfast."

"I was anxious to hit the road," he reminded her with a sly wink.

She laughed. "Whatever the reason, Lonny, you must be starving now."

She stood, glided to her closet and pulled a pink silk lounging robe from its hanger. Slipping it on, she left the room.

Lonny sat up and gazed about the room again. Who was Samantha kidding? She loved quality. She loved the finer things in life, things she'd spent her childhood dreaming about from a distance. Luckily for her, she could afford such things herself, because it would be years and years before Lonny would ever have enough money to buy nice furniture. If she was serious about wanting him to stay just as he was, she'd better think long and hard about quitting her job at LaBelle.

She returned to the bedroom, carrying a tray that held a bowl of fresh strawberries, a thick slice of Havarti on a small cutting board, and a box of whole-wheat crackers. "What?" he exclaimed indignantly. "No insects?"

She balanced the tray carefully on the mattress, then climbed onto the bed beside Lonny. "The fried grasshoppers were stale," she reported. "And you should know better than to think I'd have chocolate-covered ants. I can't bring chocolate into my house—it destroys my self-control."

"Instead, you gorge on brownies when you visit me," he mocked her. "Here, fatso, have a dietetic strawberry." He popped one of the ripe red berries into her mouth, then cut a few slices of cheese. The cutting board was roseate marble, and the knife was silver with a design of inlaid mother-of-pearl in the handle. "Pretty snazzy," he remarked. "How much does something like this cost?"

Samantha swallowed her strawberry and shrugged. "I don't know. Stephen gave it to me."

"Oh." Lonny suffered a twinge of—no, it wasn't jealousy. More like foreboding. "You didn't give back his gifts when you broke up?" he asked, his voice deceptively cool.

Samantha chuckled. "It's a cheese board, Lonny, not a diamond ring."

"You like getting expensive gifts, don't you?" he asked.

"Who doesn't? Besides you, that is," Samantha teased.

"Sammy." He placed the knife on the tray and tried to shape his thoughts into words. Why, why was it so hard to talk to her? Why was it so hard to express his apprehension?

She stared at him, obviously conscious of the difficulty he was having in trying to speak. "Spit it out, Richard Alonzo," she ordered him.

"Why should I spit it out? It's very good cheese." Damn. Now wasn't the time to hide his confusion behind a joke.

"Come on," she goaded him. "Something's bothering you. Are you upset with your father?"

"No, of course not." In all likelihood, Lonny's father was more upset with Lonny, since the old man was raring to get his son back into the Tarrytown mainstream. When Lonny announced, this morning at the breakfast table, that he wanted to give some more thought to the possibility of taking a paralegal position before he committed himself to it, Mr. Reed had nearly choked on his bran muffin. Knowing him, Lonny figured he'd probably sat up half the night figuring out a way to get Lonny a job with his firm or that of one of his colleagues.

"Then what is it?" Samantha fingered a strawberry, then took a deep breath. "Are you upset with me?"

She looked so worried, so vulnerable. He still wasn't used to the idea that Samantha could be hurt. In the past, she'd always seemed tough, impervious to emotional injury. But that had only been her facade, as he'd since learned. "No, Sammy," he reassured her, doing exactly what he feared that she'd done to him: telling her what she wanted to hear. "No, I'm not upset with you."

"You're upset about something," she guessed.

He took much longer than any dexterous man should have needed to arrange a square of cheese on a cracker. When it was centered to his satisfaction, he stalled further by eating it slowly. When that ploy ran out, he summoned his courage and faced her. "Admit it, Sammy," he said. "You like getting nice gifts from men."

"What?" Her eyes grew round with disbelief. "What are you talking about? Do you think I'm a prostitute or something?"

"No!" He reassessed what he'd said and acknowledged why she was so shocked. "That didn't come out right," he apologized. "I didn't mean to imply that."

"I'm glad to hear it," she snorted.

"What I meant..." He began to arrange another piece of cheese on a cracker, then resolutely pulled his hands away. "What I meant was that maybe Stephen wasn't your type, but you must have liked certain things about him, or you wouldn't have stayed with him for four years."

"Three years," Samantha corrected Lonny. "The last year doesn't count."

"Whatever," Lonny said, resisting the urge to waste more time by quibbling with her over the length of her relationship with Stephen. "The point is, you may want me to be myself, but you also like my haircut. You can't have it both ways."

She studied him for a minute, puzzling through what he'd said. "Can't—can't you be yourself with shorter hair?" she asked quietly.

Her unwavering gaze informed him that she knew exactly what he was getting at. One of the joys of long-term friendships was that true friends understood each other implicitly. They didn't have to explain themselves to death. "I don't know," he answered contemplatively. "I don't know whether I'm sick of my work because I want your approval, or simply because I'm working on a rough job and I smashed my thumb. I don't know anymore."

She took his hand in hers. The thumb was no longer bandaged, and she could see for herself the bluish discoloration that lingered around the joint. She examined it, then lifted it to her lips and kissed it. Releasing his hand, she turned away. "I can't tell you what you want," she whispered.

"You always could before," he reminded her. "In college, you used to tell me everything I needed to know about the girls I had my eye on. You used to tell me to study harder when I complained about some professor. You used to say, 'Stop complaining and knuckle down,' and I did, because that was really what I wanted to do."

"Fine," she said dryly. "I was your conscience. All I was doing was telling you what you already knew."

"Well, do it again," he pleaded. "I don't know what it is I'm supposed to know, so tell me."

"If you're happy building houses, build houses," she obliged. "What more is there to say?"

"What more," he replied, "is that for years you've been telling me to shape up. You were telling me that I was living the life of a hippie, that I wasn't planning for my future, that by rejecting traditional work I was throwing out the baby with the bathwater. You were telling me that I was confusing style with substance, and that I was deliberately avoiding suitable work because I didn't like the style of it. That was the sort of thing you used to tell me, remember?"

"Yes, but that was when we were friends," she argued. Then she realized what she'd said. She caught her lip between her teeth and glanced at him almost fearfully. Another tacit understanding passed between them.

He shoved aside the tray and pulled her into his arms. She rested her head on his chest, and he could feel the dampness of her tears on his skin. He stroked his hands soothingly through her hair, but he knew he wouldn't be able to console her. He needed consoling as much as she did. "We knew we were taking a big chance when we got involved," he mused wistfully. "It's hard to keep everything in balance."

"Maybe we just need a little more time to readjust," she suggested, her voice muffled by his body. "We can still be friends if we work at it."

"We never had to work at it before," he pointed out.

She brushed away her tears, and her fingertips glanced off his chest. Even that accidental contact between her hands and his skin aroused him. How could they ever be friends the way they used to be when he wanted her so much, when she couldn't even touch him without making him crave her?

"I love you, Lonny," she whispered.

"I love you, too."

"Then why can't we still be friends?"

"Friends don't pull their punches," Lonny said. "Lovers do. I don't think we can help it." He sighed, his fingers weaving through her hair again and again, trying to still her trembling. "If we were just friends, I wouldn't want to change my life for you. If we're lovers, I would."

"I would never ask you to change your life for me," she swore. "Marcy said lovers make too many demands on each other and try to change each other, and that spoils a friendship. I promised myself I wouldn't do that."

Frowning, Lonny edged away from Samantha so he could see her. "When did Marcy say that?" he asked.

"I visited her at the T-shirt shop one day when I was in Spring Lake," Samantha confessed.

He grinned, then drew her back against himself. He reflected for a while on what she'd said. "You always made demands on me when we were friends," he pointed out. "Why stop now?"

"You always ignored me when were friends," she returned. "You always made counterdemands, and I ignored you."

"Those were the good old days." Lonny sighed. He loosened his hold on Samantha in order to set the tray on the floor. Then he slid her bathrobe from her shoulders and guided her down beside him. He kissed her tear-stained cheeks, and then her lips. "Let's just love each other," he murmured. "We'll work out the rest of it some other time."

Two hours later, as he steered his truck south on the Garden State Parkway, he berated himself for having backed off just when they were finally talking again. He'd wanted to talk to her so badly, but he'd wanted to make love to her even more. No wonder their friendship was in trouble; no wonder she called him an animal. He couldn't keep himself from thinking of her in erotic terms. Sammy, his old pal, his buddy, his chum—that person seemed like a figment of his memory, a part of history. He didn't know anyone like that anymore.

It was his own fault. He'd made his choice, taken his chance, fallen in love. He'd been reckless, foolhardy, overly confident. He'd been positive that nothing could wreck their friendship, that no matter what, they'd always be able to open up to each other.

And instead, just as he was beginning to sense a crack, the merest hint of an opening, he'd backed off. Like a fool, he'd opted for loving her again.

Had he actually thought that falling in love with Samantha would be just like all the other times he'd fallen in love? Loving someone like Moira Davis had been so simple. She'd been aloof, sure, but he'd expected that. He had known people like Moira all his life. Aloofness was part of their game. She'd been aloof, he'd lusted after her, and he'd called it love. Nice and simple.

And all the other women, too—Lisbeth Whatever, and the nymphomaniac from North Carolina, and even Marcy—if it was love he'd felt for those women, it was a much easier kind of love. You loved the woman, you enjoyed her company, you did your best to satisfy her in bed, and when you parted, you did so on good terms. Never with any of those women had he wanted more.

Why couldn't it have been that way with Samantha? Why couldn't he have loved her, enjoyed her, satisfied her, and still been her friend? Why did they have to become protective of each other, evasive with each other, unsure of themselves? Why did he find himself trying to read her mind and second-guess her? Why did he feel that she wasn't being completely honest with him?

When he had been with her, he had wanted her love. But the farther he drove from New York City, the more he wanted her friendship. He wanted to be able to enter his drafty old house, race up the stairs to his bedroom, dial her number and talk to her for an hour—without once mentioning that he missed her and wanted to see her. Just like the good old days.

Lonny didn't phone her when he got home. The sun was still high, and he decided to take advantage of the late afternoon light to finish caulking some windows on the rear wall of the house. He didn't waste time unpacking but simply changed into a pair of cutoffs and a T-shirt and tied his bandanna around his head. It didn't have much hair to hold out of his face, but he wore it, anyway.

He went downstairs to the musty basement of the house and carried his ladder out through the cellar doors, which opened into the backyard. He planted the ladder carefully against the house, then returned to the cellar for his materials. "Mindless labor," he muttered beneath his breath as he climbed the ladder and started sealing one of the second-story windows. Insulating an old house was hardly an intellectual challenge; it wasn't remotely like chess, despite Samantha's claim. Had she really meant that, or had she been saying it only to humor him?

Why couldn't he trust her anymore?

Perhaps the work was mindless, but Lonny enjoyed it. He enjoyed being able to see his own progress, being able to measure it with his eyes and hands. It was tangible, physical, actual. Not like the work of lawyers.

He continued toiling on the windows for some time after the sun had set, until the shadows obscured his view of his hands. Then he packed up, went indoors and took a shower. He considered calling Samantha then, but he decided to have some supper first. Strawberries and cheese had been a snack, not a meal.

By the time he'd finished his supper and climbed the stairs to his room, he was feeling the effects of his long day. Too much driving, too much working, too much thinking. If only Samantha lived closer to him, they wouldn't feel compelled to make love twice in an hour. They might *choose* to, but they wouldn't feel so anxious about trying to beat the clock.

She'd have to quit her job if she was ever to live closer to him, though. And if she quit her job, he'd feel obligated to provide her with everything she had sacrificed for him. Which, in turn, would mean his quitting his job. And if he quit his job, he wouldn't have much reason to remain in Spring Lake, where there wouldn't be any better paying work for him. So he could move to New York, and Samantha would have no reason to quit her job, after all.

Damn. Why did it have to be so complicated?

SHE HAD EXPECTED HIM to call her that night, but he didn't. Samantha knew she could have called him if she wanted to talk to him, but she was afraid.

Afraid of calling Lonny. It seemed inconceivable to Samantha, but there it was. She was afraid.

Could they really have destroyed their friendship along the way? Was it possible that by becoming closer romantically, they had sacrificed an equally important closeness? Samantha had other friends, women with whom she met for lunch and shopped for clothes and attended an occasional movie. But none of her friendships were as deep as what she had had with Lonny. None of them were based on such abiding trust.

Now Lonny didn't trust her anymore. She was anguished by the comprehension, but she didn't know what to do about it. She resented the thought that she should have to win his trust again, when she'd done nothing to have lost it in the first place.

Yes, at one time she'd been attracted to men like Stephen, men with short hair who wore Brooks Brothers suits and looked good in them, men who shared her ambition. The first time she'd been in love with Lonny, back in college, he'd been like that, too—refined, debonair, with exquisite taste and poise. She hadn't appreciated the path his life had taken, but that was all right; she had been under no compulsion to follow him down that path.

But she was older now. She'd had the opportunity to experience the affluence she'd missed during her youth. Why couldn't he believe that she was ready to move on and try something new, just as he had? Why couldn't he believe that she loved him enough to view the world from his perspective?

The fact was, Lonny didn't believe it. He lacked faith in her. And that understanding agonized her.

She was enough of a friend not to try to reach him. She would give him the time and space he needed to work out his confusion and overcome his doubt about her. Yet her faith in him was also severely shaken. She no longer trusted him to come to the right conclusion about who she was and where she was going.

Before they'd become lovers, she had taken his friendship for granted. She hadn't fretted when weeks went by without a word from him. She had always been subliminally aware that he was a part of her life, but she hadn't devoted much thought to him from one day to the next. But now, when Monday slid into Tuesday, and then into Wednesday, and he still didn't contact her, she felt a gaping hole in her existence, a vacuum, an emptiness that only Lonny could fill.

Her work distracted her, but in a negative way. Every day she attended yet another meeting on developing the new lipstick line. One packaging proposal blurred into the next; one potential advertising campaign resembled another. Should the lipstick tubes be shaped like tubes of acrylic paint? Should the lipstick itself be the mushy consistency of acrylic, or should it be sold with an attractive stiff-bristle brush for application? Or should the design favor a crayon appearance?

As if Samantha gave a hoot. Blue lipstick was blue lipstick, and no matter how it was packaged, it looked disgusting to her.

When she was summoned to Lynette Magnusson's luxurious top-floor office Friday afternoon for a private conference, Samantha was fairly well prepared for it. She knew Lynette was going to reproach her for her lack of enthusiasm about the product. She knew that she and her boss were going to have a showdown of some sort, and she rode the elevator upstairs with a bizarre sense of relief. She was having enough difficulty dealing with the absence of Lonny from her life. She was more than willing to reach a resolution of some kind in her work. That would be one less drain on her emotional energy.

Lynette's secretary waved her directly toward the door leading to Lynette's inner sanctum, and Samantha strode unflinchingly to meet her fate. Lynette was seated at her enormous mahogany desk when Samantha entered, poring over several advertising layouts from behind her prim half glasses. "Please close the door, Samantha," she said without looking up.

Samantha obeyed, then moved soundlessly over the plush carpet to the chair across the desk from her boss and took a seat. She waited while Lynette finished examining the layouts and removed her glasses. The older woman raised her eyes to her underling and smiled coldly. "Well," she said. "I'd like to hear your opinion on the Artist's Eyes lipstick."

"You know my opinion," Samantha responded politely.

"Actually, I don't," Lynette refuted her. "You've been unusually quiet during the last few meetings. Do you prefer the tube package or the crayon package?"

"I prefer neither," Samantha told her. "I think the product looks sickening either way."

"Samantha." Lynette's smile chilled to an arctic frigidity. "This is an entirely new concept we're introducing. We need you one hundred percent behind it."

"I know that," Samantha assured her. She was amazed that she was suffering no qualms, no nervousness, not the least amount of hesitancy. "I'm afraid you can't have me one hundred percent behind it. I don't like the product, and I can't support it."

"I'm not sure LaBelle can live with that," Lynette warned her.

"Then maybe I ought to leave." There, it was said. It was done. Samantha felt wonderful.

Lynette obviously didn't. Her eyebrows arched with surprise. Apparently she'd had no idea of how displeased Samantha was with the current project. "Are you saying you want to resign?"

"I'm saying that I'm willing to."

As nonplussed as she was, Lynette had too much composure to react impulsively to Samantha's offer. She folded her hands before her and regarded the young woman facing her with a mixture of curiosity and dismay. "I'm not sure I understand," she said slowly. "This is one single product we're in disagreement on."

"Yes, and I can't give you one hundred percent on it," Samantha repeated.

"But is it worth resigning over?" Lynette challenged her. She leaned back in her high leather chair and tapped her manicured fingers together thoughtfully. "Are you having personal problems, Samantha?"

This time Samantha was caught off guard. She never discussed her personal problems with anyone at work, and even if she did, the last person she would ever discuss them with was Lynette Magnusson. She took a moment to gather her thoughts, then said, "My personal life has nothing to do with it. I've been thinking of leaving ever since we started dealing with the lipstick project. It's a ghastly product, and I can't see the point of wasting my time and energy marketing something I can't believe in."

"But you believed in the eye products," Lynette pointed out.

Samantha opened her mouth and shut it. She hadn't really considered the eye products that seriously when they'd been introduced a couple of years ago. She'd been too excited about her promotion and her new position of power in the company to philosophize on whether Artist's Eyes cosmetics were meaningful. But as she meditated on it, cosmetics weren't exactly the kind of thing any sane person ought to *believe* in. She remained silent.

"It's quite a position to give up," Lynette noted. "Have you got a better job waiting for you?"

"No," Samantha told her. "It isn't that."

"You just want to leave? With nothing else lined up? That seems rather extreme for someone like you, Samantha. You have such a good head on your shoulders."

"Then I suppose I'll find another job sooner or later," Samantha remarked serenely. She had no guarantee that she'd ever find a job like the one she was prepared to give up, but that didn't matter in the least to her.

"We don't want to lose you," Lynette went on. "You're a talented young lady, and you've done some excellent work for us. You may be willing to leave, but I'm not sure I'm willing to let you go."

Samantha was taken aback. She had been certain that Lynette would have gladly escorted her to the door, if only to fill Samantha's slot with someone more enthusiastic. "I'm—I'm not sure you can stop me," she mumbled.

"Perhaps I can make it easier for you to reconsider," Lynette suggested. "Would you like to take a leave of absence for, say, a month, and think things through?"

"A leave of absence?"

"I can put Bob Stokes on the lipstick project for now. I'm sure he can handle it. Take a month, Samantha, and give this decision the reflection it deserves. You'd be giving up a fabulous position if you leave LaBelle."

"I know that, Lynette, and..." She laughed dazedly. She'd never imagined such generosity from her boss. Even if she ultimately chose to turn in her resignation, her ego was bolstered by Lynette's vote of confidence in her. "Thank you," she managed. "I'll take a month."

"Very well," Lynette said, resuming her usual frosty demeanor. "Keep in touch, Samantha, and if you make up your mind in less than a month, do let me know." She dismissed Samantha with a slight nod.

Samantha returned to her own office with a strong feeling of liberation. A month away from LaBelle was precisely what she needed. She could use the month to investigate other employment possibilities and to see what her life would be like without the regular structure of her job. She'd learned to live—to thrive—without the routines she'd grown used to with Stephen. Perhaps she'd learn that she could thrive without the routines of her job at LaBelle Cosmetics.

And if she and Lonny hadn't solved the riddle of their relationship in a month, she might very well need her old job back, if only to keep her from going crazy. Without her work and without her best friend, she might very well find herself too bereft to function.

She packed up her briefcase and left the building for home. If she and Lonny were still friends, she would telephone him to tell him about this new development in her life. She would ask him for his advice, probably reject half of what he said, and then laugh with him and hang up feeling lighthearted and satisfied.

To hell with it. Lynette may have given Samantha a month's leave of absence, but Samantha wasn't about to be so magnanimous with Lonny. She *needed* his friendship, and she'd be damned if she'd refrain from calling him.

Upon reaching her apartment, she went directly to her bedroom telephone and dialed his number. She let it ring ten

times, then hung up. The sun hadn't set yet, so he was undoubtedly outside working.

She undressed, showered, and tried his number again.
Still no answer. By the time she'd finished eating her supper, the sky was dark, and she tried yet again to call him. No
answer.

Where on earth was he? Granted, it was Friday night. He
could be on a date. That notion didn't sadden her as much
as it enraged her. She wasn't trying to call him as a lover, for
heaven's sake. She was trying to call him as a friend, and
friends could call each other any time, day or night, Fri-
days included.

Grumbling, she stalked to her living room and switched
on the television. Before she could flop onto the sofa, the
phone began to ring. Brightening, she raced down the hall
to answer it. Maybe he had arrived home just as she'd hung
up the phone. Maybe he'd heard it ringing all the way up the
front walk, and he'd known it would be her and he was
calling her back.

Breathless, she lifted the receiver. "Hello."

"Sammy? It's Jack Rogan. Remember me?"

Jack? She sank onto the bed and groaned silently. Lord
help Lonny if he'd told Jack to feel free to make another
pass at Samantha. "Hello, Jack," she said in a clipped
voice.

"Uh . . . listen, did I catch you at a bad time?"

You made it a bad time, she almost said. *You and your
partner Lonny.* "Sort of," she admitted. "What are you
calling about?"

"Well...I've got some news. I guess you could call it bad
news," he rambled on.

Samantha's pulse began to accelerate. As angry as she
was, Jack's voice had an edge to it that frightened her. "Tell
me," she demanded.

"There's...there's been an accident, and I thought you'd want to know. Being his best friend and all—"

"An accident?"

"Now, don't panic. He's gonna be all right," Jack reported. "It's his leg, mostly—"

"What leg?" she shrieked. "Jack, what happened?"

"What do you think happened?" Jack retorted. "The clumsy idiot fell off a roof."

Chapter Eleven

"It's crazy, your coming tonight," Jack said as he backed his car out of the parking space. "There's nothing you can do here. You can't even visit him until tomorrow."

"I know," Samantha admitted with a doleful sigh. She stared out the window as the nearly abandoned train station receded behind them. Jack was right; she'd been crazy to have raced down to Spring Lake on a late train. But she couldn't have stayed in New York tonight, knowing that Lonny was hurt. She wanted to be as close to him as possible. Like Lonny, she had learned to hate being rational.

"I guess you'll want to spend the night at his house," Jack said, digging into a pocket of his baggy overalls and pulling out a key ring. "Here's his keys. He gave them to me so I could get his phone book and make some calls for him."

"I take it you called his parents?"

Jack nodded. "*They're* not coming till tomorrow," he said pointedly.

"Well, they're very reasonable people. I'm not," she declared.

Stopping at a red light, Jack checked his wristwatch. "Ten-thirty," he read. "You wanna go somewhere and get a drink or something?" At Samantha's sharp glance, he added, "This isn't a date, Sammy. I just thought we could go someplace and unwind. I don't know about you, but I'm not ready to call it a night."

Neither was she. Nor was she ready to enter Lonny's house yet. "All right," she accepted.

He drove to a smoky tavern on the main road leading into Spring Lake and parked. The bar's interior was dark and gloomy, which suited Samantha's mood perfectly. They found an empty booth and sat facing each other. "What'll you have?" Jack asked her as a barmaid approached the table.

She toyed with the idea of getting exceedingly drunk, then decided against it. "I'll have a brewskie," she said, deliberately choosing Lonny's pet name for beer. "A light one, if they've got them." If she wasn't going to get drunk, she might as well not get fat, either.

Jack turned to the barmaid. "A Bud and a Bud Light," he requested.

They remained silent, steeped in their own thoughts, until the barmaid returned with their drinks. Ignoring their glasses, they both took long draughts from the bottles and set them down.

Samantha studied Jack in the dim light. He looked concerned, but not distraught. "Tell me," she demanded. "I want to know exactly what happened."

"We were over at the Tucker house, just finishing up," Jack complied. "Lonny was replacing a few loose tiles on the roof. Tucker is such a jerk: he had some harebrained idea about putting cedar shakes on. I mean, come on—cedar shakes on a saltbox Colonial? The guy's got to be nuts."

Samantha drummed her fingers impatiently against her bottle. She didn't want to hear a lecture on architectural integrity. "So Lonny was replacing the tiles," she repeated, urging Jack to continue.

"I was out there, too, checking over the shingles. Lonny called down to me, said he needed more nails, and I turned around to get them. Next thing I knew, he was on the ground, looking like he'd given himself a new joint halfway between his knee and his ankle."

Samantha shuddered. She had to know all the details, but hearing them caused her stomach to turn. "So he broke his shinbone," she said, swallowing down her nausea.

"Clear through. Tore some muscles or ligaments or something, too, the doctor said. His leg's a real mess, Sammy." Jack took another long quaff from his bottle. "The upside is, his leg took the brunt of it. He could have landed on his head, or his back, and really done a number on himself."

"Is he going to be crippled?" she asked, amazed at how even her voice sounded, revealing not a hint of her anguish.

Jack shrugged. "Let's put it this way: he won't be doing roof work anytime too soon."

"Why him?" she asked, fighting back a sudden surge of fury. "Why was he fixing the roof? Why not you or Howie?"

"Lonny always does the roof work," Jack explained. "The guy's got the balance for it. He's got the coordination. Matter of fact, he used to get off on it. He was always saying he loved the view." He shook his head glumly. "I don't know, maybe we shouldn't have let him up there. He's been kind of distracted lately. All this past week, it was like his mind was somewhere else, miles from the work at hand. I don't know why, but his concentration was way off."

Samantha busied herself with a sip of beer. She had a pretty good suspicion of the reason for Lonny's distracted state. She'd been distracted all week, too. "He didn't talk to you about it?" she asked.

Jack shook his head again. "I thought maybe you might know what's been eating him. You're his best friend."

I'm not so sure of that, Samantha disputed him silently. What had been eating Lonny was undoubtedly his confusion about whether she was his best friend. But she wasn't about to discuss that with Jack. "So what did the doctors say? What are they going to do for him? How long will he be in the hospital?"

"They're keeping him for a few days, waiting for the swelling to go down," Jack reported. "Then they're going to operate, put in some hardware to bolt the bone back together. I don't know, Sammy. I keep telling myself he was lucky he landed feetfirst, but he sure doesn't seem very lucky at the moment."

"No," she concurred. "He doesn't."

She had many more questions for Jack, basic questions about the doctors' prognosis, about whether Lonny's insurance would cover the expenses, or whether Mr. Tucker could be held liable. And a more important question, about whether Lonny had asked Jack specifically to telephone Samantha for him. But she wasn't sure she could bear the answers, so she refrained from asking. She drank her beer instead, praying that it would still her fear.

Jack filled the silence by chattering about the bungalow in Point Pleasant. The sale had just closed, and he expected that they'd make a small bundle on the resale. "At least it's a one-story house," he joked limply. "A fall off that roof won't cost anybody more than a sprained ankle." Samantha did her best to laugh, but her laughter was as strained as Jack's.

The streets of Spring Lake were deserted when they left the bar for Lonny's house. One beer was scarcely enough to give Samantha the courage she needed to enter his house, but she wasn't about to let Jack know that her troubles with

Lonny went well beyond her immediate concern for his health. With false bravery, she swung open the car door and reached into the back seat for the suitcase she'd packed haphazardly before bolting from her apartment several hours ago.

"I'll call for you tomorrow morning, and we can go to the hospital together," Jack offered.

"Early." Samantha smiled. "Let's make him mad." She didn't dare to add that she wanted to make Lonny madly in love with her. After shutting the car door, she carried her bag up the walk to the veranda and waved Jack off.

Smothering her trepidation, she unlocked the door and stepped inside. It wasn't merely the empty darkness of the house that unnerved her, but the comprehension that the house was dark and empty because Lonny was lying in a hospital bed, wracked with pain—and the personally devastating comprehension that she might not be welcome in his home. Why hadn't he called her? Why, if he was so troubled by the state of their relationship, hadn't he opened up to her about it instead of stewing privately and letting his concentration drift dangerously from his work? Why, no matter what he thought of Samantha, had he let himself get so horribly hurt?

She stalked into the parlor, gritting her teeth at the lonely echo of her footsteps. Peering through the kitchen doorway, she noticed two unopened cans of house paint standing on the floor in the corner. She switched on the light and crossed the room to get a better look.

The cans were labeled Powder Blue, the color Lonny had intended to paint his dining room. A low sob escaped Samantha when she realized that he must have been planning to start the interior work on his house. *His* house, this oversized, rickety building that he was restoring for himself as an act of love—would he ever be able to resume work on it? Would he ever want to?

She sank into a chair and gave herself over to the tears she'd held in check since she'd received Jack's phone call. She no longer cared about the status of her friendship with Lonny. All she cared about was Lonny himself, his magnificent athletic ability, his natural confidence, his limber body. From the first time she'd seen him, dancing so wonderfully, she had been entranced by his innate grace. He was the most graceful person she'd ever known.

But his grace had failed him, and he was hurt. More than his leg had been broken in the fall.

Samantha slept little that night, and she was showered and dressed by the time Jack honked for her the following day. During the trip to the hospital, she tried to prepare herself for what Lonny would look like, how he would feel, how he would act with her. She had been impulsive to hurry down to Spring Lake. Lonny might not even want to see her, and she had to steel herself for that possibility.

They arrived at the hospital at a quarter to nine. "If I'm not mistaken, visiting hours don't start for fifteen minutes," Jack informed Samantha. "I could use a cup of coffee. How about you?"

"No, thanks," she said, afraid that if she lingered in the visitors' cafeteria, she might lose her nerve. "You go ahead and have some breakfast. I'll meet you in his room."

She walked briskly to the information desk and obtained a pass. When she headed for the elevator, nobody stopped her, so she proceeded upstairs to Lonny's room. On the third floor she paused at a nurses' station for directions, and although the nurse mumbled something about Samantha's being a few minutes too early to visit a patient, she reluctantly led her down the hall to the room.

Samantha sucked in a deep breath before entering. The room was semiprivate, and she had to pass a man watching television in the front bed to reach Lonny. The man eyed her curiously, then switched the station with a remote control device and turned his attention back to the screen.

She passed the curtain dividing the two beds and took another deep breath. The first thing she focused on was the huge white cast protruding at an angle from beneath the sheets and resting in the sling of a traction device. She tried to imagine Lonny's right leg inside the enormous plaster sculpture, but she couldn't. Not until she shifted her vision to his face.

Yes, it was Lonny, but not the Lonny she was used to, the deeply tanned smiling Lonny who bounded across roofs and sang James Taylor songs off-key. He looked drawn and frail, his eyes pocketed in shadow, his lips set in a grim line and his skin the color of ash. His arms protruded from the sleeves of his hospital gown and rested limply atop the blanket. The head of his bed had been raised so he could look out the window. He stared unmoving at the glaring morning light; evidently, he hadn't heard her come in.

Samantha was profoundly shaken by his appearance, but she determinedly forced a smile. She wasn't here to make him feel any worse than he already did. "Hello!" she said robustly.

Her voice jolted him, and he turned to her. His eyes seemed to waver slightly as his head sank back into the pillow. "Sammy," he whispered, then cleared his throat and smiled feebly. He gestured toward his broken leg. "I guess I blew it, huh."

She ventured closer to him. "The key question, Lonny, isn't what happened to your leg. What I want to know is, did you get grass stains on the rear end of your slacks?"

He laughed. Laughing obviously hurt him, but he didn't stop, even as his grin turned into a grimace. Samantha laughed, too. "Get over here," he groaned, extending his hand to her.

She pushed a chair up to the bed and sat. "I may fall more often than you," she observed dryly. "But when you fall, you do it spectacularly."

"Give me a break," he complained, then groaned again. "Bad choice of words."

He folded his hand around hers, and she was heartened by the strength of his grip. "How do you feel?" she asked.

"As the saying goes, don't ask." He squeezed her hand. "God, I'm glad you're here."

"You are?" She was surprised, and vastly relieved.

"I told Jack to call you, but I didn't know whether you'd come."

"Why wouldn't I come?"

He closed his eyes for a moment, then turned away to gaze out the window again. "You must be pretty angry with me," he mumbled.

Samantha knew it wasn't the proper time to be working out whatever was wrong between them. So she brushed off his comment with a joke. "Of course I'm angry with you. You went and fell off a roof, for heaven's sake. Did you expect me to be pleased with you?" Lonny twisted to face her again, but she cut him off before he could speak. "I came because I'm your friend," she said softly. "Nothing else matters right now."

"It does matter," he objected. "Sammy, let me say what I've got to say. I'm all doped up on painkillers at the moment, so now is the best time to say it. Then, when the drugs wear off, I can always deny everything." Samantha smiled hesitantly, but Lonny remained solemn. "I almost killed myself yesterday," he said haltingly. "It didn't hurt—when

I fell—it didn't hurt at the time, because I was in shock. I didn't feel anything. But I kept thinking, just to make sure I wasn't dead. I forced myself to keep thinking.''

Samantha tightened her hold on his hand. ''About what, Lonny?'' she murmured.

''When you come that close to killing yourself, it makes you think about what's important,'' he explained. ''Being alive is important. Friendship is important. Love is important.''

''You didn't have to throw yourself off a roof to figure that out,'' Samantha chided him.

''Maybe I did.'' He faltered, his eyes narrowing on her, lucid and piercing despite the painkillers in his system. ''Sammy...I was in love with you. I used to think that was all I wanted.''

His use of the past tense elicited a twinge of dread in Samantha, but she gamely fought it off. ''And?'' she cued him.

''When you're in love with someone, you sort of...you freeze them in your mind. You turn them into an object.'' He sighed. ''Sammy, I couldn't believe that you didn't care what I did to earn a living. That sort of thing used to be so important to you, and I fell in love with you, and suddenly there you were, changing on me. You were this beautiful, sexy woman I craved, and I'd do anything in the world for you: I'd switch jobs for you, if that was what you wanted. Anything. It never occurred to me that you'd change.''

''Lonny—''

''No, let me finish,'' he demanded. He swallowed, his eyes becoming glassy again as he succumbed to a wrenching pain, and he cursed. ''When I started thinking of you as my lover,'' he continued hoarsely, ''I stopped trusting you as my friend. It shouldn't have happened, Sammy, but it did. I was so ready to change for you that I didn't realize that you were ready to change, too."

"Not for you, Lonny," Samantha corrected him. "I was ready to change for myself." She pulled his hand into her lap and stroked it, reflecting on the enormous changes she'd undergone in the past ten years, in the past few weeks, in the past twenty-four hours. "Remember when I got my promotion, and you criticized me for being too materialistic?"

Lonny rolled his eyes.

"I told you then that it was easy for you to reject everything I'd spent my life dreaming of, because you had already had it, but that it was impossible for me to reject something I'd never had. Well, now I've had it, and it was nice, but I don't need it anymore." She let her fingers come to rest on top of his. "Yesterday, while you were pulling this stunt—" she pointed accusingly at his encased leg "—I was offering my resignation at LaBelle. Not for you, Lonny. For me. Because I've changed."

He took a minute to absorb her announcement. "You really quit?"

"Not exactly," she conceded. "My boss wouldn't accept my resignation. She gave me a leave of absence to think it over."

"That was nice of her."

"It was very flattering." Her hand began to move on his again, savoring its warmth and inherent power. She was reassured by the shape of his fingers, their flexibility and beauty. "I don't love my job," she concluded. "And I don't hate it. Right now, I don't care about it one way or the other." She lifted his hand to her lips and kissed it. "When you were lying on the ground in shock and figuring out what's important, Lonny, I notice that you didn't put careers at the top of the list."

"No." He turned his wrist to weave his fingers through hers. "Work is good. Work is necessary. But it's not as important as friendship."

The bedside telephone began to ring. He released her hand to grab the receiver. After a brief dialogue, he hung up. "That was Jack, calling from the waiting room downstairs," he told Samantha. "My parents have arrived."

Samantha stood. "I'll go down and persuade Jack to have a second cup of coffee with me, so you can visit with your folks," she resolved.

"I'd rather you stayed."

She leaned over the bed and kissed his cheek. "Don't worry, friend. I'll be back."

HER LEAVE OF ABSENCE from her job couldn't have come at a better time. Even after his surgery, Lonny was more or less housebound, and he welcomed Samantha's offer to stay with him and help out. With Jack's assistance, she moved the lumpy mattress from the "royal suite" into the parlor, so Lonny wouldn't have to navigate the stairs when he wanted to go to bed. They also moved Lonny's bureau downstairs, one drawer at a time, and the television set. She rented him a wheelchair, so he could get himself to the kitchen and the bathroom without too much difficulty. In time, his doctors assured him, his strength would be restored enough for him to use crutches.

Samantha was astonished that Lonny didn't complain about his plight. He used to boast about being a complainer, but he seemed remarkably willing to accept what had happened to him. On sunny days he wheeled himself onto the veranda to read. On rainy days he remained indoors and read some more. His father had provided him with a stack of legal textbooks, and Lonny devoured page after page of cases. "This stuff is fascinating," he would relate over dinner, sometimes carrying a heavy tome to the table with him. "Listen to this, Sammy..." he'd say, and he would read an arcane decision to her, parsing it and weighing its ramifications.

"Who would have thought it?" Samantha would tease him. "You might end up going to law school for the *right* reasons."

Perhaps Lonny wasn't growing stir-crazy, but she was. She spent the first few days running errands, shopping, cooking, opening the inseams of his jeans so he would be able to get them on over his cast. But as busy as she kept herself, as many long walks as she took on the boardwalk, she couldn't overcome her edginess.

Things still weren't right between her and Lonny. She felt relaxed and natural with him, as relaxed and natural as they had been when they were only friends. They could talk, they could joke, and they could harp on each other and help each other. But they weren't lovers anymore.

"Look, Sammy," Lonny had rationalized, "it has nothing to do with you, or how I feel about you. It's just that nights are the worst time for me. I can't get comfortable in bed with this damned cast, and the pain kicks in, and I'm a wreck. I really think we'll both sleep better if you use my bed upstairs."

She tried not to take his preferred sleeping arrangement as a rejection of her. Of course he was uncomfortable; of course he was in pain. She had no right to want to sleep with him, even if sleep was all she had in mind. To take the situation personally was egocentric. Lonny needed his rest. It was as simple as that.

Still, a part of her wondered whether comfort was Lonny's only concern. Every night she'd kiss him and then climb the stairs alone to his broad bed, where she'd toss and turn, quite possibly in as much discomfort as he was. They could talk about everything these days, everything but this strange physical distance between them. Yet she couldn't broach the subject to him, because he'd only tell her, all over again, that nights were the worst time for him and he'd rather get through them alone.

"I'm going to paint your dining room," she declared one morning after a particularly restless night.

"What?"

"Those cans of paint in the corner—they're for the dining room, right?"

Lonny peered over his coffee mug at the cans she was pointing to. He nodded slowly. "Sammy, you don't have to do that. It's a tough job, and you've done too much for me already."

"I want to do it," she asserted. "It can't be as tough as marketing cosmetics."

"Says you," Lonny shot back. She saw the gleam in his eye that indicated that he knew she was challenging him, and that he was ready to meet her challenge. "All right, paint the dining room. I'm not going to stop you."

"Great! Where are the paint brushes?" she asked.

"Down in the cellar you'll find a roller and tray, along with some stirring sticks."

"A roller? A tray? Stirring sticks?"

He snorted triumphantly. "Are you sure you can handle it, Sammy?"

"Just tell me what to do, and I'll do it," she persisted, undaunted.

It took Lonny about an hour to explain to her how to lock the legs of the stepladder, how to tell when the paint was thoroughly stirred, how much to fill the tray, how wet the roller should be before she applied it to the walls. "This color looks awfully intense," she remarked as she stirred it. She pushed up the sleeves of the paint-stained shirt Lonny had ordered her to wear over her clothing before pouring some paint into the tray. "Are you sure it's going to look good?"

"I'm sure," he answered. "What's so intense about it?"

"It reminds me of one of the lipstick colors Artist's Eyes is introducing," she grumbled, placing the tray carefully on the ladder's shelf. Lonny laughed and wheeled himself out onto the veranda to read, abandoning her to face her task alone.

By the end of the day she was convinced that the color wasn't too intense at all. In fact, it was gentle, soothing. Samantha found the actual labor of painting soothing, too. She had thought the sheer repetition of it would drive her insane, but it didn't. She liked watching the faded walls come to life under her ministrations. She liked watching the room revive. She liked being engaged in something that didn't snarl her thoughts into intricate knots.

"That was fun," she announced over dinner. Rejuvenated by her shower, she dug into the bowl of spaghetti and helped herself to a heaping portion. "Maybe I'll be able to finish the inner wall tomorrow."

"No rush," Lonny assured her, watching with amusement as she ladled sauce onto her pasta. "I see it built up your appetite."

"So I gain a pound," she said with a blithe shrug. "Seriously, Lonny, I can see why you enjoy that kind of work. It's so—so down-to-earth."

"How are your hands?" he asked. At her bewildered frown, he clarified, "The turp can really dry your skin."

"I used some hand cream I found in your bathroom," she told him, displaying her hands for him to see. "The paint doesn't even smell that bad. I'll definitely finish the wall tomorrow."

Lonny chuckled. "Here I am, finally becoming a decent adult and getting hooked on law cases, and you're going to turn into a bum on me. We can wave to each other as we pass in opposite directions."

"Fat chance of that," Samantha snorted. "Painting a room is fun, but it isn't going to lead to an office with a window."

Lonny ate, immersed in thought for a moment. "You're going to return to LaBelle, then?"

"I've got another week before I have to decide," said Samantha. "I'm thinking I probably will—but only on my terms. I don't want to be a part of any campaign for vile lipsticks. And I don't want to have to attend any more last-minute Friday afternoon meetings."

"Will your boss go along with that?"

Samantha shrugged. "She says she doesn't want to lose me. If she can live with a product manager who's revised her priorities, then she won't lose me. If she can't, I'm gone."

"I can't believe I'm listening to Ms Hustle saying such things," Lonny ribbed her.

"Ms Hustle? I'm not so close-minded I can't see that a painter's stepladder has as much to recommend it as a corporate ladder."

"Just as long as you don't lose your footing," Lonny remarked ironically.

She was still in an ebullient mood as she and Lonny cleaned up after their meal—Lonny stacked all the dishes on his lap and wheeled them to the sink for her—and when she joined him in front of the television afterward. But once she'd bade him good-night, climbed the stairs to his room, slipped out of her clothes and into a nightgown and slid beneath the blanket, her spirits began to disintegrate.

What was she doing by herself in his bed? Why, if she felt so close to him in every other way, was she afraid to confront him about this one barrier between them? They were friends, and if ever there was a time to be honest, it was now.

She tiptoed down the stairs to the dark parlor and across the room to the mattress where Lonny lay. Shoving back the covers, she climbed in next to him. He was wearing only his undershorts, and when her hand brushed along his naked ribs, they both flinched.

"Sammy—"

"Not a word, Richard Alonzo," she warned him, drawing the blanket over her and adjusting her head against his shoulder. "I came here to sleep, that's all."

"I don't think this is a very good idea," he mumbled, although his arm reflexively curved around her. "Why should we both be uncomfortable?"

"Discomfort is a state of mind," she claimed.

"You've obviously never broken your leg." His fingers floated through her hair. "I really think—"

"Shut up, Lonny," she cut him off. It felt so good to be curled up beside him, so right. The hell with his discomfort. She wasn't going to leave. She shut her eyes, and her exhaustion from her day's physical labor, combined with the familiar warmth of his arm cradling her, caused her to fall asleep almost instantly.

The morning sunlight seeping through the windows' translucent drapes roused Samantha early the following day. She opened her eyes and discovered herself still in the protective enclosure of his arm. The filtered light washed over his face in a beautiful way, and she sighed.

"Good morning," Lonny greeted her, his eyes blinking open.

She raised herself on one elbow and gazed down at him. He was smiling tentatively, staring at the multitude of tawny colors the light captured in the depths of her hair. "Good morning," she said.

"How did you sleep?" he asked.

"Never better." She bowed to kiss his lips gently. "I can't even complain about the mattress. How about you?"

"Do you hear me complaining?"

She laughed softly, then brushed a thick black lock from his brow. Her laughter ebbed as she studied him, trying to decipher his enigmatic expression. "Why didn't you want me in your bed?" she asked.

"Oh, Sammy..." He exhaled and looked past her. "I didn't think I could stand having you so close to me when I was unable to make love to you."

"We don't always have to make love, Lonny," she pointed out. "Just sleeping can be very nice."

"So can talking," he said. At her quizzical frown, he elaborated. "You were right, Sammy—once we started making love, we stopped talking. Every time I saw you, all I could think of was how much I wanted to make love with you. I forgot how much I loved talking to you. I guess I was afraid of making that mistake again."

Samantha chuckled and kissed him again. "I love talking to you, and I love making love to you, too. Wasn't it you who said we shouldn't compare apples and oranges?"

"Mmm. I've got to admit, though—sometimes I really get a craving for an apple, and an orange won't do." He slipped his hand beneath her hair to the nape of her neck and pulled her down to him. His kiss was deep and hungry, and they were both breathless when he finally eased away from her. "I love you, Sammy," he murmured. "I've just got to learn to trust myself with you."

"You were very trustworthy last night," she noted.

"Ten pounds of plaster can sure put a crimp in your sex life," he observed glumly. "How many weeks has it been, Sammy? Maybe I've begun to mutate."

"You haven't mutated," she said. "You've evolved. From animal to human being."

He nibbled the length of her jawline, then tilted her head to afford his lips access to her throat. "If I didn't know better, Sammy, I could fall in love with you," he whispered.

"But you do know better," she argued, her voice low and husky as he browsed along her shoulder. When he tugged the cotton of her nightgown upward, she clasped her hands over his. "Lonny, what are you doing?"

"Getting friendly," he answered, sliding the nightgown over her head and off.

"What about your leg?" she asked faintly as his hands closed over her breasts.

"Sammy, the last part of my anatomy you should be thinking about right now is my leg."

"I mean it, Lonny," she insisted, unable to ignore the pulse of desire building inside her as his hands moved over her belly to peel off her panties. "I don't want to hurt you."

"Then don't make any sudden moves." He wriggled his shorts past his hips, and Samantha helped him to slide them over his cast. He pulled her on top of himself, his arms wrapped tightly about her. "You know something, Sammy?" he groaned as he guided her down. "Talking can be a whole lot of fun."

Samantha opened her mouth to agree, but before she could speak, his lips were devouring hers in a subsuming kiss. And then their bodies did all the talking.

Epilogue

"It's too cold to go to the beach," Lonny protested.

"It's April," Samantha countered, zipping her windbreaker and prodding him to the door.

"It's the coldest April on record. And don't forget; I'm a gimp."

"Quit complaining," Samantha scolded. She nearly dragged him out onto the veranda. He couldn't help moving at a sluggish pace; although the cast had been removed two weeks ago and he'd begun a vigorous program of physical therapy to recoup the strength in his muscles, he still leaned heavily on a cane and favored his healthy left leg. "Come on," she exhorted him. "I want to get to the beach before it starts to rain."

"Which could be any second now," Lonny muttered, glancing up at the swollen gray clouds looming overhead. "I really don't see why we can't celebrate indoors with a couple of brewskies."

"How often do you expect to get accepted to law school?" Samantha asked, ushering him down the walk to the street. "This is a red-letter day. Or at least an acceptance-letter day." She tucked her hand around the elbow of his free arm as they approached the boardwalk. "Just think,

Lonny—someday soon, you, too, will be able to own a Mercedes with a license plate reading ESQ.''

"Heaven forbid," he scoffed. "Just because Columbia accepted me doesn't mean I'm going to accept them."

"Why wouldn't you accept them?"

He started up the ramp to the boardwalk, but Samantha steered him past it and underneath the boardwalk. He moved in a lopsided fashion beside her, his cane sinking into the sand with every step, until she found a smooth spot on the vacant beach and pulled him down to sit beside her. He arched his arm around her shoulders and tried not to shiver in the raw wind that whipped off the water. "Columbia isn't exactly the cheapest law school in the world," he remarked.

"Is that going to be a problem?" Samantha asked cautiously. "I assumed that your folks—"

"I'm not taking any money from them," Lonny declared. "They offered, but no. I'm a grown-up now, Sammy." He trailed his fingers through the sand and gazed out at the turbulent slate-colored water. "Carl Dunlap's been paying me generously for my expertise on run-down properties, and I'll be realizing some profit from the bungalow in Point Pleasant, even if I didn't do any of the work on it. I've saved up a bit, and I can make up the difference with loans. *If* I decide I want to go to Columbia."

"I could lend you some money, Lonny," Samantha offered.

He turned to her. A sudden gust tore at his hair, tousling it. "You *do* want me to go to law school, don't you?"

"Lonny, we've been through this a million times," she groaned. "The decision is yours. I really don't care."

"But . . . ?"

"But..." She sighed. Lonny knew better than to believe that she didn't care at all. "But Columbia is in Manhattan."

"Aha! Ulterior motives." He turned up the collar of his denim jacket, then snuggled up to Samantha. "So you want to lure me to New York City by offering me low-interest loans."

"Who said anything about low interest?" Samantha teased. "Actually, one thing I'd offer you interest-free is the use of my apartment during the week, while you were attending classes."

"Something tells me you've got a pretty big interest in that arrangement," Lonny said, matching her gentle kidding. "Listen, pal, I'm not going to make any final decisions untill I hear from the other law schools. So can we put an end to this celebration? I'm freezing out here."

"You once took me to the beach in February," Samantha reminded him. "Today isn't so bad compared to that day. It's springtime."

"You could have fooled me," he said, huddling closer to her. "Even the joggers aren't out today. They're probably all at home, waxing their skis."

"Well, we're not done celebrating," Samantha informed him. "I've got news for you, too."

"Oh?"

"LaBelle is going to be introducing a new line of perfumes, and guess who's been put in charge of the marketing team?"

"Not bad," Lonny praised her, giving her cheek a big kiss.

"I think they want to reward me for having been right all along about the stupidity of blue lipstick," she mused. "So far, that line's gone over like a lead balloon. At least they've belatedly recognized my brilliance."

"Your brilliance," Lonny echoed disdainfully. "As if you had to be brilliant to realize that blue lipstick is ridiculous."

"Well, if they aren't rewarding my brilliance," Samantha reasoned, "they're rewarding my guts. At least I had the courage to speak my mind, even at the risk of my job."

"You do have guts," Lonny concurred. "Maybe I ought to marry you, after all."

"Marry me?" Samantha gaped at him. "Who said anything about marriage?"

"I think I just did." Lonny maintained a straight face as he enumerated her assets. "Besides having guts, you've got a good job, a New York apartment, access to company perfume so you won't smell funny after painting my house for me..."

Samantha socked him in the arm. "That's the worst marriage proposal I've ever heard!"

"Oh?" He eyed her inquisitively. "How many have you heard?"

She hesitated, then shrugged in resignation. "All right, it's also the best marriage proposal I've ever heard. But it still stinks."

"Hmm." He pondered his words carefully. "You'll be able to take care of me in my old age. I've already seen how well you took care of me when I was in a wheelchair."

"When you're in your old age, Lonny, I'll be just two years behind you," she reminded him. "I may be even more decrepit than you."

"Hmm." He appeared peeved. "You're making this very difficult for me."

"Dig deep, Lonny," she advised him. "Surely you can come up with a good reason to marry me."

He scrutinized her carefully, then lifted a heavy lock of her windtossed hair and kissed it. "You've got beautiful hair," he said.

"That's good for a start," she encouraged him.

"And you've got great legs," he continued.

"Do I, now?"

"And the stuff in between your hair and your legs isn't so bad, either."

"What about my mind?" she asked.

"Your mind needs a tune-up. Why the hell are we sitting here on a cold beach?"

"Because it's lovely here. And I still haven't said yes to your proposal, pal."

"I want to marry you because you're my friend," he said, abruptly earnest. "I can't think of a better reason than that."

Samantha turned fully to him and caressed his face with her hands, then tucked her fingers inside his jacket's collar to warm them. "It's a damned good reason, Lonny," she agreed, then smiled wickedly. "But I'd like to hear more about my legs, if you wouldn't mind."

"You've got terrific legs," he obliged. "I've been admiring them for a long time. Not a trace of thunder in those thighs."

Samantha smiled. "Keep talking."

"Say yes, and I will."

"Yes."

He kissed her, deeply and soundly. "Let's talk about chocolate-covered ants," he suggested brightly. "We can serve them at the wedding reception."

"Brownies or nothing," she retorted.

"Brownies, but you've got to paint a rainbow over your eye when you walk down the aisle."

"Done."

Lonny kissed her again, then heaved himself up on his cane and extended his hand to Samantha to help her up. "Did I ever tell you, Sammy," he said as they headed back to the cozy warmth of his house, "that you're wonderful to talk to?"

Harlequin American Romance

COMING NEXT MONTH

#193 PLAYING FOR TIME by Barbara Bretton

Strange comings and goings, odd disappearances—Joanna's New York
apartment building sizzled with intrigue. At the heart of it was
Ryder O'Neal. She tried to maintain a safe distance from the elusive,
mysterious man, but Joanna wasn't safe—from Ryder or from the
adventure of a lifetime.

#194 ICE CRYSTALS by Pamela Browning

Monica Tye's entire life was focused on overseeing the training of her
daughter, Stacie, as a championship skater, leaving her no time to sample
the pleasures of Aspen. Duffy Copenhaver couldn't see the sense of it.
Duffy had his own prescription for happiness—it included lots of love—
but would the Tyes slow down enough to sample it?

#195 NO STRANGER by Stella Cameron

Nick Dorset dreamed of being in Abby's neighboring apartment. He
longed to sit beside her, talk to her, hold her. But when she took off her
bulky coat, Nick knew he would have to care for her, too. Abby Winston
was pregnant.

#196 AN UNEXPECTED MAN by Jacqueline Diamond

When busy obstetrician Dr. Anne Eldridge hired handsome Jason Brant
to cook her meals and clean her Irvine, California, home, she didn't
dream that he would meddle in her social life. But Jason took it upon
himself to protect Anne from her dismal choice in men. Was there a
method in his madness?

HARLEQUIN HISTORICAL

Explore love with Harlequin in the Middle
Ages, the Renaissance, in the Regency, the
Victorian and other eras.

Relive within these books the endless ages of
romance, set against authentic historical
backgrounds. Two new historical love stories
published each month.

CLAIM THE Crown

Carla Neggers

The complications only begin when they mysteriously inherit a family fortune.

Ashley and David. The sister and brother are satisfied that their anonymous gift is legitimate until someone else becomes interested in it, and they soon discover a past they didn't know existed.

Take 4 novels and a surprise gift FREE